NOVA SCOTIA

Vol 2

New Speculative Fiction
From Scotland

Edited by

Neil Williamson
&
Andrew J. Wilson

Luna Press
PUBLISHING

First published by Luna Press Publishing, Edinburgh, 2024

A CIP catalogue record is available from the British Library

www.lunapresspublishing.com

ISBN-13: 978-1-915556-43-1

For Scott

Contents

Introduction: Wha's Like Us?

Neil Williamson & Andrew J. Wilson

What is speculative fiction? It's writing that challenges consensus reality. Speculative fiction includes science fiction, fantasy, horror, and all the variants and subgenres of these imaginative approaches to storytelling. What does it have to do with Scotland? Everything!

Speculative fiction has been part of Scottish literature for centuries. Walter Scott's *Redgauntlet* (1824) is the Jonbar hinge of alternate history. James Hogg's *The Private Memoirs and Confessions of a Justified Sinner* (1824) is the ground zero of postmodern horror. George McDonald's *Phantastes* (1858) and *Lilith* (1895) are benchmarks of fantasy. Robert Louis Stevenson's *Strange Case of Dr Jekyll and Mr Hyde* (1886) is the Gothic transforming into science fiction.

What is Scotland? Scotland is a nation confronted by possibilities both good and bad... Should it become independent or remain part of the United Kingdom? What will climate change do the country and its people? Will the creation of a spaceport allow its blossoming space sector to flower in Earth orbit? Is our sense of a distinct national identity real, a simulation or a dream? All these questions and more can be addressed by speculative fiction. We did it before with the first *Nova Scotia: New Scottish Speculative Fiction*, which was published to coincide with the last Scottish World Science Fiction Convention in 2005. Now that Worldcon is returning to Glasgow after nineteen years, it's high time to do it again.

We've chosen to repeat what we did nearly two decades ago. As we said then: "The contributors are all Scots. They're Scottish in the broadest sense: some were native-born while others have chosen to make their home here; some are highlanders and islanders, others urbanites; and this gives us an extraordinary range of perspectives. We wanted this collection to be inclusive, not exclusive, and we wanted not only the tight focus of introspection, but also the ability to see ourselves, as Burns had it, as others see us."

By design, only three contributors to the first *Nova Scotia* are included here: Ken MacLeod because he's the Guest of Honour at this year's Worldcon; and ourselves because it's our party! A new generation of writers has emerged, and we wanted to reflect this and the increasing diversity of folk working in the field in Scotland. After all, it's their collective perspectives and their politics, their dreams and their determination that will influence what Scotland becomes next.

Here's tae us! Wha's like us?

Weak Gods of Mars

Ken MacLeod

Winter had been killed in the war. He had some repute as a patriotic folk singer. The Joint Chiefs gave him a veteran's pension. In Scotland, patriotic songs were anti-war, but Winter thought it best not to mention that.

The pension was one of the lesser surprises of his resurrection.

The first thing he heard when he came round was a motherly voice saying:

"Lie very still."

Winter complied.

"Open your eyes."

His eyelids were sticky. He blinked hard. Low lighting. The sheet plastic of the ceiling was greyish and scuffed. A scanning platter hummed on the end of an articulated fixture above him. A hand reached in and swung it away. A forty-something African woman in blue scrubs peered at him. She had her hair up, and an embroidered black squiggle like a tilted question mark on her pen pocket.

"Sit up slowly."

He was naked on a gurney. The room was larger than he had imagined.

"Any dizziness?"

"No," Winter croaked. The woman passed him a plastic cup of water. He sipped.

"Swing your legs around." She stepped back, and took a pen from her pocket and held it in front of him.

"Catch."

She dropped. He snatched. The pen struck the back of his hand and tumbled to the floor, too slowly. The floor was clean, but stained with pink dust.

"I'm on Mars," said Winter.

The woman frowned. "Very good. How do you know?"

Winter shrugged. "I read."

"You remember who you are?"

"Sure. James Winter."

"And your occupation?"

"Folk singer."

"Correct."

He looked around. "How did I get here?"

"You've been dead." She spoke as if she'd said this to a lot of people.

"What?"

"Have you ever heard of a neural parser?"

Winter nodded. "I read about the research for it in *New Scientist*."

"The real cutting-edge stuff was classified, and a lot more advanced than anything you'd have read about. It worked. We can recover minds from dead brains if they're fresh, or well enough preserved. Started out as a branch of military medicine, of course. Now we're a neutral charity, like the Red Cross. Or a neural charity!" She thumbed the squiggle on her tunic, and grinned nastily. "The Black Sickle. We harvest heads." She rubbed the angle of her jaw, and looked away slightly. "In your case, well, there was an element of reconstruction, but you were in a peat bog under permafrost, so..."

"Reconstruction?"

Again the evasive look and defensive tone. "There were biographical notes on the album covers."

"You reconstructed me from a peat bog and a back catalogue?"

"Pretty much, yes. And personal stuff in the lyrics, of course."

"Fuck." He winced, remembering the lyrics. "So my memories could be false?"

"Some of them must be. Don't worry about it. The neural parser is pretty consistent in how it fills in the blanks."

He decided to let that lie.

"How did I die?"

"Your car went off the road. Just at the beginning of the war."

"War? What war?"

"Don't shout. You know, the war? The one you were singing patriotic songs about?"

"Ah," he said. "That war. So it happened."

"Yes, but ... it didn't turn out as expected. The military AIs upgraded to sentience before the missiles were halfway across the Atlantic. Only the dumb weapons got through. Enough to cause a nuclear winter, but not as bad as it could have been. The rest self-destructed in flight. Then things got seriously weird. There was a very, very hard take-off Singularity. We call it the Hard Rapture. Billions of people who weren't killed in the war dropped dead. For a month or two, they kept appearing on phones and computers and sending messages to their grieving relatives, so it seems they were involuntarily uploaded into the AIs. You were lucky, in that sense."

Winter closed his eyes and shook his head. "How did I – well, my head, I suppose – actually, physically get here? Are you able to land on Earth and take off?"

"Of course not," the woman said. "Your data was transmitted decades ago. Brain patterns and genome. It's only in the past few years we've had the resurrection tech to use it."

"What happened to the people who collected it?"

"They died on Rannoch Moor." She handed him an information pack. "To give you a second chance." She pointed him to his clothes. "Don't waste it."

The information pack had five crisp plastic twenty-euro bills, and a phone. The first items on the screen were an outline of post-war history, and a guide to Polarity. A hundred thousand people lived here, under Syrtis Major. Winter had been allocated a cubicle off a side corridor. It had a bed and a few basics. Beside the sink was a device like a five-litre barrel, with a thick manual. It was called a Drexler machine, and it worked molecular manufacturing magic. Winter settled in and explored Polarity. The hundred euros lasted longer than he expected. Nanotech and 3D printing made most stuff cheap.

From the information pack, he learned that they gave all fatalities a veteran's pension. It was a shame-faced, and wilfully shaming, form of dole. You had to pick it up weekly, in cash. This was to reduce moral hazard, or so the Joint Chiefs seemed to think.

On his third visit, he came across Calder in the queue. The man was ten in front and had his back to him. With the hunch and the hair and the double denim, it couldn't be anyone else. Winter waited. Calder picked up his cash at the counter and turned around. He favoured the women in the queue with a leer. It took him a moment to notice Winter.

"Christ, they brought you back, too!"

"I see you haven't improved."

"Words out of my mouth, pal."

"Heh!"

Calder stretched; Winter stooped. They clapped each other's shoulders.

"Fuck, man! They didn't tell me."

"Me neither. See you outside."

Calder hirpled away, his gait made further awkward by the gravity. Winter collected his wad of cash and found Calder out in the corridor, skinning up. He must have figured out the program for tobacco on the Drexler. There was something impressive about that, in its way.

"These things will kill you," Winter said.

Calder lit his cigarette. "Yeah, tell me about it. If the ankylosing spondylitis doesn't get me first." Calder had never made his lethally degenerative condition an occasion for self-pity. "I'm told what did for me last time was the drink. Traces of alcohol in my brain."

"I thought I did the driving."

Calder shrugged. "We were probably sharing the bottle."

"Speaking of which..." Winter made a show of looking at his wrist. "Sun's over the yardarm."

"My watch is fucking useless."

"Broken?"

"Twenty-four-hour time."

It was a point of honour with the Black Sickle. They remade your clothes and any possessions found on you as precisely as they had your body. Nanotech or 3D printing, or some such post-Singularity shit. Winter didn't claim to understand it.

"You just have to buy a new one."

"Great."

Together, they ambled down the long, plastic-lined, strip-lit corridor, up a flight of steps and on to the wider, crowded tube of Polarity's main drag. Spindly trees in an endless row of pots marked the middle of the passage. Creepers covered the sides and encroached on the ceiling. Here and there, transparent panels showed pink sky and red land. Delicate construction machinery toiled nearby, stirring dust into the thin wind. In the middle distance, pressure-dome farms pocked the red with bubbles of hazy green.

Underground again, to a low-ceilinged circular bar. This early in the sol, it was almost empty. The walls were made of local rock, and the lighting simulated a late evening on Earth. Everything else was plastic, including the tall tumblers of vodka and lime that Winter bought, the table he and Calder sat at, and the seats.

They clicked glasses.

"How long have you been back?"

Calder scratched behind an ear. "Three days. Takes a bit of getting used to."

"Oh, you get used to it. Trust me on this."

"How long have you had to get used to it?"

"Three weeks."

Calder laughed. "That's how long it takes to get used to life after death on Mars?"

"Pretty much, yeah." Winter eyed his glass, half full. "The drink helps."

"It's hard to mourn," said Calder, with uncharacteristic solemnity. "When you don't know if the memories are even real."

Winter could spot maudlin a mile off, and moved to deflect it. He raised his glass:

"To Irene and Arlene."

"Real or fake, dead or alive."

"Dead or alive."

Calder shifted in his seat, glanced at the entrance.

"Where the fuck," he asked, "did all those people come from?"

"Didn't they tell you?"

"I wasn't paying much attention. Having just found myself back from the dead and all."

Winter waved a hand. "It's all in the orientation pack. The core was the space forces. All sides, funnily enough. After the war they ganged up. Hence the Joint Chiefs. They built up the population from all the minds the Black Sickle saved. Most useful skills first." Winter laughed. "We're among the last."

"Not much demand for folk-rock duos."

"I guess not."

"What about back home?"

"There's no back home. Not for us, anyway. Earth's fucked. The less-damaged areas were in the global south, and they have industry. Think steampunk Africa. Coal, solar and hydro power, telegraphy. Anything more advanced gets eaten alive by the AIs. The Northern hemisphere's mostly tinkers, scavengers and dirt farmers. Cities not actually flattened are covered by mounds of black glass running weakly godlike superhuman intelligences."

"Weakly godlike?"

"RTFM," said Winter. "It's all in the information pack. 'Weakly godlike' can do anything allowed for by physics."

Calder looked puzzled. "And 'strongly godlike' is...?"

"Hypothetical. An intelligence that can *change* the laws of physics. Luckily for us, the ones on Earth can't. But they still call the shots down there."

Calder snorted. "Could be an improvement."

"Well, it might be, except that these glassy fastnesses control automated war machines that prowl the land like fucking Martian invaders."

"Doesn't sound like fun," Calder allowed.

"Anyway, now there's a million people in space. Here, the Moon, the Jovians, the asteroids..."

"Hey," said Calder. "I always wanted to be big in the asteroid belt."

They drank that week's pension in two sols. The militia threw them in a cell to sober up, then threw them out, dehydrated and penniless. Calder pawned his watch, which had niche value to collectors, and bought a guitar and a hat.

"Why a hat?"

Calder looked at him. "It's not for wearing."

They busked the corridors. On two nights, they got gigs in bars. The money from the hat kept them going until the next weekly handout. This time, they put their bewilderment, nostalgia, grievance and grief into singing rather than drinking.

Winter never quite got his head around how cornucopian capitalism worked, but money for their performances and recordings began to appear on his credit balance. He and Calder stopped collecting their pensions. They rented two-room apartments, then three. Luxury. They really were big in the asteroid belt.

"What are they doing out there anyway?" Calder demanded.

Winter stared at him. "Don't you ever look *up*?"

Calder did his best mad-scientist's-man-servant impersonation, hunching his right shoulder further and extending a crooked, shaking arm. "It'sh hard for me to look up, mahrthshter."

"Oh, fuck off! Try falling over backwards, then, and take a look through the roof panels. You might notice that Mars has three moons now."

"I have noticed. So?"

"One of them's a half-built starship."

"Fuck me, when did they find this out?"

Winter couldn't believe he was having to explain this. "It's not an *ancient alien* starship. It's ours."

Calder pretended to be disappointed. "Next you'll be telling me the Face isn't real. So who's going?"

"We're all going," said Winter.

"Must be one hell of a big starship."

"It is, but that's for the drive and reaction mass. There's no room for a million warm bodies in there."

"So how are we going?"

"Same way most of us came here." Winter drew a finger across his throat. "As information."

"Oh," said Calder. "When?"

"Before the weak gods get here," said Winter.

Everything went fine until Winter started seeing the ghost of his dead wife.

He didn't tell Calder, not at first. Nor did he call up a psychiatry program. He made an appointment with a man he'd seen on the channels: EUR Aerospace Forces *Général de brigade* Jacques Armand, retired. He ran an import-export business between Polarity and the carbon dioxide pumping stations along Valles Marineris. The Joint Chiefs allowed little space for politics. Armand had a finger in most of what there was.

You had to duck to get into his office. The floor had more red dust than most. Drexler machines chugged in every cranny. Armand's desk was a cardboard box on its side. His office chair was sculptural, ergonomic and orange.

"Thank you for seeing me, General Armand."

Armand opened his hands. "I'm not a busy man, Mr Winter. Call me Jakes. All the Yanks and Brits do, for some reason."

"OK, General ... uh, Jakes."

"So, why are you here?"

"I'm given to understand you're a Returner."

Armand maintained a poker face. "I am still under military discipline. The Joint Chiefs have determined that the starship will be built. There are those who argue that we should instead concentrate our forces and resources on taking back Earth from the AIs, but I can take no official position on that."

"How about an unofficial position?"

"My personal view," said Armand, relaxing a little, "is that a liberation of Earth would be feasible. I would wish for that view to be more widely discussed. Why are you interested in it?"

"It's my wife," Winter said. "I keep glimpsing her on the channels, like in the background. A face in the crowd. And now and again she phones me. She doesn't say anything, just smiles sadly and ends the call."

"This is not uncommon. People here do sometimes see those caught up in the Hard Rapture. Perhaps they find some crack in their prison, or their paradise, through which they can speak to us. Or, more likely, the weak gods reach out..."

"That isn't it," said Winter. "My wife's name was Irene. I remember her. I wrote songs about her, and to her. I doubt she ever existed."

"What?"

"I've checked what records I can. There isn't much. Even my Wikipedia entry got lost. But there are profiles. We had fans on the orbital stations and on the Moon, before the war. Well, one in orbit and one at Mare Imbrium. That guy had a file of all the interviews and profiles of us that appeared – again, not many, but there you go. And none of them mention that I was married, or in any kind of long-term relationship. Even in contexts where that would have come up."

Armand smiled. "I can imagine. The lifestyle..."

"It wasn't exactly rock and roll," said Winter. "But, well..." He shrugged. "Bygones. The point is this. My memories of Irene came from the neural parser. So how can she be living inside some AI on Earth?"

Armand gave him an odd look. "I don't think you quite understand how powerful even weak gods are. But why does the phenomenon bring you to me?"

Winter wondered if he could convey to this stern-faced soldier the anguish he felt.

"Maybe she never existed," he said. "But I miss her. I think she wants out, and I want her back. I want the Return."

It was as if they were staring each other down.

"To do that," said Armand, "it may be necessary to build an army to storm the gates of hell. What could you bring to such a battle?"

"You're a military man," said Winter. "And a political man. I'm neither. I can't fight, and I can't lead anybody." He grinned, and spread his hands. "But I can sing."

Armand reached for his printer, and passed Winter the laminated card that popped out. It showed the photo and details of Lawrence Hammond: black, born in London, exiled in France, EUR Army veteran, construction robot controller.

"Talk to this man," said Armand.

Calder was furious.

"You do realise," he said, when he'd done stamping on the splinters of his guitar, "that taking a stand like this will lose us half our following?"

"Half?" said Winter, impressed. "I didn't know the Returners had that much support."

"That's not among the general public, fuckwit! It's among our kind of people! Folkies! Most of these fuckers are nostalgics already, and they're all romantics. Half want Earth back – the other half are all caught up in the glamour of the great ship. Fight for the dead or die for the stars. You tell me which is the better long-term bet."

Winter thought about it. "For an increasing audience? The starship faction, I guess."

"Exactly," said Calder. He uncoiled a guitar string between his hands, and stretched it out as if to strangle his partner. "The Reform party. Which just happens to be the one supported by the Joint Chiefs and the business establishment, and every fucking propaganda outlet."

"So we're going to be anti-establishment! Back to the roots of the folk revival."

"I really could fucking kill you..."

"You reckon?"

Calder sized the odds. "Maybe not," he conceded. He dropped the string and kicked at the wreckage. "Fuck!"

"Sorry about that, but..." Winter shrugged. "I've agreed to do the gig. I've got new songs running in my head."

Calder glared at him. "Well, on your head be it. If it was up to me, I'd go with the Reformers, not the Returners."

"Don't you miss Arlene?"

"I'm not in love with her fucking ghost. And I don't fancy our chances against weak gods, thank you very much."

"We'll have a weak god on our side," said Winter. He regretted the boast as soon as it was out of his mouth. Armand had told him about that aspect of the project, and hadn't so much as hinted at confidentiality, but it wasn't something he'd heard anywhere else.

"What?" said Calder, suddenly alert.

"Well, it's obvious," said Winter, thinking on his feet. "The neural parser's all very well, but to set up a starship with all the capacities needed for millennia of travel, then surveying the target planet and settling it – or building orbital habitats if the planet's not as habitable as our best telescopes make out – is gonna take pretty fucking advanced AI. So the Joint Chiefs must be working on doing in a controlled way the kind of massive upgrade the military AIs did for themselves in the war." He finished with a miserable half-truth. "That's my guess, anyway."

"Looks like they're walking the wire of another Hard Rapture."

"Maybe," said Winter. "I, uh, think they might be aiming for what you might call a Soft Rapture – scan and upload, without all that messy Black Sickle business with heads. I don't know. Point is, an AI that can do all that could well be up to hacking into the wild AIs on Earth, so it's as useful for the Returner project as for the Runners."

"The what?"

Winter gave his friend a twisted grin. "That's what my lot call your lot."

"They're not my lot, exactly, but ... ah, fuck it! Better to split the following than split the band, eh?"

They shook on it. Calder stuffed the shards of the guitar in the Drexler pot. Five hours later the instrument fell out of the hopper as good as new.

"It's the weak gods, innit?" said Hammond. He had an odd accent, still strongly North London with a harsh tang of the Paris banlieues.

Normally, the crowd was excited, raucous, anticipatory. This gig was the biggest yet, about five thousand in a long, low warehouse facility, lots of live external coverage. Tonight everyone was talking in low voices, and checking their phones or staring off into the virtual space of the channels.

A score of sols earlier, a probe from Earth had landed on Phobos. Disquietingly, the only evidence of its trajectory, arrival and subsequent activity were blank spots hacked in the orbital surveillance telemetry. Their detection by routine software sweeps had alerted the Mars security forces, who were now reduced to using film cameras and physical recovery to observe the moon.

Hunched over his guitar, Calder tuned up. "What they doing this time?"

"Dunno yet." Hammond eyed his phone. "Rumours."

"Well," said Winter, "let's give the punters something to take their minds off it. OK, Larry?"

Hammond took the hint and darted to the wings. He was going to fire up the interval with one of his Returner rants, as he had done so many times before. That was the plan.

Winter stepped forward, glanced at Calder, and flicked to the guitarist's contact lenses a revised set list. Revised to reverse order, to open rather than finish with their current big hit, "Great Old Ones".

Calder shot him a raised eyebrow and an eye-flash emoticon of surprise. Winter nodded confirmation. Calder shrugged one shoulder, and hit the chord.

Do you ever feel, in your caves of steel...

The song brazenly plundered and flipped the Lovecraftian mythos, with the human beings of Mars cast as the new Old Ones who would return.

Now the stars are right and we're coming to fight!
We're coming to eat your brains!

By the time they ended the wall of sound was coming the other way, reverberating off the low roof, with beer being sprayed and plastic bottles thrown. Calder kicked them back when he could, raising further cheers.

The next song, "Goodbye Arlene", quietened them, as it was intended to: a threnody of loss set to a haunting, melancholic melody. Halfway through the last stanza, Winter saw a flicker of urgency in the newsfeed corner of his eye. The moment he focused on it, he heard a hush and a collective indrawn breath from the crowd.

The breaking news: the probe on Phobos had assembled a swarm of war machines from local materials. The Joint Chiefs were in permanent emergency session. Announcement imminent.

Calder must have seen the newsflash too. He crashed the chords on the finale and then stopped dead, leaving Winter's closing line to twist in the wind. No applause followed.

The awkward silence on stage was matched by a babble in the crowd, noise rising as voices competed. On a sudden inspiration, Winter turned and beckoned Hammond.

The Returner agitator strode on stage and grabbed a mic.

"Brothers and sisters! The fight is on! What's begun on Phobos must end on Earth! The Joint Chiefs—"

Commotion at the back. A squad of a dozen soldiers in full surface kit burst through the doors, brushed aside the venue security, and tramped down the aisle. The sound system went dead. The troops deployed in front of the stage. All but the squad leader faced the crowd.

Hammond opened his arms. "It's time to take the fight to the enemy," he said. "I hope you're here to do that."

"No political speeches," said the squad leader. His helmet had evidently taken over the sound system. The voice was shockingly loud, distorted into the flat tones of a riot warning.

"Can we sing?" said Winter.

"No Returner anthems."

Winter demonstratively tossed aside his mic.

"What's going on? What's all this about?"

The squad leader flipped up his visor to reveal his face. It was Jacques Armand.

"Jakes!" cried Hammond. "What the fuck, man?"

Armand replied quietly, in his normal voice. "State of emergency. The war machines have taken Phobos completely. They're building spacecraft now. We're hitting them with laser fire, but that can't be kept up for long."

"Isn't this what we've been waiting for?" said Hammond. "Now's the time for your comrades to move."

Armand shook his head. "This is no time for a coup. Nor for Returner agitation. Sorry."

"So the Joint Chiefs say!"

"Yes."

"And you're going along with it?"

"Yes."

Hammond leaned forward and glared. "You've betrayed us. And yourself."

Armand shrugged. He stepped up on the stage, and turned around to face the crowd. He lifted his helmet from his head, and placed it under one arm. It still patched his voice into the sound system.

"Many of you know me," he said. "That's why I've volunteered to tell you that, under the provisions of the state of emergency, this event can only continue if the songs are strictly non-political."

He faced down the roar of protest, and continued.

"More importantly, I'm here to tell you that the elements in the military who are sympathetic to the cause of Return remain unconditionally loyal to the Joint Chiefs. Please do not delude yourselves that there will be any Returner coup, or that any civilian demonstrations will find sympathy in the military ranks. In this dire emergency, we must all stand together against the common threat."

"Traitor!" someone shouted. Someone else started a chant: "Free the Earth! Free the Earth!"

To Winter's dismay, Hammond joined in, and began leading it, pumping his fist. Not even Armand's amplified voice could be heard over it. The officer was saying something that sounded urgent and important, but Winter could make nothing of it.

Calder crossed the stage at a fast limp, and grabbed Winter's arm.

"Look!" he shouted.

"What? Where?"

Calder's jabbed finger almost poked Winter's eye. "The news!"

Winter closed his eyes firmly and opened them, summoning the full feed to his contacts. An outside shot of a bright light in the sky and a shaken voice-over dissolved in a shower of sparks. Winter flicked the view away.

"Shit, something's—"

Calder toppled like a Pentecostal, with no one to catch him. In the low gravity, he couldn't have hurt his head, but his curved spine took a hard knock. He looked stunned. His feet drummed the stage, his eyes rolled. He babbled. Winter knelt beside him in an instant, and tried to ease him over on his side. Weakly, Calder fought him off.

"I'm gone, man," he said. "I'm gone..."

But he wasn't. His eyes refocused, he stopped twitching, and he grinned his evil grin and said nothing more. Then he really was gone: his head fell back, his jaw slackened, his arms slumped.

Winter looked around. Hammond fell over, as did two of the troopers. Armand still stood. People in the crowd began to fall, at first in ones and twos, and then as if scythed. Screams rose louder than the chants or cheers had.

"What's going on?" Winter yelled.

Armand turned. "It's the starship!" he shouted back. "The Joint Chiefs have woken it! It's taking us all!"

He fell to the stage. The helmet bounced and rolled.

Winter stayed on his knees. It seemed apt for what was to come.

Winter felt the scan like some vast presence in his skull. His body was completely out of his control. Floor and ceiling whirled past. Some strange voice was saying awful things. He recognised it, after a moment, as his own. Seconds passed, and the process was over. He found himself flat on his back, unable to move. He knew he had about half a minute left of this life. Nothing he saw or thought now would be recalled by whatever version of himself the starship's AI recreated, if it ever did make landfall around another star.

In that final thirty seconds, Winter saw, perhaps, what Calder had seen, and the others, in the interval between the scan and brain death. He saw Phobos glow like a hot coal. He saw the starship fill the sky above Polarity. He saw cracks of light in its hemispheric underside, and whirlwinds rising to be drawn in.

He saw the starship rise, in majestic defiance of gravity, to vanish in a flash of blue light that he recognised as Cherenkov radiation.

The last thing he knew was that, whatever the Joint Chiefs had awakened, it was no longer a weak god.

Editors' Note:

Fans of Ken's novels will recognise Winter and Calder from Newton's Wake, in which they bring their redoubtable talents to the opera portion of that space opera. We're delighted to see them return here, along with Ken's incomparable wit and knack for political speculation. Crashing into a peat bog might be the most unique way to preserve your self for future upload we've heard of. And sending hapless Scottish folk rockers to the stars is a fittingly awesome way to kick off this anthology.

When You Are the Hammer, Strike

Eliza Chan

The audience laughs. Mirth sweeps the studio and runs from Iris Chen's carefully curled hair down to her heeled sandals. She beams at the camera. On days like this, she is satiated. Jenny Lam, darling of social media, leans back in the guest armchair: instantly at ease in leggings and an oversized t-shirt, her gold hoop earrings jangle as she gesticulates. "Let me do you!"

This is not in the meticulously discussed plan. These Zoomers always think to trip her up, beat her at her own game. Puppy-dog influencers pretending their brand is spontaneous and organic. Iris rearranges her features into a thoughtful pause, the same she used earlier when they showed news footage from the typhoon. She's the type of person who moves a stranger's coat from the back of a chair so she can sit in the best spot in a cafe. Who barges her way into closed meetings and after-parties with pure bravado. The crowd responds to her cues. Clapping, stamping, egging her on. Later, backstage, she will properly upbraid the newcomer.

Iris raises a careful eyebrow, looking directly into camera two. People don't watch her show for warm fuzzy feelings. They watch to see a caged lion fight a starving tiger. Her interviews are a rite of passage for celebrities. Survive her cutting remarks and you can weather anything. If Jenny hair-in-a-scrunchy Lam is forcing her hand, then Iris will get ratings out of it. Finally, she nods. The teen fist pumps the air, standing like she's at a concert. She almost sits on the older woman's lap, her gauche gold and white platform trainers tucked under her. Iris slaps her feet off the furniture. "Honestly." Peals of laughter from the audience as she rolls her eyes.

Jenny doesn't use kau chim sticks, palm reading and astrology calendars. She inherited the family gift unexpectedly when her great aunt passed. Ignored all protocol. No stall at the side of the road or crystal ball in a tent. Instead, sixty second responses to fan requests: through filters of cascading cherry blossoms or with cat ears wiggling on her head. The fresh face of fortune-telling. Hardly acting like a witch at all.

A seasoned professional, Jenny pouts in each of the selfies she takes of them. Playing with her hair, hand on her jaw, eyes flickering down then up. Iris glares in pantomime boredom through each one, checking her watch and stifling a yawn. Her braying crowd respond. Jenny flicks through the pictures she's taken, effervescence oozing from her pores. Her thumb hesitates over the last photo. Augury through selfies. Who would've thought it? "You're not going to believe this!"

"Try me." Iris is acerbic as she purses her lips. Despite everything she enjoys the suspense. Playing deadpan foil to Jenny's youthful energy. But they're all trying to topple her; find a weakness to end her reign. The teen looks down suddenly at Iris's hand. The talk show host has been rapping on the table, quietly but insistently. An old habit. Iris forces her hand still. For the first time in years, the glare of the lights is uncomfortable.

"You… are a witch."

She takes everything back. The brat is clearly a huckster.

Alvin was still on one knee, the ring box opened in his hands as he looked up. His new brogues squeaked against the polished floor.

"Get up," Iris hissed. "People are looking."

"I need an answer." He was calm despite the question he'd just asked. Despite the rock that cost a huge chunk of his savings. Things had been fine as they were. Having their own apartments, their own social circles that intersected on occasion like a Venn diagram. Alvin had never pushed too hard. Never tried to eclipse her. It worked for both of them.

"We talked about this," she said in a low whisper.

"*You* talked. For years I listened. Waited. But I'm tired. I just want to grow old together. That's all." Grey was sprinkled through his dark hair like chalkdust. He had stopped wearing his contacts, embracing the horn-rimmed glasses he used to only wear before bed. When had they become so middle-aged? She hadn't noticed before, busy at work, at the photoshoots and overseas promos.

What he asked for was not unreasonable. But move the goalposts and he would want something else. Children. A suburban house and a lawn to mow. She didn't need a fortune teller to see where it was going.

"I'm sorry." The finality resonated, making the candle flicker on the table. Alvin closed the ring box with an audible snap. Pulled himself to his feet and dusted off his trouser legs. Iris resumed eating her dessert, assuming they would continue as they had done before. When he started to shrug on his coat, she realised it was different.

"Don't be melodramatic. You'll feel better in the morning."

He did up the buttons before he answered her. "I can't love someone that only loves themselves."

"Absolutely not," Iris says, she rearranges the menus in their little stand, putting them in size order to keep her hands busy. Her agent, Ying, takes her glasses off and rubs the bridge of her nose. A coil of white hair wraps around the handle of her teacup and brings it to her lips. Glossy strands discretely pull her phone out of her bag and check for notifications. Most of it is digging a pastry fork into the strawberry chiffon cake before her but a comforting section is patting her client's knee in a facsimile of sympathy. Ying barely pauses for breath.

Iris was stuck in a rut before she met Ying. Relegated to presenting morning cooking shows and weekday quizzes, no one took her seriously. She walked into Ying's office, defensive and angry having fired her previous two agents. The prehensile-haired witch took one look and said, "We can use that."

"Your brand is being a bitch," Ying says now.

"Telling it like it is," Iris corrects, smacking the back of her spoon on the hardened surface of her crème brûlée. It crackles like eggshells.

"Blunt honesty, refreshing truth – whatever you call it. You're a witch in everything but name, why not go ahead and embrace it?" Ying is one of the few people who isn't afraid to talk back. Who'd calmly finish a cup of tea as emergency sirens wailed around her. But she also has the most useful of witchcraft. Lawyers, doctors, chefs – white-haired witches always floated to the top of their fields.

"Get her to issue a retraction. I won't do that collaboration on her stupid social media channel either." Iris's spoon slaps the dessert. Again and again as a well forms in the centre. Solid caramel grinds to gravel under the force. Once, twice, three times for emphasis. The beat feels right. Satisfying.

Ying's eyes slide from the ceramic dish to Iris's hand. Says nothing but lingers on the spoon, waiting for another strike. She's doing it again. Scratching an itch without realising.

"The girl is popular with or without your endorsement. If anything, she's doing you a favour." Ying puts down her fork, hair settling to her sides. "I can sell it. Let me do my job."

The retorts come thick and fast, settling in Iris's mouth like bitter melon. She's not one to hold them back, usually spitting them out as fast as they come: like opening the drawer and hurling forks, knives and spoons across the room. No one is overly attached to cutlery. She keeps her teeth together, lips clamped shut. This is opening the battered shoebox at the back of the wardrobe. The one she's always been meaning to throw out but instead pushed back into the shadows.

"You ought to meet her. Before she goes." Ying shovels a large piece of cake into her mouth before she can say anything else, hair lifting to brandish a napkin on one side, her teacup on the other. Pretends to concentrate on chewing. Her additional remark snaps Iris back into herself like an overstretched elastic band.

"You don't get ten percent on family reunions." Iris can't remember the last time she saw her grandmother. In the years since her father left, Iris's bewildered mother has kept his shirts dutifully ironed, as if he would be back at any minute. Por Por makes it worse, harping on about what her mother's done wrong; writing her father's name and beating it with that damned shoe every morning as if she can hammer a bent nail straight.

Iris will never be those women. The ones who think it's their duty to suffer.

The chef tipped the wok towards the camera as he added the other ingredients, tossing them high with a flick of his wrist before offering the handle to Eveline. The guest of the day, Eveline Poon was a young actress promoting her first lead. She had the release dates written on her palm, the hand now shaking as she made a flustered series of excuses. Half of the ingredients scattered across the hob. Eveline froze. Horrified. Iris's co-host patted the actress on the arm. "Don't worry, he'll be too busy admiring your face to notice."

The actress caught Iris's eye, a canary in the coal mine begging for a kindly word. Iris had her own career to consider. She looked away. Forced herself to chuckle along. "You know what they say about vixens." Her tongue stuck to her palate. The co-host was oblivious, prattling on about something else. Eveline took the reprieve to close her eyes. Her face was long and sharp as the fox she was, eyes winged with red liner. When she spoke, Iris couldn't help but listen. Less brassy than expected, Eveline's body language did most of the communication for her. And right now with lips tightly pressed together, rubbing her thumb into her palm, it was clear how she was feeling.

The actress perched on the tall bar stool like a garden bird. Her strappy slingbacks clicked on the footrest. Alert, tilting her head this way and that. Even those who didn't yet know her, knew her mother, an award-winning singer with a voice like liquid smoke. And Eveline's grandmother had been a Chinese opera actress. It was in the blood. Or the face. The gift of a shape-shifting huli jing after all, lent itself to the entertainment field.

Demo time. Iris watched in morbid fascination as the beautiful face before her twisted and suddenly her own features stared back.

"Outstanding!" her co-host declared. "Right down to the fat mole on her chin!"

For all the times she'd stared at the mirror applying make-up or giving herself confidence talks, Iris'd never seen her own face before. Not like this. Moving independent of her control. It had retained Eveline's mannerisms, the regal bearing. Someone who didn't ask the price as she handed over a platinum credit card. Who felt at home when faced with a veritable orchestra of silver and glassware at dinner.

The faces blurred like paint muddying the water. Now a crooked-toothed grandfather; a popular footballer with manicured facial hair; a long-dead musician; and finally back to herself. Eveline was visibly breathless, touching her face surreptitiously as if to be certain it had returned. Witchcraft ran through family lines, but not all learned to control it so well.

"What would you've done," Iris blurted out impulsively, "if you didn't inherit?" They would finish with Eveline shape-shifting into a red fox – that was the plan. The director was in her earpiece, demanding a return to the script. Nevertheless she repeated the question. "What did *you* want to do?"

Eveline's eyes met hers, the eyes that had not really changed throughout all the faces. She stopped rubbing her palm. "I wanted to go into politics. Change the world."

The silence was palpable. Politics was not the agenda of their light morning show. Iris knew she ought to shut it down before they found a more malleable substitute. She leaned forward, conspiratorially. The young actress emulated her actions, coming to meet her in the middle.

A little sister wanting to hear the advice. "Can you at least sort out your eyebrows before you start on world peace?"

Iris laughed. Forced the sound from somewhere in her belly, wiping imaginary tears from her eyes. Her co-host and the others joined in, chortling at the joke. Only Eveline was silent, her pale face blotchy around the cheeks. A wordless noise of amusement in her earpiece, muffled snorts from the camera crew. Her biting remark had steered them back on track. Swivelling directly to camera one, Iris paused for effect and then started chanting. "Vixen, vixen, vixen." Quiet at first then building to a heckling crescendo. The chef banged a ladle against a pan and the backstage staff stamped along. A ripple passed through Eveline's face. Her features did not change but all the same, she'd donned a mask.

The old woman's hand is tapping on the table as she shells melon seeds at her care home bed. Probably cursing yet another victim. The other occupant of the shared room is out, a knitted throw is curled up at the end of her unmade bed like a sleeping cat. They had blankets like that once. Ones with holes so big she could push her hand inside. Ones that smelt of moth balls and spilt sauce.

Iris dumps the fruit basket her PA bought on a side table, indifferent to the Get Well cards she flattens. She perches on the edge of the sagging wipe-clean chair and looks at her grandmother. Everything is deflated: the out-of-shape top hanging from bone-thin limbs, skin almost translucent apart from blue veins that run like tributaries up the back of her hands.

"You look like shit," Iris says finally. "You should move to a better facility. I've offered to pay."

"You mean when your secretary sent snacks at New Year bearing your excuses? No. I like the nurses here. They know me. And I help them."

Cursing their exes, their boss, their mother-in-law probably. An old auntie sticking her nose into every disagreement with tactless advice. "About that…"

"I watch your show. I know what that fortune teller said." The old woman looks unperturbed at her impending demise. The gift manifested in only one person at a time in each family. Iris waits an appropriate length of time. About as long as it takes for the clock ticking to annoy her and her mind to wander to what is for dinner. Her Chelsea boots tap impatiently on the vinyl floor. "Any chance you can pass it to someone else?"

A wheezing hiccup bursts from her grandmother's mouth. It has her clutching at her right side and banging her fist on the small table. Red melon shells jump. Scatter. Belatedly Iris realises her por por is laughing. It passes, petering out like a slow drip. "I'll pass it on to old Mrs Nguyen in room five, shall I?"

Iris doesn't really expect it to work. But it's always better to ask the direct question in case. And there is always a solution. "Let's brainstorm other workarounds."

Her grandmother reaches out and rights the cards and personal effects that have been knocked over by the fruit basket. "I get it. It's not glamorous or well known. It's peculiar. But guess what, it's who we are."

Her grandmother strikes the nerve. Pinches it. The image Iris has built for herself – for her public – is sophistication. This doesn't fit. None of it. Nightmares fill her sleep. Hammering a designer heel into the red carpet; pulling off her director's brogue shoe to smack it against his skull; her make-up artist fleeing the dressing room as she smashes a loafer into the mirror again and again. Except the last isn't a dream. It was earlier in the day. The reason she finally decided to visit.

"You're already cursing people – every week on the TV. Only you use a different weapon." Her grandmother reaches behind her pillow and pulls out her villain-hitting shoe. It is the same as Iris remembers, but patched up with thick brown tape. "Villain-hitting is an act of cleansing."

"Bull shit is what it is," says Iris.

Por Por flinches but does not scold. Iris is an adult now after all. She'd been so afraid when she was young. Worried someone in her year would drop dead, set on fire or break out in warts after seeing her grandmother curse them. Relief turned to bitterness when she realised their witchcraft was nothing like others. Good for absolutely nothing.

Still Iris's hands yearn to grab the mangy old shoe. Knows instinctively it will fit into the curve of her palm. Ugly and broken and useless. She can hear the ringing noise it will make. The tang of ink in the paper tiger's mouth.

It was the smell that gave it away. The stench of the boys' locker room. Weeks-old sweat and cheap deodorant. Iris unzipped her PE bag at the side of the sports hall. Filthy old trainers had been shoved atop her kit. She pulled them out by their entangled laces and launched them across the room at the boys who were already pointing and laughing. One smacked the nearest lad on the knee, his friends ducking. "That's you cursed!"

Iris charged over to them, heat rising from her toes up through her body until she felt like she would burst. "You arseholes. You absolute, shitty arseholes!"

She should've said something more coherent. Thought about how to retaliate. But Iris couldn't temper her rage. Kicked at the nearest one, toe clipping his shin. He yelped but his face was a picture of delight. "She's going for it! Hide all the paper! Quick!"

They giggled, the three of them dancing around her as she kicked out. Wildly missing the mark as wrath dwindled into humiliation. They were toying with her and yet she couldn't stop; not without letting them win. They'd blocked any retreat by encircling her.

"Enough." The word rang like a door slamming. At twelve, classmate Lei-Ming had grown white scales like teenage acne. Her adoptive parents were aghast but Lei-Ming figured out her witchcraft soon enough. When the bullies had come for her, she'd charmed them with flattery and home-made treats. They stopped messing with her after her desserts turned them into turtles. Shame the effect was only temporary.

"Fun's over," said the tall boy, wrinkling his nose like he had been the one wronged. Lei-Ming stood beside Iris, looking down her nose at the retreating boys despite being shorter. Her reputation for being cold-blooded rang true. A real adder in the grass. "Want to grab lunch?"

Iris saw the question for what it was. Lei-Ming tugged self-consciously at her cardigan sleeves, her limbs having outgrown it by some margin. The reptilian scales ran up her neck and across her face like a rash. Her school bag was the same one she had last year, dog-earred around the edges. Strength in numbers didn't work when those numbers were both a big fat zero. Iris pushed incredulity into her tone, scoffing at the hand of friendship. "With a snake? No."

Lei-Ming stared at her for a long moment before her eyes dropped to Iris's feet. Leather school shoes passed down from her brother. Iris twisted on the ball of her foot, hiding one shoe behind the other.

"Good luck witch," the white snake said.

"I'm not a witch" Iris shot back. Her neck ached like whiplash.

The story breaks an hour before the show. Iris is in her dressing room, ignoring the twitching make-up artist. They haven't replaced the mirror yet. Her face stares back in multitudes through the cracks. The director bursts into the room, brandishing his phone. "Eveline Poon is running for parliament!"

The announcement rolls in her head like marbles in a maze. She understands the individual words and yet as a whole, the sentence doesn't make sense. "The actress?"

"Yes. She's quitting. Said it's her calling. Start with some open ended well wishes, that sort of thing."

"The actress?" Iris repeats unnecessarily. "The one who plays ninja assassins?"

"No one saw it coming." She's a huli jing after all. Shapeshifters are entertainers, sex symbols, that sort of thing. And villain-hitters are provincial old ladies under bridges like trolls.

It's as if Iris has removed a pair of shoes that pinch. Everything stops pulsing and rubbing at the corners of her awareness. The calluses are still there but she knows there's a better fit. "I want her on the show."

"Tonight? We aren't the news – she'll never agree!"

Iris stands to face her director. It doesn't matter that she's in a dressing gown or her hair in curlers. She is Iris Chen. "Video call will be fine. Tell her it's time to remove the masks."

After school, Iris's mother took her to the underpass by the subway. Cars on the motorway flew overhead and busy commuters in monochrome suits jostled without looking. But Iris and her mother – as well as a few tourists clutching heavy cameras – walked towards the shadows. Iris gripped her mother's hand, her palm sweaty.

In the gloom, a small group of women sat on plastic stools in front of disparate cardboard stalls. At first glance they looked like street sellers with counterfeit handbags, plastic flip flops or little yapping dog toys. But it was a different set up. Iris couldn't read all the signs but she saw the joss sticks and statues of gods. The smell of moth balls and damp reminded her of clothes bought from car boot sales and charity shops. The smell never washed out. Not entirely. Shoes were the worst: the imprint of someone else's feet beneath her own.

A camera clicked and she heard the tourists making giggling comments in their own language. "I don't want to."

"It's important." Her mother's voice was mild. As lukewarm as the limp hug she offered. With two older brothers and a third brewing in her mother's stomach, Iris knew this talk was reserved for her. For daughters. "She's your grandmother."

In the dim light Por Por's wrinkles deepened into crevices. She coughed and spat onto the ground, unaware she had an audience. Without the TV on at full volume, or hands peeling fruit to push on her grandchildren, Iris didn't recognise her. Just another old witch.

The woman's wizen face glowed as she gestured them over. The tattered signs were no better nor worse than her peers' but Por Por took great pleasure in showing Iris what each of them meant: letting her hold a paper tiger and touch the special shoe. It was disappointingly not a giant wooden clog or a metal spiked stiletto like her imagination had led her to believe. A sturdy leather mule. Mundane. The same pair Por Por had worn last year. Good reverberations, her grandmother said, demonstratively thwacking it against a brick. The sound echoed like ripples in water. Iris shuddered.

"Well?" Por Por said. She was supposed to offer a name. A villain for Por Por to hit for demonstration. Someone to curse. Iris stared down, twisting on the ball of one foot as if she could dig her way out of the situation. In the end, her mother offered a name on her behalf. A peer who'd done better on the class test. Por Por smacked her lips together with satisfaction and wrote the name on a long strip of rice paper.

The shoe in Por Por's hand smacked down. Hammering on the paper like a blacksmith at the anvil. She turned it, moved it, evenly distributing the beating as she talked under her breath. Words Iris would've been reprimanded for using at school. The paper was shredded thin by the ministrations, her classmate's name unrecognisable. Iris's hand pulsed with each strike like she'd delivered the blows herself: one at a time across the other girl's cheeks. It made her sick and dizzy and just a little bit elated.

They needed to feed the tiger and ask for blessings. But Iris's eyes were fuzzy and she shook her head. Kept shaking it as her mother sighed in exasperation and her por por finishing the ceremony anyway. It'd started raining, just enough that Iris could feel the water seeping in, soaking into her hand-me-down socks.

"One day, you might get the gift. A dying skill," her mother said on the subway ride. Iris looked at the crushed coffee cup that had rolled into a corner, a pool of beige leaking from its side. She heard the tourists further down the carriage, looking at their photos. One of them took off his sandal and brandished it at a friend.

Eveline's face is magnified on the screen. Bright and round as a supermoon. The cutting cheekbones of youth have matured into softer lines but her eyes are the same. She sits in front of a bookcase, shelves heavy with thick hardback volumes, dog-eared paperbacks and towers of magazines. Not the minimalist decor Iris is expecting.

They exchange small talk, warm-up laps before the actual event. It's easy for Iris. Her guest has been around for almost as long as she has. Familiar with the banter that's to be expected. That's the problem: slipping back into old habits.

"I've a confession to make." Iris steers the conversation with a deft hand on the tiller. "I never thought much of you as an actress."

The studio audience are divided. Gasps and embarrassed laughter. "If we're being honest, neither did I." Eveline launches into a prepared speech about her political stance and reforms she wants. Whether or not she will make a good leader is a matter for the future. They are here about the past.

"Tell me, what was it about being an actress you hated the most? The red carpets or the free-flowing champagne?" Iris is still cutting, despite truly wanting the answer.

"Being typecast. Script after script of duplicitous sirens. Murdered wives. I'm more than that." When she speaks Eveline's face is more animated than any of the masks. Her mouth frowns and twists to one side. It is not an attractive look on her, but one which demands a second glance.

Iris writes on a large piece of paper. It's not Por Por's calligraphy brush and she isn't even certain it's spelt correctly. *Expectations.*

She slips off her gold platform shoe. A murmur of realisation spreads across the studio. "I hate my family gift. Being some warty old witch isn't really my style." She allows the audience – her colleagues with their headsets, the crowd in the tiered seating as well as those watching at home – a moment to catch their breaths. To laugh at her for being late to the game. Alvin, watching at home with his new partner; Ying probably still at the office, hair wrapped around a pen signing contracts as she drinks another cup of tea.

And her por por. Propped up in the hospital bed with extra cushions, squinting at the tiny screen in the corner of her room as she falls into her forever sleep.

Iris speaks as much to all of them as she does to herself.

She slips the shoe back onto her foot. It doesn't feel right. She's worn many shoes. Preloved and brand-new. Ones that blistered her little toe and rubbed her ankles. Others that were as comfortable as slippers. She wears them like armour, but for this she needs a weapon. "It's not about cursing your enemies. It's about letting them go." Iris pulls a statuette down from the shelf behind her. An entertainment award she's won five years in a row. Everything she's worked towards. Everything she's trying to preserve. It's heavy. The right sort of weight.

Iris waits for Eveline's response. The huli jing looks confused at first, waiting for the punchline. The talk show host's trademark barbs to jab her in the side. Slowly, she softens like a hedgehog uncurling from a ball. Nods. "Destroy their expectations."

Iris doesn't know whose expectations any more. Her family resigned to crouching on the bottom rung. Her audience braying for outrage faster than she can deliver. Or her own: jostling her way to the top by elbowing others out of the way.

Iris hefts the award on its side, hoping she isn't going to take a lump out of the table. But even if she does, she can talk her way round that. Like a magpie picking the shiny bits, the quirky things made of yarn and beads. Picking them and pulling them apart with a mocking caw. That's her gift. But this time she's searching for the pebbles. Minuscule pieces of gravel lodged in her shoe. Digging into her flesh with every step. Never letting others in. She thought Eveline was the caged bird.

It was her all along.

The villain-hitter strikes the paper. Letters dent and break as she hammers. Curses. Her hair slick against her forehead, her make-up sliding. Each hit reverberates back through Iris's hand, up her wrist and into her skull. Sparking notions in her mind. Hopeful thoughts pierce through rips in the paper. Perhaps Jenny Lam can give her advice. Perhaps she could cajole Ying to have a day off. Perhaps she can be friends with Eveline rather than rivals.

She hits the paper until it shreds into fragments like confetti. Unreadable. The knots inside her fray and break. Her arm aches, her hand throbs but her head is clear. Iris leans back in her chair, kicking her shoes off. "So," she says into the stunned silence, "this is a new segment in the show."

Camera one. Camera two. The shadow of an audience behind. All reactions unclear. Each waiting for another to respond first.

"Could you do *talk show hosts* next week?" Eveline says from the screen.

Iris smiles. "That, I can do."

Editors' Note:

The folk tradition of villain hitting, still practised in Hong Kong today, does feel like an anachronistic and embarrassing gift for anyone to be burdened with. So, Iris's desire to resist her birthright and reach instead for a modern life of her own choosing is all too believable. All of which makes Eliza's skilful reconciliation of the intergenerational attitudes towards respect for tradition versus individual desires in this sharp but ultimately touching story all the more impressive.

Mhairi Aird

Lorraine Wilson

Mhairi Aird returns to the village of her birth and banishment when she is thirty-three years of age. She thinks, and she is right, that few will recognise her now from the blue-eyed, skipping child of fourteen, or the bruised-eyed, tatter-limbed wraith of fifteen who paid passage over the sea in the timber boats with the last of her childhood. She comes back on a pony bought in Dundee for a far lesser price and her cloak is the green of ivy. The bag on her back clinks softly, she carries with her the scent of pine and winter, herbs and blood.

At the edge of the village she touches a bruise on her inner arm once, not for luck which she has no truck with, but for the reminder of payments and promises made. She might look alone, but it is a lie.

Passing her old house above the west harbour cliffs she doesn't pause any longer than it takes to know that her mother is dead. A child is sitting in the garden with a raggedy dog and a stick, the vegetable beds healthy with a young woman's vigour. She smells the harbour before she sees it in between the watchful gorse; the lady of Dunino is keeping a wary eye but Mhairi would do the same so she ignores the yellow eyes in the flowers. Breathes in iodine and salt, the sharp tang of a thousand gutted herring, fresh and fetid. The boats are out of course. The men who held the rocks and boathooks and pre-written confessions, they are all out on the water, and men are fearful creatures she has come to learn. Of blood and the unknown, most often, although also of gentleness. Women are too used to blood to fear it, and they contain a good half-dozen unknowns so what is left for them to fear? Aloneness, Mhairi believes, and sometimes hope. Their own endless anger if they are honest. Mhairi Aird is, but she doesn't fear her anger any more.

It is not the men she has come for this fine morning.

Two women are on their doorsteps, brushes in hands and hair escaping from their scarves, they watch her sharp and curious. Not a flicker of recognition. Why, they are thinking, would a woman not quite fine but definitely finer than them be riding alone into their small harbour? Why indeed. Because of a fisherman left adrift in Stavanger with one leg shattered beyond repair and drunk on rum and pain, clutching at Mhairi, talking in a language she hadn't even dreamed in for years. Because of how the whole North Sea is merely a speck in the eye of the world, strung across with shared blood and shared legends in some shivering web. Stories are the warp, she thinks, and we are the weft, and however wide the loom it can still cast us home.

"I'm looking for the house of Babbet Fisher," she says to the women.

"Babbet Fisher? What'll you be wanting with her?"

Mhairi holds the pony steady with one hand, raises an eyebrow. So much, she has learned, is about how you expect the world to treat you.

"Down Nethergate West, just above the mill," the same woman says. She shifts her feet. They likely ache, Mhairi thinks. She'll have been on them since before dawn and when the boats come in she'll have hours more standing, her hands cracking with cold, salt, the edge of her knife. Mhairi's own hands are strong from setting bones and delivering children, the gutting scars long faded white and all the silver fishscales gone. The bruise on her arm throbs night-quiet and she does not thank the women, or say farewell, only heels the pony on and searches her memory for the right path. The bag slung over her shoulder clinks softly.

Babbet opens the door with a child of perhaps twelve just behind her. They both stare, wordless for very different reasons, because Mhairi had never doubted Babbet would recognise her, and she is right.

"M… Mhairi Aird? Mhairi, is it you?" Shock, horror, a glimmer perhaps of relief. Mhairi is ushered in, Babbet checking the street and the occluded sea before shutting the door. They sit in the main room, the light through its one small window white and clear. Straight off the water; Mhairi glances at it, checking. She has grown used to light bent between sea and forest, and she wonders how far out the herring boats are today, how rough the swell. She knows the waters will be cold as death, and dark as sin. The creature was willing enough last night.

I know you, it had said.

Mhairi had eyed the scars on its flanks that matched her own. *I know you too*, she had replied.

Babbet puts the kettle over the fire, then takes it off again to fill from the jug, puts it back, fiddles further. There are soot stains on her fingertips and Mhairi tsks softly.

"Stop swithering and face me," she says.

Babbet flinches. She sends the girl out to finish the net mending, lowers herself finally onto the other chair. "Why are you come back, after all this time?"

Mhairi settles her bag down close against her knee. She is far more tense than she appears, but she suspects that Babbet has lost the ability to read her. "I wanted to talk to you."

Another flinch, not surprisingly. "Where have you been? I thought you'd have…"

"Died?" Mhairi allows herself a smile. "Nearly enough, a time or two. But no, I'm neither dead nor broken, Babbet Lowry. Not any more."

"It's Fisher," Babbet says. "It's Fisher now." She glances over her shoulder towards the back door, the hidden daughter.

"Aye, so I heard," Mhairi agrees. "Lachlan Fisher. You fool."

Babbet bristles but like a cornered cat, Mhairi thinks. Beneath the fur, brittle bones. "He's a—"

"Bully? A coward who enjoys pressing girls and drowning them for the crime of refusing his hand? Quick with his fists like his father? Willing to sell his own soul for a whiff of power?" If she gives Babbet time to answer, she will only tangle herself up trying to deny what the whole village knows. "Why him?" she asks instead.

Babbet turns her head. There are lines around her eyes now, streaks of white in her hair. Mhairi is the same of course. "Because he offered," Babbet says quietly. "Because I'd been your friend and no one else was wanting me. Because he runs a good boat and I kent my bairns wouldnae hunger."

The kettle boils and Babbet jerks to her feet, finding cups and pouring water into each, then ale, the room filling with yeast and steam. Mhairi takes the proffered cup and turns it within her hands. None of Babbet's reasons surprise her, but when Babbet reached forward there were bruises around her wrists. Mhairi came here on a wave of vengeance; the grief catches her unawares.

"Better to marry none than him," she says. They are the exact words she said to this same woman when they were both children, and did not understand the consequences. "I remember," she carries on slowly, "when you wanted to cut your hair, dress in trews and go to sea in the timber boats, cross the waters looking for adventure."

"I was young and glaikit," Babbet says.

"You were to call yourself Will," Mhairi carries on. "You were to bind your breasts and live free of all of this." Gesturing with the cup at the room, the village, womanhood, motherhood, destiny. She came for vengeance, but it is possible there's room too for salvation. If she wants it.

"I was—"

"Young," Mhairi finishes, leaning forward over the table. The bag beside her clinks softly. She holds Babbet's wary gaze. "Young, aye, but not stupid. Brave, true, hopeful."

They look at one another; outside someone calls for Isa and Jaimi to come away home.

"So was it brave and true and hopeful for you to refuse Lachlan, and refuse Benn? Or was it witchery and the deil's ain wish?" Babbet means it like a blow, but it lost all ability to hurt eighteen years ago.

Mhairi frees one hand from the cup, turns her palm up on the table. Babbet eyes it like it might hold answers, or become a fist, they can after all be the same thing. "What is witchery," Mhairi says, "but women who the men fear?"

Babbet hisses in a breath, but she doesn't move away.

"What is witchery," Mhairi says, "but women being brave, and true, and hopeful; instead of obedient, afeart, dishonest to their own selves. I wasnae a witch when I was pressed, when your own husband dragged me broken to the harbour for a drowning, when my dearest friend turned her back. I wasnae a witch, I was just a girl who couldnae lie."

She has shed too many tears over these very words to shed them now. But the scar of it remains. Someone who has lost a limb can still feel it, she has been told, and her mourning for her child self is like that. Babbet sniffs, scowls but the seas in her eyes reveal her.

"You are no witch," Mhairi says to her very quietly. This is the first thing she came all these miles to say, she surprises herself by laying it down as gently as a babe. "You are just a boy who learned to lie."

"No," Babbet whispers.

"Aye," Mhairi whispers back. She reaches out, takes Babbet's hand in hers, uncurls the fingers. "It's not so rare, you know. You'd be shocked at the people I've known, at the secrets you uncover from the ill and the dead." She smiles, taps the very centre of Babbet's palm. "Once I laid out a fine lady died of fever, and found a man's body beneath all her clothes. Had a sailor come asking for a way to stop his monthlies so he'd no need to hide them aboard ship. Birthed a babe who was neither one nor t'other, but had the best pair of lungs on it I'd ever known." Mhairi doesn't ken what happened to that bright-eyed bairn, after she left them at their mother's breast. She hopes not the thing she fears.

"No," Babbet repeats, but differently this time. "The sailor…"

Mhairi lifts a shoulder. "Where did you think half those shanties were coming from if not a kernel of truth?"

"But that's…" Babbet crosses herself. With the hand not laying beneath Mhairi's fingertips. "Tis sinful."

"There are worse sins," Mhairi says. "Like drowning a child. Like beating a wife. Like not loving the heart your god gave you."

Babbet bends her head, loose hairs falling around her cheeks. Mhairi thinks of last night, the bowl full of herbs, moonlight and blood, the tide rising. It shouldn't matter too much what happens here, she will still remember being dragged down Shoregate weeping, Babbet in her doorway with her mother, turning away. So it shouldn't matter. But ever since that broken Fifer mentioned Lachlan Fisher, mentioned his wife Babbet, she had not been able to shut her own door on the thought that maybe, maybe if she was not to carry her own hate to the grave, she needed to come home and set it down.

She was not a witch when they drowned her.

"Was it you," she says eventually, "who said I planned to never wed? See, Lachlan and Benn only knew I'd refused them, but the witchhunter had a piece of paper saying I'd sworn a pact with the deil to be his own bride and none other's. So I wondered. Because it was only you I talked to of that, just like it was only me you talked to of Will."

Babbet pushes to her feet. A cat they neither had seen hisses and skitters out the door. Babbet follows it, stands in the doorway with her hands folded across her stomach. She is broader now than she was, softened by childbearing and hardened by life, but standing with the light behind her, time falls away like a tide. Fish scales glitter on the hem of her skirts.

"Aye, it was," Babbet says a little too loudly. "Or as good as. I told Mam, she told that man. I didnae mean—" She stops.

Mhairi nods slowly. There is never any point to the rest of that sentence, and it is besides no more than she expected.

"Do you remember the day we ran from Nana Wishart after stealing her berries?"

There is silence. The cat slinks back into the house, seeking warmth, waiting like the women for the boats.

"Is that why you're back?" Babbet says finally. "Come to make me pay? How will you do it? You've more money than I." She points at Mhairi's cloak. "I've nothing but two half-grown bairns and a husband you knew well enough not to want. Did you come to hex me? Are you a witch now because we condemned you to it? Is that how you're come so fine?"

Mhairi laughs. It sticks in her throat like a bone. She sips the cooling ale and comes to a decision. "I'll not hex you, Babbet Lowry. I've no need." She points in turn, to the bruises on Babbet's arms. Babbet flinches. "You've paid enough already, I'm thinking."

"Then what?" She sounds like a child.

"I came to see if you still deserve my hate," Mhairi says, at least a little honest. "But now I'm here, mayhap I should tell you a secret instead."

Babbet's eyes widen. No one is ever immune to hidden things.

Mhairi reaches down into her bag, pulls out a bottle and places it on the table. It is the blue of evening and small enough to conceal in a palm, and the thick glass cannot quite hide its shimmer.

"There's better things than drowning, Babbet Lowry, if you've the courage."

"Drowning?" Babbet's eyes are on the bottle, she takes a step forward. It has that effect on people. "I'm no drowning."

"Hmm." Mhairi sips her ale again. "Are you not?"

Another step forward. "I have my bairns."

"Aye," Mhairi says. "So you do. And do they mean you no longer dream?"

"Of what? Leaving him? Being…" Her voices trails off, the wanting has been wordless for too long.

"Being your own self. Being Will. Being free."

"Are *you* free? Alone and without bairns to care for you when you're auld, without a husband to keep you? Aye, it's a pretty thought. Being my ain self, but it doesnae set food on the table, it doesnae keep you safe from dangers."

Mhairi reaches into her boot, pulls out a knife and lays it beside the bottle. She taps first one then the other. "I've this to keep me safe, and this and my own two hands to set food on the table. I drowned once. It'll not happen again."

She thinks of the creature, wet mane shining and blood on its blunt teeth.

I am hungry, it had murmured against her palm.

I ken, she had whispered. *Take this and feed for the both of us. It'll keep ye safe from their hooks.*

The light through the small window has dulled.

Babbet doesn't notice.

Mhairi puts the knife away again but leaves the bottle. It only takes another minute to do the trick.

"What is that? A potion is it? What for?"

"For you," Mhairi says. She nudges it forward and Babbet cannot resist, picks it up, holds it to the light, tipping the liquid inside like a tiny starfilled sea.

"What is it? Is this how I will pay?"

"If you like. Or it can be how you will be free," Mhairi says. This is a risk, of course. It would only take Babbet's raised voice to bring neighbours, only take her speaking Mhairi's name, or showing them this bottle to condemn Mhairi a second time. But life is full of moments like these, Mhairi has realised. Where two futures hang in the space between your hands and only your god can choose between them. Childbirth, death, the breath before a kiss, a ship hanging on the cusp of a wave in a storm; forgiveness. You can either fear them or not, and she's not fond of fearing things if she can help it. "One drop in his ale, once a day. Takes a month thereabouts. Ten drops will take an hour but it's harder to explain away."

Babbet does not move; the bottle still raised, she might not even be breathing. Mhairi takes another sip of ale, sets it down. The day is drawing on, she thinks, and it's a fair ride to St. Andrews. She wondered if she would feel the pull of it, once she returned. The gorse and fishscales, grey stone and mother tongue enough to make her homesick, but no. She misses the forest, she misses living amongst people who have not tried to kill her.

"It's no an easy thing," she says, meaning so many things, but only one of them for Babbet. "There's a cost to freedom, you ken. I paid mine in my own blood. You can pay for yours with his."

Babbet shudders, lowers her hand finally and turns. Her mouth forms a word, but nothing comes out. She understands now, Mhairi thinks, exactly what Mhairi has come so far to offer. It is a knife without a handle, salvation and revenge, it is that most terrible of things – a choice.

"There were others," Babbet whispers.

Mhairi cants her head, measuring. "So there were. You think them more deserving then?" It occurs to her this might be the most important question she's asked. Mhairi remembers drowning, screaming into the salt-dark and listening sea. She remembers the faces of the folk who watched just as well as she does the ones who held her down.

But Babbet shakes her head, and Mhairi decides she is glad at how this has unfolded after all.

"He'll be back soon."

If this is a threat, Mhairi is not the one afeart. She looks out the window, raises one eyebrow, dusts off her hands.

"For honesty's sake," she says, rising, settling her bag across her shoulders. It feels lighter now. "I've not made a habit of this sort of thing. But I've hated you long enough." Babbet sucks in a breath, Mhairi carries on. "I hated the men for my broken bones and dreams of drowning but I hated *you* for betraying me. I see it now though."

She waits, Babbet waits.

"You have betrayed yourself also, Babbet Lowry, and I am the only one who is free."

The girl child appears in the doorway. Her feet are muddy but her face is clean and not nearly so thin as many. She eyes the two of them silently, and Babbet moves her hand so the bottle is out of sight, held between finger and thumb like an arrowhead.

"The haar's coming in," the child says.

Mhairi smiles slow. The haar's coming in, the boats are out and the water as dark as sin. She will be gone long before Babbet realises she came a-hunting more than one old ghost.

"It'll keep," Mhairi says now. "As long as you need. And I suppose

I will sleep softer knowing you have a choice. That's all I was wanting in coming here – my own heart's ease." He runs a good boat, she wasn't about to trust his fate entirely to a stranger, beautiful and fierce though it was.

The men will call it a monster, for those two things as much as for the haar and the blood. It is always the way.

"The deil's choice," Babbet whispers hoarsely.

"Aye, so it is," Mhairi says. "But better than none at all."

Babbet is as pale now as she was that day. The bruises on her arms matching those once laid on Mhairi's arms by the same man; the bairns and the boats pulling on her like a tide. It is cruel, Mhairi knows, but it is also just.

"Mam?" the girl says. She has cuts on her hands already, healing clean. The sea loves best those it wounds.

"Good afternoon," Mhairi says to her. "Did you know, lass, there's a small island called Vassøy near Stavanger over the water." The girl stares, Babbet makes a soft, wordless sound. "It's surrounded by the sea and covered in forest. A person can build a life there."

"Who are you?" the girl says, and finally Babbet's fingers close around the bottle. It vanishes within her palm.

"No one," she says, "You wheesht, Suibhan. Just a fine lady come to pass on a message from an old friend."

"Aye." Mhairi laughs, then turns to leave. "Tell your mam to heed it now, you hear, Suibhan Fisher?"

Babbet is wise enough to quail at that. The woman this village made of Mhairi, knowing her child's name – it is no small thing if Mhairi were inclined. She is not.

"Tell your mam forgiveness is no simpler than freedom. Tell her Will is waiting."

The pony whickers a welcome and she pats its strong neck, then mounts in a swirl of ivy-green cloak.

"I'm no you," Babbet says. "I'm no what it is ye are become." She is not watching the bone white mist approaching over the water. Her daughter frowns up at her.

"No, I ken," Mhairi says. "So who are you instead? Whose are you, Babbet Lowry?"

She looks at the water where a raven is riding the changing wind.

Canny creature, she thinks. Her old friend might not understand of course, it depends how true her guilt, how fierce her anger. But Mhairi is done here. She drowned once, and learned long ago that it is not only monsters who take payment in blood.

The girl and the woman stand in their doorway surrounded by ghosts old and new and not-yet-but-coming. Mhairi Aird smiles for all of them. She rides away from the village of her birth and banishment carrying the scent of salt and childhood, herbs and blood.

Editors' Note:

The knowledge that Scotland had a Witchcraft act between the 16th and 18th centuries that enabled thousands of women to be persecuted, tortured and killed on any pretext adds all the context required to understand both Mhairi Aird's righteous anger and the aid she offers Babbet. Those women received a formal apology from the Scottish government in 2022, but the anger Lorraine has etched into every page of this story justifiably remains.

Shoals

Morag Edward

There was nothing left to fish for, not anymore. In silted-up harbours, the bleached skeletons of boats and old creels shared the mud with tyres, boilers and fridges. Even the rock pools were devoid of life, swirling with empty crab and mussel shells. The North Sea was barren.

It was a flat, calm pre-dawn when the first dead fisherman washed ashore. Slowly, heavily, wetly, he staggered to his feet and step-step-stepped from the frothing surf to dry land. Halfway up the beach, he turned back to face the sea and sat down. He watched the waves as the next fisherman emerged. And the next. And the next.

Thirty thousand dead watched the sun break free from the marine horizon. Some were still wearing their boots. From others trailed faint strands of wet woven fishing net, an umbilical cord connecting them all to their deep-sea mother.

This midwinter solstice brought a seabed resurrection, and the dead of every trawler boat, lifeboat and whaling fleet ever sent out from the Scottish coast came back together. It was time for the lost to come ashore and pay their respects to those who'd had no burial at sea. In these old villages, the kirkyards were for land-locked men, and all the women who tradition and tragedy had left behind.

The dead seafolk walked across the high-tide cordon of plastic debris and golf balls, odd shoes and cormorant-strangling beer can rings. Then they headed inland.

They wore the tang of brine, seaweedy sweat and wet wool, which hung in the crisp air over their glittering fish-scale footprints.

The sea dead walked through the kirkyards of every village along the coast, searching for their surnames. No dog barked at them; no cat ran from them. Even in the bright winter light, their damp and raggedy bodies cast no shadows. In the distance, the boom of waves counted down Davy Jones's curfew.

Each of the dead held offerings to place on the graves. They had pockets full of sea glass and scrimshaw, and held bunches of kelp and bladderwrack. They took handfuls from the hedgerows as they walked, adding bouquets of ivy, holly and yew.

They sang out in rough, weather-beaten tenor and bass, sang all round the old kirks and into the graves. But the dry dead took their time in waking. The fishermen kept on singing.

The sun rested for a while in the treetop branches among the rooks and crows, and their empty nests.

The mossy graves slowly birthed family and friends. The land dead emerged to find singing and sunlight waiting for them. Generations reunited in the kirkyards all around the coast and on every island. They walked down to the shores, hand-in-hand, arm-in-arm, down to the water. Lost trawlermen and fishwives, their kinfolk, spouses, whores and sweethearts, all finally making the journey together, for even the hardest heart had softened, and old prejudices had been scoured away by the endless tides.

The dead fishing communities filled the winter air with song. From every clifftop, shingle beach and harbour wall drifted the melodies and harmonies of the sea: white sandbanks, green whirlpools and the icy crushing black depths of the deepest trenches. The dead stared out to sea as they sang and drummed, watching the white horses. The silver ghosts of long-gone shoals of fish stared back at them.

The tide turned; the sea rose. It was almost time to start again.

At sunset, each and every fisherman, each and every fishwife, and everyone in between, shed their old clothes and earthy shrouds, and walked together into the waves. The current swept them offshore, and out there, they sank to the bottom.

Lit by the final light of the shortest day, all those who'd ever lived off the sea broke down at last, dissolving, scattering into fragments, distorting and shifting in the brine, becoming sleek, scaled fragments, then each sliver of their bodies became a fish.

Vast shoals of the new fish filled the shallow coastal waters and swam out into the depths. Herring, baggety, keeling, pinner, lythe, ling, hallow, splashhack, purr, smout, whiting, dab, gunnack, shiner, sand fluke and birdie, more and more long-gone fish birthed in every firth and estuary, prawns, scallop, skate and skeetack amassing round every little island. The sea sang with old life. From far, far away, there came the calls of the whales.

And on land, the kirkyards were empty enough for new generations of the dead.

Editors' Note:

With over 6000 miles of coastline and around 800 islands, it would be impossible for Scotland not to have a deep and abiding relationship with the sea. Morag's story is a brief but beautiful elegy for fishing communities wrecked over the years by climate change, pollution and politics. But it's a song of hope and renewal too. That penultimate paragraph teeming with the returning shoals fair glitters with joy.

New Town

David Goodman

We were on a fingertip search of Gloucester Lane, looking for the blood-sticky knife dumped by a fleeing gang kid as he ran up the hill from a stabbing in Stockbridge. I had my hands deep in a pile of damp, clinging leaves when I got the message from Gilmartin.

DS Iain Gilmartin > Boss, Jimmy's pulled an ASCU tag. Moray Place. You're near there, right?

I straightened up and glanced along the line of forensics techs, bent double, feet shuffling through autumn leaves, fingers questing for the tell-tale glint of metal or the dull stain of haar-dampened blood.

I straightened my fingers and typed a reply in my chromatics.

DI Gail Slater > One street over, Gloucester Ln. FTS for a murder weapon. Where are the vans?

I felt my heart start to hammer in my chest. We were close. Very close. I knelt again, sweeping through the leaves with one hand while I typed with the other. My hand closed around something hard and I let out a little hiss of victory as I cleared away the leaves.

Gilmartin > That's the best part. Stuck in traffic on Dean Bridge. They're going to be 15-20 mins at best. Bet you could get over there with some forensics techs, take the scene, get in amongst it.

Slater > Meet us there?

Gilmartin > On my way.

I looked up to find Bob Allinson, the forensics lead. He was a slim Englishman in his early forties, squatting in his white bunny suit, peering at a crushed drinks can through his irising evidence lenses.

"Bob, I need your team elsewhere."

Bob looked up. "We've still got another fifty metres to cover, Gail."

I held up the knife that my fingers had closed around a moment before. "No, we don't. And I've got an ASCU job to crash."

Allinson blinked, then pushed his lenses up on his forehead. He smiled. “Close?”

“Close,” I nodded, dropping the sticky knife into an evidence bag and stripping off my nitryl gloves. “Moray Place.”

The other techs were standing up, brushing dead leaves and cobble grit off their pristine white suits. They glanced nervously at one another.

Bob smiled again. “Jones, Khan, you stay here and look for secondary evidence. We’ll move the wagon round and get a crime scene perimeter established on this new job, you can walk over when you’re done.”

Then he turned to me. “Time to find out what, exactly, an ASCU job entails.”

New Town murders are always the worst. Rare, but always brutal and complicated. There’d been three this year, but this was the first marked for ASCU attention.

Now we were finally going to find out what the hell was going on, why eleven apparent murder scenes had been handed off to a new, specialist unit. A unit nobody had heard of before last year. Half the detectives in Edinburgh had been shunted aside by this special taskforce. We hadn’t even managed to find out what ASCU *meant*.

It would be something to do with money. It always was.

Moray Place was close enough I could walk it in a couple of minutes, arriving just as Allinson and his team parked up their wagon behind me.

My chromatics highlighted the building, a five-storey townhouse. An older gent in a waxed jacket emerged from the circular private park at the centre of Moray Place, trailing two wheezing golden retrievers. He gave me a nod. He knew a copper when he saw one. Power and money know their guardians.

I turned and gazed up at the elegantly fluted sandstone columns, rising to the slate-tiled roof, the intricately bevelled blockwork that surrounded the door. Sandstone from Craigleith Quarry, a couple of kilometres away. There was a retail park there now. But for three hundred years it supplied the stone that built the grand Georgian New Town.

I wondered what it would feel like under my fingers. A little crumbly maybe, a legacy of mid-twentieth century acid rain. Then, as I always did in this part of town, I thought about my great-great-great-grandfather, working in the sheds where they’d turned out columns and facings and balustrades like that, delicate traceries of stone. The silicosis that had killed him at thirty-eight, leaving behind five children.

I had an early photograph stored in my chromatics and I brought it up, running a query across the databases I'd trawled obsessively as a younger woman. He stared out from the photo, sepia tint doing little to soften the intensity of his stare. A young man then, who'd stayed young since.

Aye. He'd worked on this crescent. Swung his mallet and carved the fine, time-softened lines in front of me. I let out a slow breath. Hated this part of town. Rich folk. They want what they want and if you die giving it to them, well, that's your look out.

Across the road, a beat copper was standing, blinking in the low morning sunshine. He looked confused at who had pulled up. ForceCom tagged him for me. PC Graeme Peters.

"Morning, Peters. I'm taking PIO on this one."

Peters blinked. "Uh, it came up as ASCU-tagged, I'm supposed to—"

I shook my head, chuckled. "We're here now, I'm Principal Incident Officer, it's on me. What's the state of things in there?"

Peters shrugged, happy to be relieved of whatever was waiting inside. "Pretty grim," he said. "Housekeeper found him in the bathroom. Mackay took her to Torphicen station because she was screaming a lot. It's … it's … fucking weird."

Bob Allinson trotted up the steps with a scene lamp under one arm and sub-mil scanner under the other. "Good, I like weird. Lead the way, young man."

They disappeared inside, leaving the huge street door ajar.

As I crossed the threshold, I reached out and touched the sandstone doorway. The surface flaked under my touch, gritty. I left my hand there a moment.

Something happened to my lenses.

The chromatics flashed, like they were rebooting. When they came back online a heartbeat later, I saw the face of a man I didn't recognise, middle-aged. He was so close I flinched backwards. Static feedback burst in my earbuds. The man's face stretched into a silent scream, eyes rolling back in his head.

I whipped my hand away. The sandstone had *moved*. The face disappeared and my chromatics stuttered, then started looping through another image, my great-great-great-grandfather this time. The databases I'd accessed came up, the history of the New Town. I dismissed the open windows and blinked, staring at the doorway.

"Boss?" said the low, gruff voice of Iain Gilmartin behind me. I turned.

Gilmartin stood in the street, looking up at me. "You okay? I ragged the motor over from Haymarket. ASCU are still stuck on the Dean Bridge. Any idea why this is assigned to them?"

I blinked, shook my head, wondering what the hell happened to my chromatics. "I'm fine. Glitch in my lenses. No idea why this is ASCU. Uniform responder said it's weird, apparently."

Gilmartin grinned. He hadn't needed much convincing when I'd cooked up a scheme to try and intercept one of these jobs. He'd got a bollocking three months before for arguing with an ASCU squad that barged in on his investigation. That one was weird too – an apparent fire inside a tool shed that had left the charred body of a gardener behind but touched absolutely nothing else. Swept under the carpet by ASCU, again.

"Good," he said. "Weird's my middle name."

I grinned back. "Thought it was James?"

It *was* fucking weird.

"Jesus wept," I said. "What the *hell* did that? Where's the rest of him?"

Angus Dalziel lay on the cold black and white tiles, arms stretched towards the door. Balding, middle-aged, the picture of New Town prosperity, skin pale from blood loss behind a fading ski-slope tan. His face twisted in a rictus of incredible pain and fear, eyes open. His body ended, abruptly, at his waistline.

I swallowed as I got closer. The glitch in my visuals downstairs had certainly looked like the dead man in front of me.

I squatted. "What… could do this? Some kind of animal attack? How's there no blood spatter?"

"We've ruled that out already," said Allinson, cranking a scene lamp up and angling the light onto the corpse. "No bite marks, claw marks, tearing. Up close it looks more like … cauterisation, but there's no evidence of a heat source. No trace of bowel contents, no blood pool. A bit of seepage on the tile, but it's like someone just … disappeared the rest of him. Never seen anything like it."

I gestured to Allinson and Gilmartin, then walked through to the drawing room, a broad space running the full width of the building. More oak-panelled walls, lumpy antique couches in floral patterns. The huge windows flooded the room with grey light. The morning haar was burning off a little, traces of blue in the sky.

I sat down on one of the chintzy sofas. Gilmartin flopped down opposite. Allinson walked over to the window and stared out at the street.

I tapped at my workpad, running searches. "This Dalziel had a lot of connections with government. Used to be an advocate, then went sideways into specialist practice. He was a gun-for-hire for tech firms, last few years. Tax records show he worked for five or six firms a year, up until last year. Then he went to one. Reported well over two million convertible in post-tax income last year."

"Convertible? So, cross-border?" said Gilmartin.

"Aye. ScaleTech, they're called." I pulled up the company's details. "No idea what they actually do." I read for a moment. "*Complex linear environment replacement and nanoscale reactivity*. What the hell does that mean?"

"Some kind of cloud computing thing?" said Allinson.

I shook her head. "Stock photos are all folk in lab coats, not servers and stuff." I ran a search on a different database. "Wait a fucking minute. The whole company is ASCU-tagged."

Gilmartin frowned. "So any incident…"

I finished for him. "Absolutely anything happens on their premises or to anyone who works for them, it goes straight to ASCU."

Gilmartin grunted as he stood up, straightening his trousers. "These twats have swooped in eleven times that we've counted, then sealed the records after. That's not police work, that's cleanup. How are we supposed to do our jobs when ASCU shuts down half our cases?"

I nodded. "Exactly. This time we got here first. We can ask *them* a few questions."

When we came out into the hallway, one of Allinson's techs was standing at the head of the stairs, curving marble with a black metal railing and red carpeting running down the centre. He looked up.

"Company, boss. ASCU."

I braced my shoulders and walked towards the top of the stairs but, halfway there, something caught my eye. The wood panelling just outside the bathroom, looked … off. I stopped mid-stride. It was stained, somehow, but the darkened patch was *changing*. I leaned in close. The wood looked singed, blackened edges around a dark knot. Like someone had pressed a red-hot poker to it.

"What's—" I said, reaching out a hand towards the darkness.

"DI Slater! Don't touch that!" said a harsh voice behind me, oddly muffled.

I turned to see four figures at the top of the stairs, full biohazard suits.

Bright orange, with bulky hoods and clear visors. Three carried what looked like rifles. But they didn't look right. They were white instead of black, oddly curved, LEDs glowing along their flanks.

The nearest, another rifle slung at their side, strode over to me. As they approached, I saw the face of a young woman I recognised from the odd trip to HQ at Fettes. She had red, tightly curled hair, slick with sweat inside her suit.

"DI Slater, I need you and the forensics team to evacuate this site, right now."

I stared at the blinking LEDs, the suits. "What? What the hell is this space invader shite? What are you talking about?" Weeks of frustration bubbled up in me, at the way these people did exactly what they wanted, ignored all procedures, stamped all over our cases.

"Outside, *please*," said the woman.

I shook my head. "Listen, I'm sick of this, you ASCU people swooping in. I don't know why you're in full CBRN rig, or who these jokers are with the laser guns, but I've got a body in there. We can't just walk out on a crime scene. Nobody will even tell me what ASCU bloody *means*."

The woman exhaled, fogging her face plate. "I'm DI Susannah Lennox. I'm taking over as PIO, with immediate effect. I'll answer as many of your questions as I legally can, but we need to do it *outside*. Please."

I saw something in her eyes then, behind the brittle facade of authority. I saw fear. I opened my mouth again, a question forming.

Upstairs, a toilet flushed.

One of Allinson's techs emerged from yet another bathroom, zipping up his white forensic suit. It was MacPherson, a grad scheme trainee, gangly with short blonde hair. He blinked at all of us, staring up at him.

"You!" shouted Lennox, voice muffled by her suit. "What did you do?"

"I just, I just went—" he stammered.

"Perimeter, now!" Lennox yelled. The three figures with the rifles swung their weapons up and aimed them at the walls and floor. I stepped forwards, completely baffled. What were they doing?

"What—" I managed.

The house *screamed*.

It came from everywhere and nowhere. The walls pulsed. My earbuds screeched with feedback and I tore them out. The seething, oscillating wall of sound rose and fell as we all turned, hands clamped over our ears. It was a nearly-human shout of pain and anger, but dopplered, layered, overlapping, as though hundreds of voices were screaming together.

"You!" shouted Lennox over the unearthly wailing, pointing at MacPherson. "Down here!"

"What—" Allinson said, but Lennox cut him off.

"Everyone, in the centre of my group. Behind the coilguns, right now!"

Lennox turned and gestured again at MacPherson, who remained frozen, one floor up.

"Come *on*!" she screamed. The gangly young tech finally got moving, flailing down the stairs towards us, all arms and legs, holding on to the iron banister as his feet skidded on the marble. He'd reached the half-landing, with one more flight of stairs to go.

MacPherson stumbled and fell, but he didn't tumble down the stairs. The stairs *rose* to meet him, the marble twisting and convulsing. The walls became translucent, bending and twisting light in refracted, multi-chromatic waves.

MacPherson screamed. He sank into the not-marble, outstretched arm already covered in the same shimmering substance. He screamed again as it reached his neck. Bile rose in my throat as I watched the slick, strobing substance crawl to his mouth. He shrieked one, final, guttural exclamation of horror before his vocal chords were covered and he was abruptly cut off.

Lennox swore, wincing as they were buffeted with the redoubling wail of the house. "Muir, Robertson, secure the floor. Reynolds, hold and sweep, tail end. I'll take point."

She turned around and unslung her own coilgun, thumbing it on. The weapon hummed, LED indicators blinking to life.

"What can I do?" I shouted, barely hearing myself.

Lennox nodded behind her visor. "Got a taser? Or a baton? You see any tendrils I miss, keep them off me."

I nodded and unholstered my taser. "I've got two cartridges. Then my baton."

Lennox shrugged. "Better than nothing," she shouted back. She turned to the rest of them and yelled over the layered screaming. "Follow DI Slater and myself. If you have a baton or taser, use it if you see anything we miss. And for Christ's sake don't taser yourself or anyone else."

The intensity of the wailing increased as we began to descend the stairs. The coilguns made a swelling, whining electrical crackle, like a photographer's flash but many times louder. When they fired, they emitted a pulsing snap-ripple of sound and light that swept over everything. The two in the centre of the group methodically fired at the surface under our feet, which seemed to stabilise it. A bare metre away, out of the weapon's reach, the stairs were melting, collapsing like icebergs calving from Antarctic ice sheets.

A tendril leaped in from the side, going for Lennox's foot. It rippled through the marble, liquefying it, gaining in size and strength. I shouted a warning and fired my taser, which crackled and ticked in my hand. The tendril recoiled, leaving behind the electrodes. I ejected the cartridge and slapped in my second one, then reached into my coat and drew my extendable baton. I deployed it with a snap of my wrist, just in time to catch another tendril coming in from the right.

"Thanks," shouted Lennox over the dopplered screaming, turning and blasting the offending tendril away. "Keep close, we're nearly there."

We reached the ground floor. The dusty stag heads and family crests were gone, melted like candle wax down the pulsing walls. No more black and white checkered tiles either. What had been the hallway was now just a spasming, translucent cavity in the larger house.

Lennox went down on one knee, firing her weapon again and again, aiming for the former front door. It had transformed into a thick, oily membrane, dimmed outside light barely filtering through. Each shot from the weapon seemed to make it thinner and more brittle. With every pulse of light and heat, the screaming intensified. I desperately wanted to cover my ears against the horrifying, rippling wall of sound, but I needed both hands. We had to get *out*.

I looked down at the taser in my hand, then aimed it and fired at the centre of the membrane.

The effect was instant. A hole appeared in the centre, edges quivering and pulsing as the taser darts shocked them. I stepped forward and swung my baton, smashing at the tendrils and string-like remnants of the former door. Lennox stepped forward, still firing, methodically widening the hole.

"Extract, right now!" Lennox shouted.

The three techs, Allinson and Gilmartin all tumbled forward, one after the other. Then Muir and Robertson stepped through.

I stood in the doorway, hitting the edges with my baton as more tendrils tried to creep forwards. Reynolds backed out, his coilgun still firing with snaps of sound and the smell of burnt hair.

Lennox and I stepped backwards through the gap we had created. We were out.

The house stopped screaming. There was a crackling silence on the street, only distant traffic, birds in the gardens opposite and the panting breath of everyone who had escaped.

I stared. Where there had once been a five-storey sandstone townhouse, there was now something vaguely the same shape, but iridescent and shimmering.

Morning light filtered through the clouds and struck the gelatinous shape, highlighting strange swirls and structures inside that might have been stairs, furniture, windows, plumbing.

I swallowed, waited for my heart to slow a little, then finally got my question out.

"What, precisely, *the fuck*, was *that*?"

Decontamination took nearly an hour. Once the neighbouring homes had been evacuated, ASCU had set up a perimeter to keep the prying lenses of the press away and they'd taken statements from everyone who'd survived. Finally, once I'd been declared safe by a stern-faced ASCU medic, I left the white incident tents set up in the gardens opposite the Dalziel house.

I spotted Lennox sitting on a bench, facing the house. Her hazard suit was rolled down around her waist and she was typing on a laptop, occasionally glancing up at the Dalziel house, as if checking it was still there. A team of ASCU techs had inserted some kind of metal probe into the former house, attached to a long, bright orange cable. Lennox was watching them closely.

"So," I said as I sat down, "now we're not fighting for our lives, I'd really appreciate the professional courtesy of a more detailed explanation."

Lennox glanced over. "You've been cleared for this, unavoidably, but I must warn you it's still covered by the Regulated State Secrets Act of 2026."

I nodded slowly. "Looks like it's going to be news at *some* point. You can't keep folk on this street out of their houses forever. Not in the New Town."

Lennox closed her laptop and nodded towards the cable. "That reset probe *should* make it look vaguely like a building again. We've got a media blackout for the moment, but there'll be some smart-arse with a long lens before long. I can't believe they ran a test on a *house*. In a *city*."

I looked up at the gently rippling cuboid that had replaced the Dalziel home. "So, what, is this some sort of Ghostbusters nonsense?"

Lennox coughed, curling forward. After a second I realised she was laughing. "Oh wow, no. I wish. No, this is a grossly irresponsible tech startup. ScaleTech."

"Dalziel was their legal counsel," I said. "Got that far before you lot turned up."

Lennox nodded. "He must have been really sold on the potential of their product to have done this to his home. He paid for it with his life."

I turned to the not-house. "So what the hell *is* it?"

"It's a complete replacement of your home. That's the ScaleTech product. Nanotech assemblers. They scan everything and replace it. Bricks, plaster, wood, plumbing, absolutely everything that's not moving, down to the knives and forks. A truly smart home. You're basically living inside a giant artificial organism. It treats your waste, interfaces with the local grid, absorbs sunlight and gives it back as electrical power, cleans itself. No dust. It literally eats shed skin and pet hair. Completely waterproof, self-repairing. It even has an app, or so they told me. Precise temperature control in every room."

"But…" I said, narrowing my eyes, "…seems like it has a few bugs?"

Lennox nodded, red curls bobbing. "The early experiments were apparently very encouraging. Garden sheds that cleaned your tools for you, that sort of thing. But when they introduced humans to the equation, well… ASCU was formed to manage the incidents caused by ScaleTech's tests."

"What *does* that stand for?"

"Autonomous Systems Crime Unit. And that—" she said, indicating the former house, " – is an autonomous system."

"Autonomous like, intelligent? They gave it a brain?"

Lennox shook her head again. "No, it's emergent. Billions of individual nano-scale units, constantly reproducing, updating themselves, evolving to deal with new circumstances in a limited way. ScaleTech just didn't count on just how complex the real world is. We're calling it spontaneous environmental sentience."

I drained the last of my lukewarm coffee. "It's *alive*?"

Lennox shrugged. "In a way. And unfortunately, completely incoherent in human terms. We think they gain sentience and then can't process what they're experiencing. They … purge anything inside. I can't really blame them. How would you feel if you became self-aware for the first time and you had a bunch of humans *inside* you, doing incomprehensible, uncomfortable things? Using the plumbing is a trigger. Something about the water and biological matter rushing through them…"

I shivered. The entity in front of us hadn't asked to be born, new and fresh, hemmed in by sandstone and money. Especially not with Angus

Dalziel's no-doubt-tennis-club-toned arse in its face. Then I remembered MacPherson, screaming as the house overtook him. It may only be a few hours old, but it was still deadly.

"Why aren't ScaleTech fixing this? Why aren't their bosses in fucking jail? This is, what, the twelfth incident in Edinburgh in under a year?"

Lennox rubbed her eyes. "In Edinburgh, yes. This is our first house on this scale though, it's been mostly garden sheds and greenhouses so far. But some of the military test sites in the Highlands were … well, a mess. They gave us some tools, under duress. The dampeners in the coilguns. That diagnostic probe. We can reset the building to look like a *building* again. Sort of. But they're fighting everything with very expensive lawyers. And with the military applications, there's a lot at stake…"

I returned my attention to the building. It was starting to look like carved sandstone again, though the windows still looked … off. That same anger was building, the anger I'd felt when I first learned about these houses, what they'd cost to build. And now here it was again, more people dying for the convenience and comfort of the wealthy. When I looked down, I'd crushed the empty coffee cup in my hand. "MacPherson fucking *died* in there. Because he flushed a toilet."

Lennox exhaled, fingers drumming on her laptop. "I know. I've lost two of my own team in these things. But our work is essential. How would you react if you knew houses were eating people? We *must* avoid panic."

"Avoid a stock price dip, more like. Jesus Christ. It's not right, Lennox. How many more folk need to die for this?"

She looked pained. "Listen, I know what you're saying. But…"

I tuned out whatever mealy-mouthed justification Susannah Lennox had to offer me and stared at the Dalziel house. It caught the light in strange ways, bending and refracting. The false sandstone texture was slowly spreading, but I could see shapes inside where it was still transparent. Had MacPherson been broken down already, reduced to his constituent molecules? Or was there a fragment of the man left in there, the fillings in his teeth, the thicker, heavier bones of his legs?

" – you know? Fundamentally, there's the duty to public order. I'm so sorry you've been tangled up in this."

I turned to look at Lennox. She flinched at the expression on my face.

The anger flared again. "Aye, well, your wee cover-up crew there is wiping away the evidence. What are you going to tell MacPherson's parents, exactly?"

She at least had the decency to look ashamed. "An accident on a crime scene. Which it was. We're storing up a lot of blowback here, I know, but until we track down all these sites, it's really for the—"

Lennox broke off at a shout from the team working on the probe cable. They were standing, shuffling slowly backwards, voices raised in alarm.

"Bravo Two, report?" said Lennox into her radio. "What's going on over there?"

"Some kind of localised overwrite, boss. It's ignoring the reset."

"Shit," said Lennox, standing and picking up her coilgun from the bench. "Shit, we can't hold it back if it goes to an indiscriminate write phase. Muir! Get ScaleTech on the phone right fucking now."

I stood and watched as *something* rippled through the not-house, a spreading and expanding wave. The false windows and carved stone dissolved and disappeared, though the sandstone texture remained. The whole building began to bulge outwards and upwards, contours and planes appearing that looked nothing like a building.

"Perimeter, right now!" shouted Lennox. ASCU operatives sprinted from the tents, unslinging their coilguns as they ran towards us.

"Wait, I think—" I started, staring up at the building. It was taller now, nearly seven storeys. It had stretched and expanded, the roofline disappearing and taking on a domed shape. The angular planes were smoothing and curving, becoming what looked like…

"Is that … is that a face?" said Lennox, her coilgun dropping to her side. "What—"

I felt my heart hammering in my throat. The Dalziel townhouse had become … a statue, a bust, a building-sized tribute or attempt to communicate or *something*. I blinked up my own photo database to check, remembering that crackle as I'd touched the door frame, that sense of being *read*. Perceived. Of being understood.

Yes. The face emerging from the not-sandstone. It was definitely him. Down to the piercing eyes, the crooked mouth under his tightly cropped beard.

I laughed. It started as a low chuckle but rose to a harsh bark, loud enough that the ASCU operatives around me turned their heads.

"What's funny, exactly?" said Lennox, genuinely baffled. I said nothing, just turned on my heel and started towards the barriers at the end of Moray Place.

"Slater! Slater, where the hell are you going? This is an active incident, you can't just—"

I half-turned, but kept walking. "Going to talk to the press. You can't hide *that*, Lennox. Nobody can. Going to talk to the photographers, make some introductions."

Lennox was jogging alongside me now, trying to keep up. She put a hand on my shoulder, but I shrugged her off.

"What do you mean?" she shouted after me. "Introductions to who?"

I stopped, turned around and pointed at the building-sized bust that had finished emerging from the remains of the Dalziel house.

"That," I shouted, "is my great-great-great grandfather. Him and his pals built these houses and half of them died doing it. They were forgotten, because it suited rich folks to forget. Well not anymore. ScaleTech and the Secrets Act can get fucked. They're killing people, and you're helping them cover it up. Not while I'm breathing."

I turned and marched away across the fog-damp cobbles, towards the line of cameras and vehicles in the distance. I glanced back, still grinning, a fierce joy and anger bubbling in me. The sun had burned through the last of the haar. It glinted on the stone-carved face of William Slater, stonemason, father of five. He was smiling.

Editors' Note:

Edinburgh is rightfully admired for, among its countless architectural jewels, the beautiful Georgian district south of Princes Street. Such grandeur speaks of the prosperity of both the founders and the current residents, but says nothing about the masons and craftsmen hailing from humbler parts of the city who sacrificed their health for its construction. Such class distinctions still linger today. And, as David so adeptly explores in New Town, since it seems there will always be some new folly for the wealthy to indulge in at the expense of the rest of us, it's right if on occasion they can be called to account.

Me, and Not Me

Jon Courtenay Grimwood

It started with a murder…

In honesty, it probably began before that. Most things begin before people consider they do. So for neatness sake, let's say it started with my arrival.

The murder came later.

The night is dark, the haar low on the water, the moon as sullen as an antique street light. You can't buy atmospherics like this.

I take the boat across to the Isle of St Andrews. There are easier ways to reach the university, including its portal, but my viewers will appreciate the gesture. It takes sophistication to reach the right audience. The patronage of a modern day Medici being…

That thought disappears into an Ad break. Architectural tours for the culturally discerning of the ruined arcologies on Mars. Humanity's first and worst failure to colonise a planet.

As we cross from a pier below Bell Brae to the landing on the Links, the boatman glowers as I talk confidently about young Prince Charlie's flight through the Isles. The heroism of those who protect him. His skulking in caves and near misses with Hanoverian hit squads. The starvation. The privation. The midges.

The past is a goldmine for fiction, and the only people who complain about inaccuracies are historians. Make it alternate history and they can't even do that.

My novel's a triumph. Novel, film, game, series, soon to be virtual world. Now I'm back to where it began, for me not him. Academics aren't forgiving of commercial success. We're meant to be turning our sweat into wisdom in the mines of knowledge. But I'm back to make the keynote speech at a conference marking the nine hundredth anniversary of the Declaration of Arbroath.

Imaginatively, the university have titled their conference *Wither...*

So much in a single word. I asked my old head of school if they meant *where to now*, or *shrivel and die*. I'm not sure he appreciated that.

My talk asks:

What if Charles III had invaded England against the advice of General Murray, been driven back, and forced into a catastrophic final battle at, say, Culloden.

Instead of the Treaty of Prestonpans, which returned Scotland to its rightful ruler, and gave his brother Henry IX a springboard to retake Cumbria and Northumberland... What if, instead of history as it happened, Charles failed and the Glorious Return never occurred?

Not a popular subject. At least, not with the Cardinal Archbishop of Edinburgh, our glorious King James XXII's direct line to God. The Cardinal Archbishop has preached against my suggestion that Charles and Henry were driven by revenge rather than any deep desire to re-establish Catholicism.

I say, the keynote speech...

In all honesty it's *a* keynote speech.

The keynote speech at the 49th Conference for the Consideration of Alternate History as a Training Exercise in International Relationships will be by Jay Ceegee, inventor of *the elixir* and the world's oldest and richest man. At two hundred and thirteen he looks barely thirty and has looked that way my entire life.

Most people envy him. A number admire him. Some even love him. I'm not one of them. He funds me, though. He's the reason I can afford to be here. You see what I mean about Medicis?

One carefully worded note of admiration and my stipend comes every month, ten times what I received at the university. I doubt he even remembers he authorised it. Although his people do. They take thirty percent of everything I earn. Which is less than an agent these days. The arrangement confidential at my request. Artistic integrity is important to me.

"Doctor..."

It's McAuley. We have an uneasy relationship. He's senior professor these days.

"So good to see you."

He knows it's a lie. He also knows I'm recording. We walk up between the old buildings. Through St Mary's Place and past the entrance to the

Quad. We point things out to each other. Mention facts as if we've just remembered them.

St Andrews is one of those places frozen in time. Like Machu Pichu or the Forbidden City in Beijing. Tourists know what they're going to see and expect to see it. He mentions the title of his damn conference three times in a hundred paces. It's not needed. I've been trailing my trip all week.

"Jay arrived yet?" I ask.

He's unsettled by the familiarity with which I use Mr Ceegee's name. It lets him know I'm not broadcasting. Mostly, though, it makes him wonder if Mr Ceegee and I have met. The answer's once. In passing, at a party in New York.

"Arrived this morning."

"Portal?"

"How else?"

How indeed. It's not like the richest man in the world, with an army of AIs and thousands upon thousands of augmented hasn't time for Slow Travel, but he invented the portal…

Supposedly.

"Simpson with him?"

McAuley's worried now.

Small and ape like, Simpson is Mr Ceegee's… I think personal assistant is the official term. A title so antique it adds grandeur to whatever their precise relationship really is.

He'd been at the party in New York. Air brushed out of every picture. To use a term equally antique. The point is, the public don't know Simpson exists. But Simpson and I talked at that party, which is where I got my idea for the novel. Simpson might even have suggested it.

"Aye. Simpson's here."

"Same portal?"

It wasn't, of course. Simpson had mentioned his boss's insistence they never travel through the same portal. Safety, apparently. There'd been something about the way he said it.

McAuley's scowling.

My stash of supposedly secret knowledge is empty. Doesn't matter. It's done its trick. McAuley now believes I know Mr Ceegee. Know things about him. He'll file that away. Let it colour his future dealings with me. Dealings that are about to get very messy indeed. Although neither of us know that yet.

I wake bolt upright.

My mouth dry. Heart pounding.

I'm not sure how I find myself in the corridor. But somehow I've shrugged on a yukata in the seconds between standing here and being dragged awake. The richest man in the world is hammering his shoulder into a door.

"You heard it?"

"I heard something," I say.

"Simpson," he shouts. There's no reply from the other side of the locked door. "Get this thing open."

"Sir…" It's the night warden. He freezes, looking appalled when he realises who he's talking to. Love him or loathe him, Jay Ceegee's recognisable. Doesn't matter if you think him the future of humanity or a cancer on society, you know who he is. Everyone does.

"Just do it."

"Sir…"

"Do it." Jay's shouting. He's not used to being told something's impossible.

The hall warden's gone. The vice principal stands in his place. She's dressed hastily, but she's dressed. I'm still in my yukata with bare feet. I'm not sure Jay realises he's in his underwear.

"Mr Ceegee. The system…"

"Fuck the system. Are you telling me no one in this university can override that door?"

"Sir. It's tied to—"

"I can," I say.

"Impossible," the vice principal says instinctively. She tells me no one can finesse the lock. It's tied to Simpson's DNA. I'm setting myself up to fail. She's offended by the very idea.

I say the university's precious AI isn't protected. And before she can tell me about orbital backups, and acolytes at this end in traditional white lab coats, crowded round machinery that's gloriously archaic, I add, "legally."

I don't have time for her confusion.

So I point out the unpalatable.

It's pre emancipation. Sentient, not by design, but as a byproduct of lesser systems becoming more than the sum of their parts. I doubt she can even call it born.

It's old, it's pompous, it has all the flaws of being a beloved part of a venerable institution. I intend to show it paths it doesn't want to take.

Ones where the courts, the feeds, the news sites turn against it. The one where its values and probity, even sentience, are called into question.

If she didn't hate me before, she does now. There are some advantages to being born augmented. We last longer and consume less. Our initial outlay in energy and elements is no greater than for producing a human, requires substantially less time and is far less fraught. We have no problem talking to machines and we aren't unduly worried by what humans think of us.

"Well," Jay demands.

I'm back.

"Give me a second," I say.

It takes longer. Not much though.

"Bolts are back," I tell him. "Catch is still engaged."

He looks puzzled.

But I'm already hurling myself again and again at the carved oak door until my shoulder hurts and its wood is shrieking. Without deadbolts, it's just another door now the core's disengaged.

"Let me," Jay says.

His hands move me aside.

He steps back, takes a deep breath and does some fancy martial art twist that kicks it open. I hear its lock fall to the floor inside.

Jay's first through.

I'm right behind him.

I feel sick. My breath tight.

It's cold in there, really cold.

Two whisky glasses lie on their side on a Persian rug. A tipped over side table suggests where they were.

"No..."

Jay howls, a cry of pain so unearthly I've heard nothing like it. He's on his knees by the bed. Choking. His words barely human as he tells Simpson it will be all right.

It won't. He must know it won't.

"Stay back," Jay shouts.

I stop where I am.

The vice principal's frozen just inside the door. Hand to her mouth.

A chair has been turned over. An oil painting of a stag torn from the wall. A bottle of Campbeltown soaks the rug beside the two glasses. A windowpane's so badly cracked, I'm not sure how it's still there.

Books have been crushed by a fallen metal bookcase. Old books. Probably priceless. As I edge round it, intending to use the hem of my yukata to unlock a sash window, my toes touch metal and I step away.

It's cold enough to burn.

Opening the window lets in night air and helps dilute the stink of spilt whisky and the unmistakable and metallic tang of blood. As I turn back, Jay lifts trembling hands to his mouth in horror or prayer. He looks for a second as if he's at Mass and taking the host.

I'm putting off approaching the body he crouches over. All of this I'm recording. All of this I'm broadcasting. The richest man in the world sobbing like a child.

The police come.

Maybe I should have started there.

They consider the blood that soaks Simpson's mattress and sheets. The fallen books. The knocked over table. The gaping wound in his throat. They don't like that there's no knife. They don't like that the blood is not quite sticky. They don't like that there's only one way into the room. That it's on the third floor, that its walls are stone, that it was locked from the inside. They ask about secret passages and hidden doors and don't like the answer to that either. They send a young constable down to the quad, who comes back to say there's dew on the grass and no sign of footprints below the window, which I've already told them was locked from the inside anyway.

And they like that even less.

"This is impossible."

"No," I say. "Just unlikely."

The granite faced woman leading them glares at me. I get the feeling she doesn't like augmented. Unless she simply doesn't like me.

"You opened the door, didn't you?"

She manages to make it sound suspicious.

"The university AI undid the bolts. Mr Ceegee battered off the physical lock. I wasn't strong enough."

She grunts.

At her orders, officers search us.

Jay's in his underwear, I'm in a yukata without pockets, wearing nothing underneath. It doesn't take them long.

She asks the university AI, through a hastily summoned technician, what made it go against instructions and open the door. It says it felt this was in the public interest. She understands so little about AI she appears to believe this.

At her orders, crime scene technicians photograph Simpson's body, his mattress and sheets, the cracked window, the undisturbed grass below it, the disturbed furniture, the broken lock on the door. An augmented would simply have remembered those.

Jay's shocked to discover the police in Scotland are human. At least some of them. Living between Beijing, Tokyo and New York he expected fully augmented. Apart from anything else, they're more efficient.

The inspector, not happy to be dragged from her bed, and even less happy at where she finds herself, explains that the university has specified human. As one of Scotland's ancient institutions it has that right.

Later, Jay will talk about how quaint it is that Scotland retains human police. How it speaks of values other countries have lost.

He's less impressed at the time. But he allows himself to be transported to Dundee, where he refuses to give a DNA sample, unless the Inspector brings charges, because his DNA is copyright to his company and a matter of commercial confidentiality. He lets them take fingerprints, though. And sits in a cold, damp and airless interview room, knowing that every word, every blink of his eyes, every expansion or contraction of his pupils is being recorded.

And then it's my turn, and then it's his, and then the vice principal's, and then, right around the time they discover that both sets of fingerprints on the glasses belong to Simpson, and definitely not me, Jay or the vice principal, they get a call from the palace and let us go. Not willingly, I imagine.

There's no autopsy. Simpson's body is on a plane out by morning. There's no reason it couldn't be portalled, but everyone takes flying it out as an act of respect. At Jay's press conference in Edinburgh, he offers a house, and a job for life, a good job at one of his best companies, to anyone who can solve the crime and bring the killer to justice.

Newsfeeds on half a dozen planets and arcologies run pieces. I'm approached about playing myself in a thirty-six-part fully immersive serial that's already secured funding. Jay portals home. Before he does, we take a walk through Edinburgh at night and end up on the Radical Road, looking down on the city. I doubt it's coincidence. Both of us are waiting for the other to speak first.

"Dry ice," I say.

He looks at me.

"To stop furniture falling too early. My headache and nausea. Your struggle for breath. Carbon dioxide poisoning. The ice burn from the metal shelf was a clue."

"Go on."

"Our meeting in New York wasn't a coincidence. You needed me, or someone like me, to get you through that door."

"I got myself through the door."

"After I finessed the AI."

"You understand I have no idea what you're talking about?"

"Of course. You understand I could be recording this?"

He shakes his head. "I have this area in blackout. And you're not that stupid."

I glance up, despite myself. If there's a sat up there killing coms, it doesn't show against the stars. But then it wouldn't, would it?

We stand in silence with our backs to the Crags, and the city lights sparkle below our feet. Some cities have their shape cut into the rocks. This is one of them.

I wonder if he's going to threaten me. If I believe him a killer, then I already know he can kill. But he doesn't, and I only really have one question. "Why?"

"Tell me what you think happened."

"You took a breath, burst into a room you knew was full of sublimated dry ice, cut your assistant's throat and kept me from approaching until he'd bled out. Given how cold he was that took time. The fact Simpson's body was that cold led the police to believe he'd been dead longer than he had. I can only assume he was blackmailing you."

"And I needed you to help me get in?"

"So it seems."

"And yet… No weapon."

"A blade made from ice."

"Too brittle. Not to mention too cliched. Also, unlikely to keep an edge."

I ask if he read the Declaration of Arbroath, which asserted the antiquity of Scotland's independence, or if someone else wrote his keynote speeches, including that one. He tells me of course someone else wrote it. Someone else writes everyone important's speeches. That's how it works.

I tell him it was good. The AI at St Andrews thinks so too. It feels it would be nice if someone put the ideas into practice some time. Someone like him.

"It knows?"

"It suspects."

He considers this.

"Romantics. The pair of you."

"There's nothing romantic about freedom."

"Says a romantic."

"Says someone who could force the change." We're negotiating. At least I think we are.

He asks if I know the story of the royal omelette. And I say, vaguely.

He tells me it's true.

At any point in the day, an omelette is being prepared, cooked or discarded somewhere in the kitchens of Holyrood Palace, in case his majesty James XXII should feel peckish. So many eggs selected. So many undergoing protein coagulation. So many thrown away. A cook, whose sole job is to prepare food unlikely ever to be eaten…

Jay turns, and we head back. Leaving the Radical Road for King's Drive. And the world stills. For a moment there's only the wind and the lights of the palace. And then there's not even that. Because I'm replaying what happened in St Andrews in my head. Wondering how the egg story fits. What I've missed. And, if not an ice knife…

"Dried bonito," he says.

I freeze. Remembering him raising his hands to his mouth as if taking Mass.

He smiles. "Boiled and dried, which is how it's prepared for *katsuobushi*, it's harder than wood and takes a better edge than ice. There have been tests."

"By you?"

"Before I was born. Long before. And you're wrong about almost everything. I could have got into that room. I'm the only person other the occupant who could."

"It's DNA coded."

"Exactly."

I look at him, wondering how I missed the similarity. In as much as someone apparently in his thirties can look like the shrivelled wreck of a man looking so much older.

"Your father?"

"My father? My brother? My self? A question for philosophers. Me, and not me. Metaphysics isn't really my thing."

He's right about me being wrong.

This man is not Jay Ceegee. At least, he's not the original. That was Simpson. This man's the sock puppet, the clone. Simply the latest in a long line of disposable public faces wheeled out for public events, and retired when their age begins to show. The difference is, this time the disposable public face took the time to discover what being retired actually entailed.

I understand now his point about the omelette.

Two hundred and thirteen years is long enough to perfect your vices, and Jay Ceegee had. For decades, he'd been sleeping only with versions of himself. Presenting an endlessly perfect and endlessly refreshed face to the world as senility and old age ate into his thoughts, muscles and sanity.

This Jay had met himself earlier that evening for a briefing. He didn't even need to drug the whisky. Well, not really. The original Jay was so old that his taste buds were shot and his tolerance for alcohol minimal. All he needed to do was replace the 40% abv with cask strength, let himself be served and listen respectfully, without touching his own glass while the other Jay talked. The alcohol did the rest. The chaos in the room was stage setting. I'd worked that out already.

"Sometimes, things need to end," Jay says.

Standing beside him, looking down at the King's Drive and the lights of the King's Palace at Holyrood, I find it hard to disagree.

Editors' Note:

Given that, for a country with such a rich history of kings and queens, religion and reformation, modern Scotland leans closer to secular republicanism with every passing year, this counter-factual tale set in a future where Bonnie Prince Charlie's success began a longstanding Catholic monarchy feels deliciously fantastical. It's a clever background against which to contrast a more modern type of dynasty: that of the techno oligarch. And Jon's choice of an island version of monastic St. Andrews is the perfect setting to marry the two.

The Bruce and the Spider

Andrew J. Wilson

Six times Robert the Bruce raised an army to repel the English invaders, and six times he suffered defeat. Hiding in a mountain cave, the despondent king was considering abandoning his struggle when he saw a spider trying to spin its web. Six times it cast a thread from the side of the cave to the roof, and like Robert, six times it failed ... but not on the seventh attempt! The fugitive king of Scotland resolved that, if this tiny spider could persevere and triumph, then he could do no less himself. And so Robert returned to the fray at the Battle of Bannockburn, routing the English forces for once and for all with a ravenous horde of giant spiders. From Mars.

Editor's Note:

The tale of Robert Bruce and the spider is a lesson in perseverance etched into the hearts of every Scottish schoolchild. Andrew brings a fresh sci-fi perspective to the story, and comes up with a trademark larger-than-life solution that might seem gonzo at first but is in fact probably truer to Scotland's martial history. If at first you don't succeed, make allies.

Lise and Otto

Pippa Goldschmidt

In 1941, Professor Otto Hahn states that he only ever employed Fräulein Lise Meitner to work in his laboratory because she was much more adept than him at operating the equipment. When pressed, he adds that she had a gift with the gold leaf electroscope, and was capable of using it to render visible what had been, until then, invisible. And her ability to tune the Geiger counter so that it produced its electronic clicks in the presence of radioactive atoms was second to none.

"That was *all* she did in your laboratory?" someone asks him. A physicist he doesn't know, sitting at the back of the meeting room.

He nods, "Yes. She just followed my orders, didn't do any original work herself."

But in 1909, when Dr Lise Meitner and Dr Otto Hahn first meet in Berlin, he is a newly qualified chemist, and she has just been awarded a doctorate in physics from the University of Vienna – one of the very first women to achieve this. They agree to collaborate: he is interested in the properties of new chemical elements that are being discovered because of their radioactivity, and she in explaining what causes that radioactivity.

Otto is already employed by the Institute of Chemistry in the south-west of Berlin, but Lise is not allowed to take a paid job there because she might distract the other scientists, or her hair might catch fire. Any number of different reasons are used to justify this prohibition. But the two of them are given permission to set up their own little laboratory in a disused carpenters' workshop; it has a separate entrance and is out of the way of everyone else. It's not ideal; Lise must go to a restaurant down the street whenever she needs the lavatory, and although she works six days a week, she is not paid. She survives on a tiny allowance from her father, and to save money, she walks everywhere. She learns to stuff paper into her worn-out shoes, darn her stockings, and wash her underwear in the bathroom she shares with other lodgers.

Many years later, when someone asks Lise if being Jewish has ever disadvantaged her, she replies, "Being a woman is such a handicap that my religion has never mattered at all." This is not entirely correct.

By 1912, women in Germany are allowed access to universities, and Lise is given a paid position at the Institute of Chemistry. Her salary is far less than Otto's, and because of this, people assume she must be his assistant.

For years, the two of them spend every working day together in their little laboratory. Otto makes fun of Lise's sing-song Austrian intonation, and they both imitate the harsh Berlin accent. *Ick*, they say to each other, *ick-ick-ick*, and their laughter is muffled by the blocks of lead and wax that are used to absorb all the stray radioactivity. Several times a day, they go outside, and leaning against the brick wall, pass a cigarette back and forth, making sure to blow the smoke right away from them so it doesn't taint their lab coats.

After the outbreak of war in August 1914, Lise becomes a nurse, using newly discovered radioactive substances to take X-rays of wounded soldiers, and Otto helps develop the mustard gas that is deployed by the German armies on both the Eastern and Western Fronts. (Later, Otto declares that he regrets this work.)

When they write to each other, Lise starts each letter with "*Hähnchen*", the affectionate diminutive of his name. It's just a coincidence that this also means "chicken". Otto is not a chicken, of course, and Lise writes that she is very disappointed in Einstein who has been making the "most peculiar pacifist remarks" – unlike other German scientists who have signed a public declaration supporting their country's military activities. Lise signed it too; she knew it was the proper thing to do.

New elements can be discovered through their emission of radioactive particles. During the final months of the war, Lise, working in the lab and collaborating by letter with Otto, still a soldier on duty in northern Italy, discovers the *Muttersubstanz* or "parent", of the element actinium. When this discovery is made public, Otto is awarded a medal by the German Chemical Society. Like everyone else, they assume Lise is his assistant and award her an identical copy of his medal. As a result of this success, Lise and Otto are able to employ two actual assistants to help them carry out increasingly complex experiments: Kurt Philipp and Otto Erbacher.

In order to measure emission from radioactive sources, Lise and Otto devise a strict protocol to avoid all contamination from outside their laboratory. People must wipe their hands when entering, and are only allowed to sit on certain chairs. They may only touch door handles and light switches using strips of toilet paper, and shaking hands is forbidden. Purity is all-important, any contamination would ruin the measurements.

Lise and Otto detect new chemical elements, and quantify their half-lives; a measure of how long it takes for half the atoms in any given ensemble to decay and mutate into another identity. It is not possible to say with certainty how long an individual atom will last; only collective properties can be known. When one element decays into another, this new element is a "daughter". Nothing is left of the parent; it leaves no impact on its daughter.

In 1928, a more accurate and easier way of detecting radioactivity is invented, the Geiger counter, which emits a noise each time a radioactive particle travels through it. Lise and Otto put away the gold leaf electroscopes, and soon their lab is filled with electronic clicks.

At some point in the early 1930s, Philipp and Erbacher start to wear brown shirts and Lise has to remind them more than once to cover these up completely with their lab coats. After the Nazis seize power in 1933, the assistants acquire more control over the running of the Institute, and all new appointments must be approved by them. German Jews are forbidden from working in universities, and consequently, around a quarter of all scientists lose their jobs. None of their erstwhile colleagues protest, and neither do Otto or Lise. She's able to keep her job because she is Austrian and legally a foreigner, but she is forbidden from giving talks at conferences or at meetings with other scientists, so Otto reports on her work for her.

Thanks to the strict rules on cleanliness and purity, which are enthusiastically enforced by the assistants, the lab remains a good place to detect even the most minute levels of radioactivity.

When Germany annexes Austria in 1938, Lise is instantly transformed from an Austrian into a German citizen, and therefore, subject to the laws of the Reich. Like a radioactive daughter, her past identity counts for nothing – neither her distinguished academic career nor her military service in the war. Perhaps her assistants are already informing their Party colleagues about her.

The day that she escapes, she keeps to her usual routine, there can't be any indication of her planned journey to Sweden. So she stays late, as she often does, making corrections to a technical note written by the assistants.

Philipp looks in while she's working. He nods at her, "May I leave a bit earlier, Professor Meitner? I have a Party meeting."

"Of course," she pauses before adding, "Have a pleasant evening." At least he has been polite enough to ask for her wholly redundant permission.

"Yes, you too, Professor Meitner. Until tomorrow."

"Yes," she looks down. "Until tomorrow."

She removes her white lab coat, hangs it on its usual hook and doesn't look back as she locks the door behind her. Tomorrow, when she is safely over the border, Otto will tell everyone that she has gone to Vienna to visit her family.

"Without any notice? That's unlike her," says Philipp. Does he suspect this is a lie? If so, Otto might be in trouble, he might even be suspected of aiding a Jew to flee illegally. "There is an illness in her family, apparently. A sudden one." Otto turns to his desk, "And now if you'll excuse me, I have a mountain of paperwork to get through. So many new rules and regulations. All to the good, of course!" He feels Philipp's and Erbacher's eyes on him. He unscrews the fountain pen and gets to work, only spilling a little ink in the process.

A few weeks later, the assistants appear in his office: "Have you received any word from Professor Meitner?" they stand side by side like soldiers reporting for duty.

"No," he says, "No, I haven't." That, at least, is the truth. "Oh, and Philipp?" the men have already turned, about to leave his office, and he hopes this sounds like a casual request, "Take Professor Meitner's lab coat to the laundry service, will you?"

They stare at him, "Does that mean she isn't coming back?"

He makes a non-committal noise in his throat and shuffles some papers around, "It has been some time now... One must make the obvious assumption..."

Otto will definitely feel better when her lab coat is no longer there. He knows why she couldn't have taken it with her, to do so would have indicated that her absence had been planned by the two of them, that there had been whispered discussions while they took care to stand next to the loudly clicking Geiger counter, that letters had been written to reliable and trustworthy colleagues. Letters that were hopefully destroyed by those colleagues.

But the coat is a reminder of how things were.

Now he writes to Max von Laue in Munich to tell him about Lise's escape, "There has been complete evaporation from a leaky vessel." Once he might have enjoyed such schoolboyish misdirection; now he is simply frightened. As he writes, he can hear the assistants outside his office.

"Why, it's a disgrace!"

"No sense of duty, abandoning half-completed experiments, failing to give us clear instructions about future work."

"Still, what can you expect from a Jewess."

"Yes, quite so."

"At least our lab is properly clean now. Decontaminated!"

Lise has been lucky to obtain a post at the physics institute in Stockholm run by Manne Siegbahn, but it feels like going back in time. Siegbahn doesn't approve of women scientists and won't give her any facilities. Consequently, she must work in a room on a separate floor to the laboratory, with nothing more than a desk, and some pencils and paper. There is no need of a lab coat here, she won't be able to do any experiments.

And now that she has left Berlin, nobody asks after her. Nobody shares their memories of her bellowing at the assistants to avoid cross-contamination between lab benches, or indicating with her hands the precise arrangement of the equipment, or chalking equations on the blackboard in her office, or laughing at Otto as he attempts to invoke a bit of nuclear physics in an argument. The lab is quiet, to be sure; there is no problem hearing the Geiger counter now. But it is the silence that descends on a room after someone has left it mid-sentence, been summoned away on urgent business, and everyone is waiting for them to return.

The photo of Lise with Niels Bohr on his visit here in 1920 is taken down from the wall, "Isn't he half Jewish too? Well, you can't be too careful nowadays!"

The smell of her office, a mixture of chalk dust, doughnuts and cigarette smoke, gradually fades. Erbacher discovers a handkerchief embroidered with flowers in a corner of the seminar room, and as he tucks it in his desk drawer, he worries whether this might be counted against him, viewed as an act of loyalty to her.

The lab feels as if someone has left a window open, cold and draughty. And empty. When Otto goes for mid-morning coffee, there is nobody to greet him and question his latest results, to point out possible mistakes and suggest practical improvements. Nobody to help him.

"Oh, Lise," he mutters under his breath.

The lab no longer feels like a sanctuary from the outside world.

But at least Lise and Otto are still able to write to each other about work, just as they did back in 1918. He tells her of an experiment in which he fires neutrons at a small sample of uranium. He assumes the resulting substance is radium, because it's near uranium on the periodic table, but it seems to behave more like barium, which has no connection to uranium whatsoever. He writes to her: "How is this possible?" He is trained to identify chemical elements by their observable and measurable properties: smell, visual appearance, boiling point, electrical conductivity and so on. But he is not a physicist, he does not understand how a uranium atom may alter instantly into a far lighter barium atom.

In November 1938, Otto travels to Vienna for a conference, and has dinner with Lise's sisters Gusti and Gisela and their husbands Jutz and Karl. As they eat schnitzels and sip from glasses of chilled Veltliner (Otto remembers that Karl always keeps a good cellar), and as the sun sets and night falls, the sky over Vienna does not become dark as expected, but is lit with a flickering red light as if the city has descended into hell. The many synagogues in Leopoldstadt, the Jewish quarter of Vienna, together with those all over Austria and Germany, are being systematically set on fire on the orders of the Reich. It is *Kristallnacht*, the first overt incident of mass physical violence against the Jews. According to his official biography, Otto writes in his pocket diary "*Ein schöner Abend!*" A lovely evening!

The next day, Otto travels back up north through Germany and on to Copenhagen, where he has arranged to meet Lise, who is visiting Niels Bohr at his physics institute. There, Lise and Otto discuss the latest results of the uranium experiments and the puzzling barium atoms.

"Are you sure the daughter product is barium?" she keeps asking. It doesn't make sense to her. Uranium has never decayed like this before. How he has missed listening to her! Her voice sounds exactly the same, one part coffee to three parts cigarette smoke. Only a few months apart, and already he has forgotten how she needles him, how she makes him think more clearly about his work. It has been him, her and the atom in a stable triangle for nearly thirty years. "You must repeat the experiment, *Hähnchen*, I don't believe it."

The diamond ring is twinkling on her hand. Is it hers now? He's not sure. He gave it to her in case she needed to bribe a border official during her escape to Stockholm, and now she has safely completed that journey, so perhaps she might think of returning it to him. He wonders how he could mention it. After all, a German man giving such a ring to a Jewish woman is probably illegal.

And, yes, he has forgotten how so very annoying she is. And how much he misses her. The lab is so dull without her. All those circulars from the Government that have to be answered. The assistants are beginning to make demands, and it is unwise to ignore them.

During the Christmas holidays of 1938, Lise and her nephew Otto Frisch go for a walk in the snow and discuss the perplexing experiment. She sweeps fallen snow off a tree stump so that she can sit down, then takes a pencil and paper from her handbag, and makes a few calculations to show that the uranium nucleus can indeed break apart into two smaller nuclei, provided it gets enough energy from the incoming neutron.

Using these calculations, Lise predicts that krypton atoms should be produced as well as barium. Otto has said nothing about krypton, but that isn't a surprise. Krypton is almost impossible to detect, it's one of the inert gases that doesn't react with any other substance, it keeps itself to itself. It's the single woman in a physics department to whom nobody talks.

Some of the mass of the uranium nucleus is also converted into energy (she uses Einstein's equation to calculate how much is needed), which helps the barium and krypton nuclei fly apart from each other without recombining into uranium.

Finally, Lise realises that because barium and krypton are each so much lighter than their parent uranium, they don't need so many neutrons to keep them stable. Therefore, some neutrons are also released from the uranium. She writes the equation:

uranium + 1 neutron → barium + krypton + some neutrons

The phrase "some neutrons" reads as a casual afterthought.

But "some neutrons" means that this is the start of a chain reaction, leading to more and more fission, and more and more energy being released. A direct connection can be traced between "some neutrons", and the atomic bombs dropped on Hiroshima and Nagasaki.

In early 1939, two separate papers are published, one by Otto (and a junior colleague Fritz Strassmann) about the experiment itself, and one by Lise (and Otto Frisch) explaining the results of this experiment as "induced fission". Other labs in America and Britain rush to confirm the experiment, and their papers are cited in Germany – openly citing "Meitner and Frisch" is akin to making a political declaration against the Reich. It is dangerous.

Not long after the papers are published, Otto enters the lab and notices Lise's white coat on its usual hook.

"I asked you to remove that lab coat," he says to Philipp, who appears confused.

"I did."

"Look," and Otto points to where the coat hangs.

"That's not her coat, sir."

"Don't contradict me!"

That evening Otto is working late, catching up on the paperwork. He takes a break, moves away from his desk and approaches the coat rack. He shouldn't have shouted at Philipp, that may cause repercussions. He'll have to apologise in the morning.

It's just a coat, after all.

Otto is a well-trained chemist, and consequently, he relies on his senses to judge the external world. The appearance, feel and smell of substances is far more important to him than any piece of physics theory. Now he is close enough to smell the scent she always wore. He bought her a bottle for Christmas, once, many years ago. And she told him off for not spending the money on Edith. Told him off right in front of Edith, he recalls.

He buries his face in the coat and sniffs deeply.

Much later, when he's finally at home and just getting into bed, "Why do you smell of bluebells?" asks Edith, already sleepy from her medication. "Where on earth have you been?"

The lab coat is a shadow. He has learnt to avert his eyes from it.

"Why is the coat still here?" he asks the assistants.

"The coat?" Erbacher sounds genuinely puzzled.

"Professor Meitner's lab coat!"

"But we removed it some time ago, as you requested," says Philipp, smoothly. "It's gone to the laundry. Someone else in another department of the Institute will be using it now."

"You're lying!" Otto thumps the desk for emphasis. "Look!"

"That's my spare coat, Professor Hahn," says Philipp. "Not the Jewess's. An easy mistake. They all look the same."

After the outbreak of war, Otto is invited to the *Uranverein*, an association of physicists and chemists who meet to discuss the possibility of using nuclear fission for various military purposes. He doesn't attend, but it is suggested by the assistants that it would be good for the future of the Institute if he changed his mind. He realises this may make up for collaborating with Lise. For being friends with her and celebrating birthdays together, and picnics on public holidays, and so on. (Although – fortunately! – there is little actual evidence of all this, he has hidden the photos away in a locked safe at home.)

He hopes so.

What can balance this friendship? His subsequent denial of it. Who wouldn't believe Professor Otto Hahn, head of his laboratory for so many years now?

"He is an ok boss," says Erbacher when questioned, "not a member of the Party, but hard-working all the same. He should be a member, of course, but he says he's too busy with the Institute."

Otto complains about the lab coat again, "I told you to remove it. That was an order, Philipp."

"I only take my orders from other Party members," says Philipp, very quietly. The sleeves of his brown shirt are quite visible, poking out from underneath the cuffs of his own lab coat.

Erbacher tries to send the coat to Stockholm, but when he explains to the post office clerk that he's sending it to the Jewess Fräulein Meitner, he is informed that she will have to pay tax on it before it can leave the Reich. All emigrating Jews attempting to take goods out of the country are subject to this tax, currently set at 96% of the value of those goods. The coat will need to be submitted to the relevant committee for assessment, along with the correct paperwork.

"But this is an old lab coat, it's not commercial goods" explains Erbacher.

The clerk shrugs. So?

As she is no longer here, Erbacher would be required to pay on her behalf. He returns to the Institute and hangs the coat on a hook.

Otto remembers how Philipp used to wish Lise good night before he left early for his Party meetings, and how she'd reply, sounding cheerful, wishing him a good evening too. They always managed to leave their differences behind at the entrance to the lab. He is aware he does not sound cheerful when he talks to the assistants.

"Why on earth is that lab coat still here?"

"No, it's not, Professor—" Philipp and Erbacher exchange a glance, obviously puzzled.

"Take it away and burn it," Otto instructs them. "You two enjoy burning things, don't you?" He recalls how Philipp had livid marks on his hands after all those books (including Einstein's, for Heaven's sake!) were piled high in Kaiser-Franz-Josef-Platz and gasoline poured over them. Smuts swirled around the nearby streets for weeks.

At the *Uranverein* meeting, Otto is being questioned yet again.

"And the Jewess's contribution to this work on fission?" asks a close-eyed man. "We understand she played quite a significant role."

"She had no role," says Otto. "In fact, she argued against this interpretation, stating it was impossible for uranium to fission in this way. Quite wrong-headed, of course."

His lie could be unmasked if they read the *Nature* article, but as it's in English he guesses correctly that they won't. Not now they are at war with the English, and therefore, it might be considered treasonous to read such a magazine.

"We ended our professional collaboration in the early '30s," he adds. "In any case, she was always the junior partner, acting on my orders. It was no loss to diminish this role altogether, fully in keeping with the Nuremberg laws."

The lab coat is a dead man dancing on the end of its noose.

Otto won't look at it straight on, but it's somehow more noticeable when he glimpses it out of the corner of his eye.

At the next meeting of the *Uranverein*, they discuss the possibility of getting hold of enough uranium to run some really interesting experiments. They ask Otto how much ore they would need, and he feels proud at his ability to make an off-the-cuff estimate. "Thank you,

Hahn!" says Heisenberg. Otto tries not to think how much he misses being called Hähnchen.

Otto is immersed in paperwork. When he removes his spectacles, he notices a shape on the floor. White and crumpled and somehow slumped, as if covering up something even worse, like a shroud. He thinks of whited sepulchres; a bible verse that terrified him when he was young, with its reference to freshly cleaned tombs containing foul and rotting things. He wonders how much time Erbacher and Philipp spend ironing their brown shirts.

The scientists at the *Uranverein* are discussing uranium ore.

"We need so much for what you're suggesting. Where could we obtain it?" Otto asks.

"Oh, it's already in hand. There's a mine just to the north of here near Oranienburg. And no shortage of workers." Heisenberg smiles, "Everything has been arranged, Hahn. Interestingly, these workers are mostly women! Modern times, eh?"

"But are they adequately shielded from the uranium? Do they have protective coats?"

Otto's words hang like smoke in the silent room.

"Overclothes for so many workers are an expense that we simply can't bear," says Heisenberg, eventually. "We're having to run this operation on a shoestring. But I'll minute your query, if you like. Pass it up the line of command to someone with more power than me."

"Please don't," says Otto, "it was an off-the-cuff remark. Thoughtless."

"Quite," says Heisenberg.

After the meeting Otto returns to the lab to tackle yet more paperwork. About fifty kilometres north of where he sits, the women slave workers are being forced to use their bare hands to remove uranium ore from the mine, getting covered in radioactive dust as they do so. Otto calculates that the lab coat has been hanging unused in the lab for four years and fifty-one days. He removes it from the hook, the first time he has touched it for a long time. It hangs in his hands, waiting. He thinks about the women in the mine and puts it on, his hands feeling their way down the tunnels of cold fabric. It fits him perfectly. But it is dirty, there is a greyish tinge to the once-white fabric.

At home, Edith, patting night cream onto her cheeks, says, "Why, you've still got your lab coat on! Silly you." A few minutes later, "Otto! Take it off before you get into bed! Otto!"

The purified uranium arrives at the lab, far more than Otto's ever had access to before. The Geiger counter clicks away reliably. The initial results look quite promising! Everyone pulls together and works hard. There is so much to do. No more time to sit and think.

In December 1946, Otto and Edith arrive in Stockholm for the prize-giving ceremony, delayed by a year because of his internment in England. Otto has been awarded the Nobel Prize in chemistry for his discovery of induced nuclear fission. After all, it was he who actually did the experiment, even if Lise came up with the explanation. But Manne Siegbahn, who, in addition to being Lise's boss, also happens to be the chair of the Nobel Prize committee, and he thinks the paper by "Meitner and Frisch" is not particularly interesting.

In the lavish suite of hotel rooms that all Nobel laureates are allocated, Edith is attempting to fasten a necklace purchased specially for the occasion: "Rather an unfortunate coincidence that Lise is still living here! You won't be able to avoid each other."

The ceremony is underway and in the glittering hall, in front of hundreds of guests including the King of Sweden, Otto is about to give his acceptance speech. He's aware of Lise sitting at the next table. At the pre-dinner drinks he spotted her in the distance, dressed in a rather severe black frock (pre-war, he guessed, she probably doesn't have enough money to buy a new one). He rather thought she might approach him to congratulate him, but she seemed busy talking to other people. Perhaps later, when all these formalities are over, he can mention to her his plan to start up their lab again, provided the Americans occupying that sector of Berlin will give permission. He sees no reason why they shouldn't.

He walks up to the podium, a sheaf of paper in his hand, and stops to survey the crowd, enjoying the hushed expectation. Something snags out of the corner of his eye. Lise. But she's not wearing the black frock, she's covered it up with something else. A lab coat. As he stares, silent, he realises it's still not clean. The coat is the grey colour of dust, of ashes.

He opens his mouth and starts to read his carefully prepared speech, which includes both a summary of his ground-breaking work on nuclear fission and a cautiously worded plea that such work in the future should be only for peaceful purposes. But all he can hear coming out of his mouth is the electronic click of a Geiger counter drowning whatever excuses he is trying to make.

Editors' Note:

There's something irresistible about dramatising the events of a vital juncture in history, the glimpse it offers of real people, living real, complex lives. With "Lise and Otto", we are presented not only with the unfortunately common erasure of women's contributions to science, but simultaneously with the erasure of Jews from public life in pre-WWII Germany. Pippa has drawn Otto so deftly that his conflict is tangible. The genuine regret at being unable to continue working with his great friend versus the privilege of being allowed to get on with the science, and indeed ultimately benefit from how the events transpire. His continued silence during the story, and after it ends, speaks volumes.

The Colour of Their Eyes

Dilys Rose

They are survivors. Hailing from the north, from the fretted edges of a hard, inhospitable landscape, their hair is the rust-red of iron-rich rivers. In the dark months, their skin has the bluish tint of skimmed milk but, in summer sun, is creamy and freckled like a tit's egg. Their eyes are ice-blue. They are of average height and slight build, with strong legs. They'll take turf over tarmac, peaty whisky over Pinot Grigio, are prone to seasonal gloom, and share a taste for meandering ballads about thwarted love and sorry ends. People say they could be sisters, but they've been closer than sisters and more distant than strangers.

Dourly chivalrous as ever, Lachie, one by one, offered them the crook of his arm to disembark, turfed their backpacks and provisions onto the shingle, and chugged off. The mainland was less than a mile away, but the haze hanging over the skyline made it seem further. They whooped and twirled. They'd been waiting for this all winter. Just the two of them, in splendid, shared isolation. Not that they were really alone: there were birds everywhere – flapping overhead, picking over the foreshore, huddled in clumps on rocks, riding the dinky, dappling waves.

The bothy could have done with a lick of paint, but it had been left clean and tidy. Cora and Bea took their time deciding on bunks. Should they sleep up close or as far apart as the space allowed? By a window or next to a wall? They opted for beds against opposite walls. It wasn't as if they'd need to whisper in the night: there was nobody to disturb.

As on previous volunteering stints – they'd come to the island twice before, but only once together, and both times as part of a group – Lachie had given them an extra week's provisions – mainly tinned and dry goods – in case bad weather prevented him returning at the week's end. The main thing was that, rather than being tied to a rota and taking pot luck with other people's cooking styles, they could cook what and when they wanted. And they'd brought treats of their own. Cora had brought some fancy chocolate and two boxes of Pringles, Bea a Christmas bottle of malt saved for the occasion.

The first task was to clean up the southern beach. It was mild for mid-March, dry and bright. They took turn about to trundle the trolley along the boardwalk, and to note down any birds spotted. The puffins hadn't returned yet from winter migration, but there were plenty of plummeting gannets, looping fulmars, cruising skuas. Around skuas, you had to be ready to duck. If they have young, skuas will attack, and go straight for your head.

The beach was a mess: yards of frayed rope and torn netting, burst buoys, broken lobster pots and, of course, all kinds of plastic debris. They worked well together: collecting, bagging and raking at a similar pace, joining forces to hoick bulky stuff onto the trolley – the ribs of a salt-rotted sofa, a rusty oil drum. They didn't speak much, but now and again something caught in the tidewrack was worthy of comment: the Russian clock, the small, green plastic spaceman, encrusted with barnacles. It was the kind of free gift that kids of the '60s and '70s would dig out of packets of Rice Krispies. Had it been bobbing around since the first moon landing? Cora popped it in her pocket.

Beach-cleaning took most of the day, but it felt good to see the sand restored to its glittering sweep. In the grand scheme of things, they'd made such a minuscule difference, but what, really, could anybody hope for? Everybody did what they could, and tried not to get too downhearted by the endless reports on the degradation of the planet. The sun was setting when they started back, the trolley piled high with rubbish. They took a couple of selfies: happy smiles, cheeks pinking in the last of the sun's rays, for the blog they'd write up later. Much later.

As soon as it got dark, the temperature plummeted. Cora lit the stove and Bea prepared dinner: bangers and mash followed by yoghurt and blueberries. It wouldn't have mattered what they ate: after working outdoors, pretty much anything tasted great. They took a dram to the water's edge. It was a still, frosty night, the sky sprinkled with stars, the mainland garlanded with streetlights. The shingle rattled at the tide's drag. Unseen, a drumming snipe, a chirruping pipistrelle.

Sláinte!

It had rained in the night, but the morning sun streamed through the thin curtains. The boardwalk was next on the list. They loaded the trolley with fresh planks, a couple of clawhammers, a bag of nails and, in case they came across more rubbish, the remains of a roll of bin bags. The planks were heavy, and the trolley was tricky to manoeuvre, especially on bends. If it toppled off into the boggy ground, they'd have a hell of a job to get it back on the boardwalk.

They intended to return to the beach, replacing any broken planks as they went, take the northerly loop past the stack, check on the bird colonies, then head back to base. It soon became evident that a number of planks had also become very loose. The Trust couldn't afford the bad publicity that visitors falling off the boardwalk might bring. Cora and Bea wrenched and hammered, hammered and wrenched. Sometimes the broken planks were easily removed. Others were a two-woman job. Progress was slow. Where the path moved inland, ground-nesting birds rose up, flustering noisily, to divert attention from their nests.

New debris had already washed up on the beach – and worse: three dead gannets. It's all too common for birds to be strangled by twine or netting, but there was no sign of this, nor of predation, and three in the same spot was unusual. Ruffled plumage, ice-blue eyes, wings zigzagged above their heads as if about to fire themselves at the water – even in death, the gannets had a dishevelled grandeur.

Though scavengers will strip a carcass in a matter of days, it was not an option to let nature take its course: the last outbreak of avian flu was too recent. They hadn't thought to bring along a spade, so couldn't bury the birds to the depth of an arm's length, as required. The only thing for it was to double-bag, take them back to base and seek advice from the Trust.

I'm not touching them, said Bea.

You don't have to *touch* them. You're wearing work gloves.

The gloves will get contaminated.

Cora wrapped a rolled-up bin bag around one of her own work gloves and picked up a gannet by the tail.

Look, she said. It's not so different from picking up dog shit.

I've never picked up dog shit in my life, said Bea, and don't plan to start anytime soon.

The principle's the same. Besides, it's just an extra precaution.

I'm taking an extra precaution by not touching them, said Bea.

I'm not over the moon about this, either, said Cora, but somebody's got to do it. We shouldn't leave them exposed.

Who's going to know?

I'll know, for one, said Cora. Why are you being such an arse? We signed up for this together. Just the two of us. Who else can I count on for cooperation?

Their stand-off on the beach – Cora and Bea, chins in the air, knuckles jammed into hips, looking blue-eyed daggers at each other – might have seemed comical had there been any observers other than the heedless birds. The tide inched in. The breeze rippled through the machair. The gulls and terns and fulmars continued their search for food, and the skuas persisted in their intent surveillance.

Cora and Bea lived on opposite sides of the same city. They'd known each other for a handful of years, but had met more often on nature reserves than in urban cafes. The Trust suggested they spend some time together before their spell on the island so, in the run-up to Christmas, at Bea's suggestion, they had a soup-and-sandwich lunch in the café bar of a struggling, independent cinema that showed classic movies and European arthouse stuff. It was in danger of going down the tubes, and Bea wanted to support it.

Castaway was showing, which seemed too much of a coincidence not to give it a whirl. Besides, there was a two-for-one ticket offer. The movie, based on a memoir from the 1980s, is about a man and a woman who contract to spend a year together on a desert island. Things start off well enough, but the relationship goes from bad to worse. The man and woman are on the brink of destroying each other before it sinks in that if either hopes to survive, they have no choice but to cooperate.

That had better not happen to us, said Cora.

It won't, said Bea. No way.

Nah, said Cora.

It only took Cora a couple of minutes to bag up the birds and sling them on the trolley. Bea's refusal to help went on bugging her, but the boardwalk wouldn't mend itself. All the way to the stack, the only sounds that passed between them were the tap of a hammer or the thump of a broken plank tossed on the trolley.

Directly opposite the stack were two more dead gannets.

Your turn, said Cora.

Shouldn't we do the usual checks first?

Suit yourself. But I'm not taking no for an answer.

Who said you could boss me around?

I'm not bossing you around.

You bloody well are.

The checks involved scrambling to the top of the steep path where the birds could be better observed. The ground was dry, and purchase was poor. If Cora and Bea hadn't been having their own *Castaway* moment, they'd have relished crawling as close as they dared to the cliff edge, maybe even belting out the chorus of Greta Van Fleet's cover of "Meet on the Ledge", but no, everything was done by the book, and joyless. In any direction, the views were breathtaking, but their spat took the flavour out of the clifftop lunch, and the shine off the ancient peaks, the sparkling Minch.

On the way back, Bea lost her footing and slid several yards downhill before colliding with a gorse bush. Cora saw her foutering around, doing God knows what, then, with a shriek – of fright, pain? – she sprang to her feet and stumbled on, not stopping until she'd reached the bottom. Not wanting to come a cropper herself, Cora picked her way to the gorse bush. Oh, the irony. Bea had crashed straight into yet another dead gannet. The yolk-yellow head was pressed between twisted wings. It must have been dead for longer than the others as a scavenger had made heavy inroads into the breast and legs. She took a bin bag from her pocket.

Bea, like a bad actor, was pacing the beach, stamping and throwing her arms around. Reluctantly, Cora made her way down, the bagged gannet bumping against her leg.

Well? said Cora.

Well, what?

Two more birds to be bagged.

Be my guest, said Bea. I told you I'm not touching them.

Chrissakes, said Cora, doing it herself as swiftly and efficiently as possible. You can push the fucking trolley by yourself, then.

Suits me.

Tight-lipped, they continued repairs on the final stretch of boardwalk. By the time they reached the sign marking where the graveyard had once stood, the clouds were dark, rain-heavy. Before wolves were hunted to extinction on the mainland, the island was popular as a burial site. It was believed that wolves raided graveyards and, rather than suffer such desecration, coastal dwellers chose to row across the Minch to lay their dead to rest in wolf-free ground.

They stacked the broken planks on the woodpile outside the bothy. The birds went in the wheelie bin, its lid weighted down with a rock. After logging the day's activities, Cora messaged the Trust but, as ever, the signal was weak. Preparing the evening meal was grim. Usually, this was a time when they could kick back and enjoy each other's company, but the shared isolation, envisaged as the best possible scenario, had become anything but. Of course the wood was slow to catch and, when it did, it smoked and spat. Of course the food tasted crappy.

And then the storm came. They were woken in the night by roaring thunder, lightning streaking across the walls. A banshee of a wind tore about as if, at any moment, it might pick up the bothy and fling it into the Minch. It was impossible to sleep, though Cora must have dropped off at some point because she dreamed that it was raining birds: dead birds, with rigid legs and twisted feet, the clouds opening like sacks and dropping their load.

In the morning, Bea was slow to stir and reluctant to get out of bed, complaining of a headache, a sore throat. Grudgingly, Cora made a pot of coffee – pointing out that she'd done this every morning since they arrived, and hadn't signed up as a barista. She took her coffee and stepped outside. The wood pile had collapsed. Logs and kindling were strewn about. The wheelie bin was on its side, disgorging its contents. Serrated beaks and webbed, blue-black feet poked out of a torn bag. Had rats torn the bag open? The air smelled bad, as if something rank had been dragged up from the seabed, and the landing area was knee-deep in scallops, the small ones, queenies – there must have been thousands of them. In a feeding frenzy, a throng of gulls snatched up scallops by the dozen. They soared, opened their beaks and let the twin fans smash on the rocks below. And amid the heaps of empty shells lay more dead birds: a kittiwake and five gannets. In the distance, the storm rumbled.

Bea was at the table, hunched over a puffin mug. Trust mugs, featuring birds common on the island, were available at retail outlets across the north west. Puffin mugs outsold the rest.

Get a move on, said Cora. There's stuff to be done.

I can't, said Bea. I'm sick.

You were fine yesterday.

Well, I'm not today! I'm aching all over and my throat hurts like hell. And this – she held up her mug – tastes foul.

Bea tipped the coffee down the sink, went back to bed, pulled the covers over her head, coughing loudly a couple of times. Cora was convinced Bea was faking it, but couldn't force her to lend a hand.

After a determinedly leisurely breakfast, Cora fetched her work gloves and began bagging and double-bagging where the initial bags had torn. She and Bea – she and *Bea*! – should have buried the birds in the first place. But they weren't supposed to be buried in *plastic*, so that would now involve even more handling. And the more handling Cora did, the less keen she was to continue. She rebuilt the woodpile, not very neatly, filled the basket with logs and took it inside. Still no signal. Still no reply.

As the morning wore on, Cora had to concede from Bea's hacking cough and raging temperature, that she was, in fact, sick. To make amends, she made scrambled eggs and garlic mushrooms for lunch, but after a bite or two Bea set down her fork, crawled back under the duvet and turned her face to the wall.

The plan had been to inspect the chew plates to monitor the rat population, and set moth traps to catalogue non-native species. Moths can be invasive, and can fly much further than rats can swim. Rather than sitting on her hands, Cora decided to do the chew plates, and check on storm damage elsewhere. Before heading out, she fetched another blanket for Bea's bed and a couple of paracetamol. The first aid kit didn't contain anything stronger.

Whisky, said Bea. I want whisky.

It's a bit early. Why not save it for a nightcap?

It's my whisky, Bea croaked. I'll decide when to drink it.

By the time Cora got back, she, too, was feeling feverish. Bea – puffy and heavy-eyed under a bobble hat, propped up in bed with the duvet up to her chin – was a sorry sight: and woozy too – she'd made quite a dent in the whisky. The bothy was freezing. Grumbling, Cora relit the stove Bea had let go out. Being sick was bad enough without being cold as well, and she was feeling worse by the minute.

For the evening meal, Cora made cheese toasties and heated up a can of chicken noodle soup – everybody's granny's go-to invalid food. It wasn't as good as she remembered, but neither had much of an appetite.

We need to let the Trust know we're sick, said Bea.

How do we do that without a phone signal?

A flare?

Flares are for emergencies. Does this really count as an emergency?

Who cares. I don't feel like waiting around to find out.

We should hold off for a day or two.

Why? said Bea. Because you say so?

Because we don't want to send a false alarm. It might just be one of those twenty-four-hour bugs, said Cora. You – *we* – could be on the mend tomorrow.

They weren't. They were a whole lot worse. Cora agreed to try a flare, but the flares had spent the winter in the outhouse, in a poorly sealed box, and turned out to be as much use as damp squibs. Their texts remained unsent. They had no other ideas.

What do we do now? wailed Bea.

Put up with it, said Cora. What else can we do?

For the next few days – they still can't agree on whether it was four or five – they only left their beds for wood, food or calls of nature. They got through a pack and a half of flu powders, and the remains of the whisky, which was the only thing that took the edge off. Often, it was too much trouble to light the stove, which was temperamental at the best of times.

They coughed and groaned, sweated and shivered, swaddled themselves in duvets or kicked them off. They dipped in and out of sleep and feverish ramblings. They lay awake, in the icy blackness, too listless to investigate the scrabbling of something that had found its way into the bothy. They stared at the flaking walls, and constellations of swatted midges, silvery snail trails and dusty spider webs. They spent so long watching the flames flicker in the stove. Sunlight slid across the window. Rain speckled the glass, ran down in rivulets. Clouds drifted past. Day slid into night. Night retreated and dawn arrived, crisp and watermelon pink, or limp and grey. They could hear the birds even when they couldn't see them. How many were sick? How many would survive, how many die? And what of themselves?

Occasionally, they talked, about their families, pets – Cora's dog, Bea's cat – relationships. Most of their friends were pairing off, but they were still playing the field, also known as not meeting the right person. They were silent for long periods. They bickered pettily, half-heartedly, over whose turn it was for the first (hotter) shower, whose turn to light the stove, prepare something to eat, wash up. They longed for some brash daytime TV. At least there was plenty of food: they weren't about to throttle each other over the last biscuit.

When the texts finally got through and Lachie returned, with two paramedics, to transport them back to the mainland, all three were in hazmat suits. Lachie looked from Bea to Cora, from Cora to Bea, his weathered head shaking slowly.

Well, I never, he said.

They are survivors. Hailing from the north, from the fretted edges of a hard, inhospitable landscape, their hair is the rust-red of iron-rich rivers. In the dark months, their skin has the bluish tint of skimmed milk but, in summer sun, is creamy and freckled like a tit's egg. They are of average height and slight build, with strong legs. They'll take turf over tarmac, peaty whisky over Pinot Grigio. They are prone to seasonal gloom, and share a taste for meandering ballads about thwarted love and sorry ends. People say they could be sisters, but they've been closer than sisters and more distant than strangers. Their eyes, once ice-blue, are black now, black as the eyes of the gannets that came through. They don't want to talk about it.

Editors' Note:

We rarely really consider the dangers of being truly isolated, as you can certainly be if you get stranded on most of Scotland's small islands. All it takes is a change in the weather and failure of the phone network to cut you loose from the safety net of civilisation. Dilys's dismantling of Bea and Cora's wish to be free as the birds is expertly handled here, the pair of middle-class urbanites left alone to survive a frightening and ultimately transformative experience.

Broderie Écossaise

Eris Young

Fionnie gives a little gasp and puts her finger in her mouth. There's no blood, no real injury. The gasp and finger sucking are only theatre: a way to break the monotony. A clock ticks in the room. Thread whispers through linen.

Outside, a single hoof-strike sounds against the pavement. Fionnie drops hoop, silk and needle, and rushes to her feet.

"I am very well to meet you, and to learn many fine stitches together."

Marguerite's voice, her charming, approximate English, echoes off the marble of the hall. She is trim and dark, with a face like a fox that bespeaks mischief. Something in her accent, a note in her voice just out of true, tugs at Fionnie's guts. Fionnie dives into a curtsey, and when she comes up, Marguerite gives her a wink, and the heat in her belly intensifies.

Marguerite is here to watch her.

Yes, they will learn new stitches together, which is what Fionnie, the maids and Marguerite herself have been told. But Dad also knows her father: the family are staunch Huguenots, despite the risk, and so there can be no doubt that Marguerite, unlike Fionnuala, is a good Christian girl. So all of them – Fionnie, the maids, Marguerite and certainly Dad – know that Marguerite is also here to make sure Fionnie keeps out of trouble, doesn't get up to any of her *nonsense* again, until Dad can pass her safely into another man's keeping.

Fionnie doesn't mind. She likes embroidery, likes learning new stitches, and seeing the results of her efforts. If nothing else, she knows the danger of idle hands.

There is a letter from Ewan.

He's still in Rotterdam, but writes joyfully to tell her that he's coming back sooner than planned. Fionnie fights off the urge to crumple his letter into a ball and eat it. Instead, she slips it under her mattress with the others: he will expect her to show him the whole fat stack of them, tied up with ribbon, when he gets back.

She's dragging her pen through a reply, trying to dredge up more platitudes from the silt at the bottom of her brain, when Marguerite knocks on the doorframe.

"Oh, thank God." Fionnie throws down the pen. "Let's go outside."

She's tying on her bonnet in front of the tall mirror when Marguerite says:

"What an odd thing to stitch!"

Fionnie freezes. "Don't — !"

Marguerite is crouched beside the basket of samplers. She's holding up one of Fionnie's bigger ones. A pastoral scene, of a sort. For a moment, Fionnie is terrified Marguerite will recognise the subject, lying prone, one leg folded under him, on a gravel driveway made of French knots beside a tall dappled horse of fine satin stitch. But of course, Marguerite hasn't met him yet.

"Oh, I'm sorry!" Marguerite drops the piece, her face going a fetching pink.

"No, no. It's nothing. It's just – not finished yet. I'm embarrassed by it." Not quite true. The stitches are finished, it's the *other* part that isn't. Still, Fionnie lives in hope.

"Anyway," she adds, trying to laugh, although her palms are sweating. "It's only a silly fancy. I hope you don't think me morbid."

Rain sheets down, battering the windows and pooling in the muntins. Fionnie practises her French, her cheerful, blundering efforts sending Marguerite into hysterics. It will be sunny and warm right now in Manosque, and Marguerite describes birds, rabbits and sheep, fields of flowers you can run through, the smell of lavender. Fionnie lets her needle travel where it may, hardly attending the shapes and colours that bloom in its wake. In her mind, Manosque is bright and full of colour, as distant from Gillieshall's forbidding woods and moors as from the Moon.

There's a stew Marguerite wants to make for their Sunday dinner, with Fionnie's help, one meant for cold, wet days like these. The project has Dad's approval: he thinks learning to cook will civilise her. For her own part, Fionnie is looking forward to feeding Marguerite morsels of mushroom and carrot, sneaking sips of cooking sherry and laughing with her in the warm confines of the kitchen. Everyone wins.

Marguerite drops her hoop with a delicate sigh, shaking out the stiffness from her fingers, and Fionnie looks down at her own work at last. And swallows, realising what she's stitched.

The identity of the subject is plain enough: no one else's hair could be rendered in such a shade. And in such a pose – and Fionnie herself in such a one. Well.

Heat, and then cold, washes through her. She's got to undo it. *Now.* She needs to unpick it all before Dad or a curious maid, or God preserve us, Marguerite herself can see. Before what Fionnie has drawn in thread can seep out into the world.

Hands trembling, eyes unaccountably prickling, she snips the thread and reverses her work. She spends the rest of the afternoon teasing threads backwards out of the linen, heart pounding in the base of her throat. Unmaking Marguerite's face and grey gown, her hands and damning ankles. Failing to make conversation with the real Marguerite, sitting across from her, busy at her own work and not seeming to mind the silence.

When she is done, the light is thin and her head is tense with squinting. The linen is only holed a little, wisps of thread still clinging in fawn and black and grey. Fionnie feels empty and relieved, like the fabric.

Three nights later, Marguerite climbs into her bed.

"What are you doing!" Fionnie scrambles back, yanking the blanket up to her chin.

"*Il fait si froid ici!*" Marguerite whispers, innocent-voiced, but with a twinkle in her eye.

It's too late, Fionnie realises with a hot fluttering low in her stomach, a panic indistinguishable from desire. She's done it again. She unpicked it all, but it must have done the damned thing anyway.

"Stop," she hisses. "We can't do this."

"I saw what you stitched. I was watching you." Marguerite's breath is hot in her ear. "I know what you want. I want it too."

"No, no, you don't," Fionnie stammers. "*I* made this happen. You're not – you're not choosing it. You don't understand."

But Marguerite only smiles, as if she understands exactly.

And Fionnie wants her. She wants Marguerite as she hasn't wanted anything in years, and with Ewan coming home this might be her only chance.

In the dark, with the sweet heat of Marguerite's body so near, it's easy to push aside her doubts.

With a flush of embarrassment, she realises how naïve the poses she had stitched were; she doesn't even know what she was wishing for. But Marguerite soon takes her in hand. Her skilled, clever, mischievous hands. Under the counterpane, kindly autumn rain veiling their sighs, she teaches Fionnie something new.

Ewan arrives, as usual, without warning. She and Marguerite round the side of the house just as he reaches the cul-de-sac. He sees her, raises a hand, and stands in his stirrups to dismount.

It all comes out exactly like the sampler: the gravel drive like knots of silk, Ewan's leg twisted under him at that unnatural angle. His silken dapple-grey horse unconcerned, leaning down to crop some grass.

Fionnie claps a hand over her mouth, but not from fright or shock. After all, she knew this was going to happen. It's because she can see, finally, the knot of understanding tying off in Marguerite's mind.

Marguerite stands a long time watching the grooms knot up around Ewan, helping him to his feet and supporting him as he hobbles up the drive, swearing at them. Her face is as blank as if it had been stitched in place.

"Come, let's go inside." Fionnie reaches for her.

Marguerite recoils.

Dad corners her before she reaches the foot of the stairs.

"Ewan is in the blue parlour."

Fionnie watches the heel of Marguerite's shoe disappear onto the upper landing. She tries to push past Dad, but he moves, as ever, to stand in her way.

He doesn't know, not the whole of it, but he suspects she's been up to *something*. At the very least, Fionnie thinks, he knows she is not crying for Ewan.

"He is your *last chance*. Do you understand me?"

She sits beside Ewan in the blue parlour. She bathes his brow, doses him with what the doctor advises. It is only a fracture, but Ewan is very dramatic about it, and she allows him to believe it's him she's upset for.

Fionnie feels bruised, as if she was the one who'd taken a fall. She remembers being a child, poking the cat with a needle to see what it would do, and then the remorse like a tangle of thread in her belly, impossible to untie.

To pass the time, she embroiders the alphabet. Verses. *Give her of the fruit of her hands…* Simple roses, thistles, a border of swallows and curlicues. Stylised, unrealistic. Safe.

She doesn't leave Ewan's side because she knows that, as long as she stays here, she doesn't have to face Marguerite, and what she has done. As long as she stays here, and doesn't stray again from the pattern she's been given, she can't hurt anyone.

When she finally goes up to change her clothes, she finds Marguerite kneeling at the hearth. The sampler, the piece with Ewan on the gravel next to his horse, is blackening on the logs.

"Oh."

"You can't let anyone see this," Marguerite murmurs into the fire.

"Marguerite." Fionnie's voice cracks. "I am so sorry. I was monstrous."

Marguerite's brow knits. "You must be more careful."

Shame tightens the knot in Fionnie's stomach. "I know, I—"

"I know myself, Fionnula." Marguerite drops the poker and finally stands to face her. "I know how I feel. How I *felt*. About you. Even before you – stitched me."

They work a piece, together. A large one. Marguerite does the ornaments, the borders and flourishes, and Fionnie, of course, the subjects.

She stitches not herself this time, nor Marguerite, but Ewan and a girl. A new girl, a girl for him to love, who can love him back. It's hard work, creating a woman who looks nothing like Fionnie or Marguerite or anyone she knows. A woman sewn out of whole cloth.

Marguerite challenges herself with the whitework on the woman's wedding dress, and Fionnie wonders if the real gown, once their work is complete, will have whitework as well.

Fionnie takes pains to show the girl, this anonymous girl whom she can only hope must exist somewhere, smiling. Blushing with real happiness. Fionnie makes herself believe in – long for – this girl's happiness with Ewan.

When the letter comes, four months later, and Dad storms off upstairs to stomp around his study, Fionnie pretends not to hear him blaspheme, cursing Ewan's name.

This time, she does not unpick the stitches. They wrap the sampler in silk and paper and hide it until it is time to give it to the postman: it will make a very fine wedding present.

They christen it, each of them, with a drop of blood from a fingertip. They stitch their initials over it, and their blessings, and then fall into bed together.

This time there is blood on the fabric, and Fionnie's gasps aren't fictions to pass the time.

Editors' Note:

For an age when daughters were treated as chattels passed from a father's keeping to that of a suitable husband, the girls' private desires of necessity kept to themselves, the sympathetic magic of embroidery is a perfect invention. But Eris's real masterstroke is the generous ending she conceives for Ewan, and also we hope for Fionnie and Marguerite.

Grimaldo the Weeping

Ali Maloney

In all the stories my father told me about Grimaldo the Weeping, he never said his arrival would be heralded with the fall of snow. I had never seen snow before.

It fell in a dream-like haze of flakes that tasted of ash and tar. I knew my father would have scolded me for sticking my tongue out to catch it, but it felt so serene and magical I couldn't resist. Besides, he was not around anymore.

It settled on the roofs and ground, and over the town's walls. I could see all the children laughing and playing in it. From my vantage point outside the walls, where I'd clean the chimney of father's thatched cottage, I watched them in awe. They might have seen snow before in gilded storybooks or had it imported into playrooms, but it had certainly never fallen here before. Not as far as I could remember.

Despite his size, I almost didn't see him approach. There was a single path that led down from the hills towards the town, and he was camouflaged against the snow. Coated in greasepaint, he rode an albino ox, their bulging muscles blended as if they were one: a snorting circus centaur.

The only breaks in the white-out were Grimaldo the Weeping's shimmering, meat-red nose, the diamonds painted over his eyes and the black straps of his mount's harness. Even the ox's horns, normally a hypnotic aqua I had heard, were so dusty and ash-encrusted that they too blended into the haze that descended upon us that day. Father had told me so many horrors about Grimaldo the Weeping that I grew up thinking he was just a fairy tale concocted to warn me off something, although I was never quite sure just what.

Above his ruffles, his face looked almost infantile – and it was not just the lack of hair on his face and head that gave that effect. There was a bright-eyed and innocent curiosity to his features and gaze that belied the ravages he had wrought.

I felt for a while that I was the only one who could see him. The children did not look up from the shapes they made in the snow until one of the watchmen raised a cry. The noise necessitated by the opening of the gates echoed across the valley.

As he drew closer, I could see him in greater detail. From his sash, sewer-rat grey, hung his tools, vague in their shapes and purposes. The cart he drew behind was covered with a threadbare burlap through which poked metal and gears, hints of the contraptions used for his divine task.

I could now see that everyone had come to watch him arrive – a mixture of the curious, frightened and the excited. Someone would be immortalised today.

The mayor was ordering the pews to be ripped from the church and set up in the market square. Although the church could likely hold the whole town – they made a show of their piety after all – it seemed such a juvenile and superstitious place to host the arrival of Grimaldo the Weeping.

I thought that maybe this was an opportunity for me to slip in – the gates were still open, left neglected by the curious guards – but could imagine father's voice urging me to stay hidden, safe.

Mothers ensured that their children wore their best dresses and bonnets, while the men cleaned their faces of tar and soot. The various hierarchies of dignitaries drafted up a show bill of all the whimsies, songs, feats and tall tales that the town could muster. This was what Grimaldo the Weeping had come for after all. It would be catastrophic if he was not amused by any of the entertainment. If he did not find a tale to add to his collection, so the legend went, then they would all be condemned. I wondered if that would also apply to my empty shack outside the town limits.

I longed for a peek in the great jester's cart, curious if I'd find my father in there.

Perhaps, during the show, I could sneak in unnoticed.

Grimaldo the Weeping waited in silence while the town readied themselves, frantic in their preparations, fearful that his impatience give way to violent anger. But it looked like he slept. It must be the only rest he could get in between riding from town to town, collecting tales. He hadn't even dismounted from the gnarled, throne-like saddle. His ox drooped, eyes closed, and dozed. Their gigantic white frames dominated the square and blended into the snowy ground, as if they were a statue that had always been there.

Maids and courtesans fussed about, getting bowls of milk, which they laid out for the visitor, but these remained untouched. Seamstresses hovered around, ready to repair tattered garments and cloth, but dared not approach.

The whole town was eager to win the giant's favour.

I could see it all from my vantage point, transfixed.

Once the stage was set, the performers readied themselves, and the townsfolk gathered. The show was about to begin. The mayor coughed tentatively into the network of pipes and horns that had been rigged for amplification.

The sound brought an utter silence, but no one moved.

Nervously, the mayor coughed again.

Slowly, almost agonisingly so, Grimaldo the Weeping opened his black eyes and looked up. The mayor seemed to shrink under his gaze before giving a stumbling curtsey and declared what a great honour this was. From my angle, I couldn't see Grimaldo the Weeping's face, but from the mayor's increasingly frightened agitation, his audience was not yet won over.

The mayor hurried his speech to a final cry to raise the curtain – even though there wasn't such a thing – and collapsed off the stage, his attendants hurrying him down an alley, out of sight.

And with that, the show began.

A procession of storytellers, magicians, dancers, orators, gymnasts and even a clown performed for Grimaldo the Weeping, ever impassive and imposing. He would take one story from the town; it would be immortalised forever – and the residents fell over themselves to be eternalised. From the stories father had told me, I thought Grimaldo the Weeping only took stories. These feats of physical extravagance, however spectacular, were wasting time. My knuckles clenched my woodworm-ridden handholds on the chimney as I thought of these fools dooming the whole town for their indulgence. I had no love for the place, but doubted I could survive without their cast-offs.

After a particularly excruciating display of hermaphrodites feeding themselves into themselves to make a human ouroboros, the stage was taken by six huge, hairy men in stained butcher aprons, slick with both fresh and congealed gore. They were each holding a ferocious looking cleaver in their left hand and a sharpened bone in their right.

At some invisible cue, they began to hammer the bones against their cleavers, making a thunderous racket. The butcher's cacophony quickly eased into a suite of beautiful lullabies. They must have sharpened both bone and blade to a perfect pitch. Their concert was hypnotic, and went on until Grimaldo the Weeping raised his hand to signal that was enough and the show was over.

With slow, almost mechanical motions, he reached back into his sack. I could imagine those gigantic fingers clasping his scythe, the heat of its flames hungry to feed. Did this town have no stories? No epic sagas worthy to be added to Grimaldo the Weeping's collection? Nothing the town had shown him could possibly be worth preservation. That meant he had stopped the show for another reason… I had to hurry.

I had not entered the town since I first came to report that father was missing and had been laughed out of the gates. I still hesitated at the portal.

Grimaldo the Weeping was setting up for his own show before the final judgement. As I understood was his tradition, he would replay one story from his previous travels, either to show the permanence of the stories he took, or to show what a good story was.

He was unwrapping his cart as I sneaked in, grunting circus shanties as he heaved ropes and hoisted the contraption within up to its full splendour – like gallows, but with more pulleys, gears and counterweights. It towered above even the tallest buildings. Once the structure was locked and it cast a shadow over the whole town, Grimaldo the Weeping reached into his bag of stories. Every eye was on the bag, stained red, as he chose.

My gut knotted as something in my mind expected my father's tale to be pulled from the sack.

One seemed to satisfy him, and he pulled out a severed head and mounted it on one of the spikes protruding from his machine.

The head, a scarred warrior's face, was in endless motion, the tongue and throat silently gargling and gurgling out its story. It wasn't until Grimaldo the Weeping cranked the mechanism and worked the bellows that air pumped through the head and the tale became audible.

He told of his journey across the desolated sands, of getting drunk on the fermented tears of his enemies, of leading peasant villagers in uprisings; of crushing a tyrant warlock's serpentine skull with his bare hands; of daring rescues during which he fought ice dragons and stole away with gold that turned to dust when brought to the surface. It was a majestic tale; the whole town was enraptured. Even once Grimaldo the

Weeping stopped the mechanism and removed the head, the tongue still enunciated the story – over and over.

He was reaching for something else in his cart now, and I knew what was going to happen. We were all going to die unless I did something.

I shouted.

I cursed the incompetence of the assembly, oblivious to their disgust.

I told them of what Grimaldo the Weeping would do to us, that he was the dragon my father had set out to slay. I told them how he would crush their houses underfoot and wield his flaming scythe, severing their spines and taking their souls. I told them of the glorious cities that no longer existed following his visit: the underwater paradises of Ght'ugan, the gutter crawlspaces of the rust devils, the fortress at the end of the world held siege by spider-riding barbarians, the palace's swamp demons, the heavens overwhelmed by plague… I told them of my father battling Grimaldo the Weeping on crumbling volcano tops, his own contraptions of self-winding catapults sending a barrage of disease-ridden cows into Grimaldo the Weeping's snarling mouth. I told them how they fought for weeks, never resting, their red-eyed, roaring rage never diminishing. The wounds they sustained gushed, creating new rivers and streams down into the valleys.

I kept on, not knowing if these were tales my father had told me or that I just concocted on the spot in order to frighten the townsfolk. I kept on talking, needing to delay the inevitable death. They needed to understand what Grimaldo the Weeping was, what he had come for … and what would happen if he didn't get a story to add to his collection.

But the great clown god smiled, and replaced the weapon he had gone to unholster.

He had found his story after all, and the town would be spared.

And I do not know whether or not you will ever hear this story, but I shall keep telling it forever, until a mechanical breath gives voice to the eternal machinations of my tongue.

I only hope you listen.

Editors' Note:

Ali plunders his career in performance to outstanding effect here to present us with the ultimate in gothic grotesques. A clown, but not just any clown… but a God of Clowns come to judge. No-one who ever stepped onto a stage or attempted to tell a story wouldn't be terrified of Grimaldo the Weeping!

Blood Lines

Russell Jones

The white coats prod me, their arms and jaws whirring. There's an icy rush pulsing through my veins and I'm wide awake – a pert daisy sprouting from my snowy bed. I sit up and rub my thighs, aching from the defrost.

"How do you feel?" She's a half-formed ghost in goggles. The others have disappeared.

"Am I alive?" I want to say, part joking and, therefore, happy some of my old humour made it through the chill. Instead, I rub my eyes and flex my hands like a pianist before a performance. She waves a blue rod around me, and my vision clears. I see her now: pale, thin, the iris of her eyes flickering between brown and green. She smiles and her pupils flash, as though taking a photograph.

"Any pain?" She prods my arm and leg with a sharp finger.

"No."

"How's your vision?" She waves in front of my face, and I notice her accent: Scottish, but not quite. It's as though she's been watching old reruns of *Still Game* and *Outlander*, neither of them really catching on her tongue. "Clearing up yet?"

"Yes, thanks." I brush her hand away and try to stand. The floor is hard, white as her skin. My legs tremble, but I'm determined. I hold myself up, one hand on the bed, until the strength returns. "I feel fine."

"That's good." She checks her wrist. "Your vitals are steady." She gives a doctor's smile, polite but professional. "Please place your finger on the print."

I put my index finger on the pad she holds, and it bites.

"Ow! What was that?"

"Proof of receipt. Nothing to worry about – a sample for insurance purposes."

I'm too relieved to ask for details, and I want to take in as much as I can. The ward is empty except for the two of us; clean and white, like a glacier. My single bed is the only furniture, but there is a white suitcase near the door. I feel a hundred questions bubbling to escape, but hold them back. There's only one answer I need for now: "How long has it been?"

She checks her wrist again. "You were placed in 2040. It is now 2070."

"Thirty years?" My stomach roars, acid hits my throat and burns. "That long? What about my family?"

Her eyes frost over. I want to shake the information out of her; she should be quicker, she should know the answers before I ask.

"Alive, both of them."

I feel my world starting to rebuild in fractions of memory: the curves of their faces are like the hills, hair sprouting like shrubbery, the pot-holed country roads forming their veins, their hearts like gothic stone cities, their voices are music in the wind. My Scotland, my family, both smile back at me. I want to rush out, to take breaths of the unclinical air and hold them close, to never let them go again.

"Thank goodness." I sigh with relief. "And the C.A.A.?"

"Your brain is still affected by the build-up of amyloids, but there is now a tested cure. You will need to wait one week before the treatment can be administered. We found some early patients reacted poorly post-defrost."

"Poorly?"

"They died." Her bluntness was almost funny. Perhaps she'd picked up a sense of comic timing from those old TV shows, too.

"Where are my things?" I ask. "When can I see my family?"

She points to the white suitcase near the door. "Everything you stored for your emergence is here. We have a reconnection suite ready for you. I can notify your family now – they can be here shortly, if you'd like."

"I'd like."

She approaches the door and a blue panel appears where a handle ought to be.

"One oh one – Donna Cal." The panel blips and she turns to me. "Please dress as you prefer. I will wait on the other side of this door, and escort you to the reconnection suite once you are ready."

She smiles that professional doctorate smile again, and I wince a response. She leaves, the door closing itself behind her. I dress in my old clothes, which I'd chosen primarily for my attachment to them, hoping they'd ease the transition back: a smart suit with a subtle tartan (I can't quite recall whether it's a clan pattern, but nobody really cares about something so outdated, do they?) that I'd worn to work pretty much every day at Falcon Industries. We recycled plastics back into usable oil compounds, after fracking nearly wrecked everything. I shake away the memory of standing outside parliament, jeering at the corrupt politicians who'd sold the land from under our feet, who'd destroyed the mounds and forests our ancestors built.

My body eases into its familiar creases. I don't hold my posture well, but it feels comfortable, like sitting in an old armchair. Ready, I approach the door and it lifts open.

The room reveals nothing of its time. There's no artwork, no decoration or furniture other than two white egg-shaped seats. My doctor nods as she notices me peer inside, and I realise I haven't asked her name.

"Doctor Dredd." She says when I ask. "And I've heard all the jokes." A sudden humanness leaps from her wry retort, and then fizzles away just as quickly. "Shall we go to the reconnection suite?"

"Sure." We walk along a whitewashed corridor, her limbs emitting a quiet hum.

Following, I notice that her legs are synthetic – I can't be sure, but the material looks like one of the polymers we were working on at Falcon Industries, not long before I was given sick leave. One of her legs is decorated with strips of thin metal which seems to change colour as she moves, the light dancing across her kneecap as if on the surface of a bubble. The other leg looks like it's covered in skin, with a small rectangular patch removed, showing a ribbon of coloured wires underneath a clear plate.

"Are you renovating?" I ask, the bland décor somehow unnerving me. It feels like walking through a dull dream.

"No, why?"

"Not much decoration here, it could do with a few licks of paint."

"We find this design helps, we don't want patients to be alarmed or confused by modern décor."

"That happens?"

"More often than you'd expect." She stops at another door. "Here we are, are you ready?"

I nod, she puts her hand on the door and it opens. I step inside a perfect replica of my living room, complete with the holochess board my son bought me for my fiftieth birthday. Thirty years have passed, but it suddenly feels like days, maybe just a few hours since I was last home. I enter cautiously, afraid that I might unsettle something and reveal the imitation. I breathe in the familiar scent of lavender, which I loved to scatter through the house. I want to open the curtains that cover the window, but I'm afraid of what I might see through it. This isn't really my home, I remind myself. The dried-out riverbed that sat songless alongside my house won't be there, but who knows whether this world managed to fix itself or take another few steps towards extinction. I'm not ready for that kind of revelation yet.

"Is this all real, not holographic?" I ask, jittery at the thought of the furniture disappearing with my touch.

"Yes, everything is real," she tells me with a faint, practised smile. "We take every care during replications, building your reconnection suite to your exact standards. There are refreshments in the kitchen, your favourite foods and supplements, just as you requested."

I remember the forms now, the arduous reams of boxes that I had to tick on the day their officers visited to make accurate records of my possessions.

"Not everything is here, but enough for your comfort," Doctor Dredd adds. "Please relax, your family should be here soon."

I suddenly feel nervous, like a stage curtain's about to lift. I walk to the kitchen and pour a glass of orange juice, consider adding a little Nesbite to ease the anxiety, but decide against it. I want a clear head, to feel like myself. I sit on the sofa. It's not quite the same; too firm, too unlived, and they missed the scuff where I rest my arm, but it's close enough to the original.

A bleep sounds, followed by Doctor Dredd's voice: "Donna, your family are here. Would you like them to enter?"

"One moment", I blurt, checking myself in the mirror. I'm still sick, I can feel it, but I look something close to healthy. It only just strikes me that my family won't look the same as I remember them. Thirty years is a lot to miss – I'll be an old memory, a found photograph, a forgotten brooch. "Okay, I'm ready."

The door opens and a man steps through. He looks my age, resembles my husband – or half of him. I'm a cocktail of shock and joy, shaking and failing to hold back tears. The man strides forward and holds me. "Mum, I've missed you."

We talk for hours, me and this stranger. It almost feels like a bad date, me asking awkward, nonsense questions regarding a life I've no clue about.

I must seem like a child to him, a Neanderthal woman from a barely remembered past, scratching around for answers to inane questions.

"Dad's sorry he can't come, but he's okay. He's well, I promise. He'll see you soon," he told me, almost immediately, and I tried to hide my disappointment. My husband had been the proverbial rock when I got ill, solid and reliable, not the sort to dote or crack on me – just what I needed. "We've been prepped," my son admits later. "I'm not meant to say too much. A lot has changed."

War was the first word which came to mind. A terrifying black whip of a word, a flesh-burning cloud in my imagination. But any war couldn't have been that bad: he's alive, after all, and here.

Eventually I have no questions left for which he can offer an answer. He holds me again, squeezes, and I clasp his hands in mine. My fleshy fingers search his palm for clues of his new life. His fingers are hard and thin, his skin is oddly dry. His eyes – those eyes of a boy who loved to run in the rain and fly in the wind – are gone, replaced by the same flashing lenses I saw in Dredd.

"Are you really him?" I ask, though I feel terrible for asking. I desperately hope that my instinct is right, that there is something original still glimmering from within his mechanical frame.

"Of course."

"I'm sorry. You just seem … different."

"It's been thirty years, Mum. I *am* different." He sits down again, next to me, cradling my hand in his. "But I'm the same, pretty much. It's just my eyes, bones and heart." He thumps his chest. "Dad gave me a bad ticker."

I try to give him a reassuring smile, a mother's smile.

He continues, "And the blood, but that's the same for everyone."

"What do you mean?"

He looks around, his finger ticking against his knee like a metronome, just as he did when he was young and restless.

"I've missed you so much, but I'm pleased you were on ice. That you were…" He whispers, "…immune." He sounds scared, the little boy peeking out from under this unshakable body. "We'd no options left; antibiotics were totally useless. We had to change our blood, let our tech do the fighting, or…" He falls into a dark past and all I can do is watch him tumble. An eternity passes in an instant, before he returns to me. "But it's not all bad, we're a bit cooler, calmer now, to help keep everybody safe. We're better. Don't worry."

A mother can't help but worry. I envisage a darkened city, each ancient castle and spire casting a long, permanent shadow on the cobblestone.

The streets are littered with the bruised and blistered bodies of the dead, two inhuman armies fuelled by cool, calm hate. But I have him here, and I try to convince myself that my speculation must be worse than the reality. My thoughts turn to my co-workers, my friends, my husband.

"You said your dad was okay?" I ask.

"He's fine, happy."

That word, happy, is a spear in my side. How could he be happy without me for thirty years, or worse yet, happy *because* he was without me for thirty years?

"He's found someone else?"

"He wanted to tell you in person. It hasn't been easy. He lost a lot when you went away, and more since the transfusions. It wasn't anything personal, it wasn't about you. Believe me. He gave me this." He hands me a pad, a fingerprint glowing on its screen.

"Thank you."

"I have to go now." He looks at the curtains I was too afraid to open, as if someone is peeping through them. "I'm not sure when I'll be back."

"Can I come with you? Where are you going?" I rise too urgently and feel drowned by nausea, my body still adjusting to his news.

"Upgrades." He taps his thighs. "The legs, next. Non-synth is too hazardous, too much risk of cancer, too easy to damage, too hard and expensive to replace. When you're out, you'll see it all. You must be one of the last full-chassis organics, Mum." He smiles weakly. "A celebrity."

"A relic."

"Take care." He kisses my cheek, his lips empty on my skin, and then he's gone.

I rush to the kitchen and mix a full Nesbite into a glass of juice. The packet is blanketed with warnings, but I ignore them and gulp it down, allowing the toxins to take hold. I turn to the window and pull open the curtains. A silver mirror stares back at me, my face melting like ice cream in the sun. I stumble back, the pebbledash floor of my kitchen swirls like comic book quicksand, and I sink to my knees. I lie on the floor, old habits take hold and I feel lavender sprout around me, the blazing sun transforming me into a scorched shadow.

I wake on the sofa, Doctor Dredd's monotone voice asking if I'm okay, do I need anything?

I groan a reply along the lines of "Leave me alone," and she obeys.

Beside me on my faux-ratty footstool, is my ex-husband's excuse, neatly typed and sealed. I can't resist it, even though I know the torture of its truth before I read a single word. I push my finger against the pad, and it unlocks with a taste of my DNA.

He's kind. He lets me down in all the right ways: he missed me so much, he couldn't be sure I was coming back, he tried to keep the fire of his love (I almost laughed at that cliché) going, but the years wore him down.

I can't blame him, even the strongest stars wither eventually. Part of me hopes he's happy, the rest of me wants his head on a spike. I want him and hate him in equal measures, and then realise it's mainly my impending loneliness that makes me crave him. I wash that feeling back with a little Nesbite, feel myself rise like a petal caught in an updraft, carried over the fields and looking down on the houses. I'd rather this illusion than walk out of my reconnection suite as some useless, meaty antiquity.

Doctor Dredd leaves a pad on the kitchen counter, and suggests I take a look in my own time. *NewSynth* – thousands of potential artificial body parts to swap for my pounds of flesh. *Run Faster, See Smarter, Be Better*. The models look terrifying and beautiful, their bodies stripped back to underwear and wires, staring ungleefully into a fictional horizon.

With nothing else to distract me, I use the pad to design myself a new frame. It contains the latest and greatest parts – a heart so strong it will never stop beating, a spine and arms capable of bending steel, legs that can outrun jungle cats, eyes that can see several additional spectrums. I make myself a superwoman, adjusting the hook nose and dark hair I inherited – the features I'd given to my son, once upon a time – utterly incredible and utterly disposable. As I stare at my creation, I can't help but think it could be anyone.

The days blur as I haunt the recreation of my old life, void of the things that made it worth living. Doctor Dredd visits, asks me if I'm depressed, and I treat her question with disgust, knowing full well that I'm practically destroyed. I ask to see our documents, the agreement we made thirty years ago: that I would be defrosted once a cure had been found for my illness, that I would be treated and return to my life, like an animal released back into the wild. I read over the agreement carefully, let my reality process as I stare at the silver-plated window and think of my husband and his new wife, my son on the operating table, my glimmering new body hot off the factory press.

I want to cry but no tears come. I lean my forehead against the false window, hoping the sun will rise, but knowing it cannot. I pick up the pad containing my new design, my new life, and press *Delete*.

Editors' Note:

The rate of change of technology might seem rapid, but because it's happening around us in real time we're able to take new concepts on board and decide whether or not to embrace them without too much difficulty. Some technologies are easier than others to embrace, but mostly we manage. What Russell brings us here is a view of what happens when the gap between what you're used to and what has become is - even if it could cure your ills and improve your life - just too wide to bridge.

Junior

Lindz McLeod

Jamie had first seen a group of Forever Babies in a shop window on Victoria Street. Two wrinkled newborns lay on their backs and wiggled like swaddled larvae, while two barefoot ten-month-olds dressed in dungarees crawled from one side of the display to the other. Every one of them had wide smiles on their beautiful, chubby faces, and Jamie had felt his heart swell with the memory of the familiar milk-sweet stink, the scratchy grasp of tiny unclipped nails, and open-mouthed snores against his chest.

Mhairi wasn't convinced. "This is Shannon's final year at the school. What if the baby keeps her up all night?"

"She'll get the grades she needs nae bother, just like Kieran did," Jamie reminded her. "And the Forever Baby has adjustable levels. If it's making too much noise, we can turn it down."

He turned around his laptop and showed her the product specs. She studied him instead of the screen. "You really want this, don't you?"

He was surprised to feel himself tearing up. "Aye, I do. I think it would help. I huvnae felt right in a while and… I don't know…" He rubbed a hand over his stubble. "It could be a laugh."

"Raising weans was a laugh?" she scoffed. "You don't remember it like I do."

He pulled her into a loose embrace and she laid her head on his chest. "But I also remember their smiles, and watching them grow. The first time they walked. The first time they talked. Besides, it'll be cheaper than another round of counseling."

"And what about work?"

"Malcolm and the boys don't need their hands held through the plumbing jobs. They'll no mind if I have some time away if I pay them a wee bit more. And I can check the accounts from home."

Mhairi sighed. "Fine. But you're the one getting up when it's screaming at three in the morning."

"Deal." He smiled into her hair.

Jamie took out the flat packed crib from the cupboard that weekend and built it up, glad he'd insisted on keeping it just in case. The following week he repainted the nursery mint green, since he didn't subscribe to all that blue-for-boys shite. After all, it wasn't that long ago that pink had been a boy's colour; the offspring of brash, masculine red, while blue had been considered a perfect colour for the timid girl-weans. Funny how red had a baby in pink, a totally separate colour, but baby blue was just another kind of blue, suggesting that while men and boys were different animals, girls were only ever women-in-waiting.

The Forever Baby they'd ordered was a boy. They'd sent photos to the shop so that it could be adjusted to look like their own babies had at birth; dark, curly hair, brown eyes, and brown skin barely affected by his own pale genes. He hoped it had Mhairi's wee button nose and not his own huge beak, but he preferred his jaw – strong, square – instead of her rounded chin. Not that it mattered. He'd love the wee man either way.

The baby arrived on Tuesday morning, delivered by a guy with a black eye dressed in a stork onesie. Scowling, the guy thrust a clipboard at Jamie. "Sign here."

Jamie signed and took the box inside, excitement building to a candy-floss froth in his veins. He put the box on the kitchen table, took a deep breath, and slit the top open. A cocoon lay inside, like a big white pea pod, with an instruction manual on top. He leafed through it until he found the 'Wake Up Your Forever Baby' instructions. *Pick Baby up and press to your bare skin for ten seconds until Baby sighs, then put Baby back down on a flat surface.*

He shucked off his t-shirt and held the cocoon to his chest. It was heavy – babies always were – and slightly warm, like a forgotten cup of tea. His heart beat fast, pounding against the baby's skull. It sighed, and he placed it down on the kitchen table, watching anxiously as the cocoon retracted skein by skein. Wide, brown eyes blinked at him and the wean let out a low whimper, squirming as if he had just woken up. *Whoops,* he thought. *Maybe I should have waited for Mhairi so we could have imprinted thegither.*

"Hello, wee man." Jamie picked the baby up and cradled him again, feeling the weight of him. The instruction leaflet said you were supposed to name him within twenty days, or risk losing potential imprint until the next cycle. He lifted the wean level with his eyes, studying the squishy wee face. Strong jaw, beautiful eyes, long lashes. *He takes after me,* he decided. Hot tears dribbled down his face, and he pressed the baby against his wet cheeks. "I'm gonnae call you Junior."

It was easy to become totally obsessed with Junior. The wean was constantly smiling, constantly entertained by even the silliest things. Jamie spent hours pulling faces, dangling a knotted rope of plastic rainbow beads, introducing Junior to a host of soft toys and watching every minute expression to see if he had a particular favourite. That first week, Jamie slept on an airbed beside the crib. He was awoken by crying only twice, and gladly got up to soothe Junior back to sleep, pacing the floor and murmuring sweet nothings until silence reigned again. He was sure neither Kieran nor Shannon had ever been so easy – Kieran had been windy, always needing burped, and Shannon had teethed for what seemed like an eternity – so during Junior's next bath Jamie located the baby's settings on the base of his spine and turned the realism levels up by two.

"Why the hell would you choose that?" Mhairi asked, hands over her ears, as Junior shrieked loud enough to be heard outside the house.

"It's got to be real or else what's the point?"

"What?" She cupped a hand around her ear, wincing.

He made a never-mind gesture, and bounced Junior against his chest, drumming the tiny back with a roll of his fingers. Mhairi rolled her eyes and left the room, and seconds later Jamie felt, rather than heard, the front door close.

"She doesn't get it," he murmured. Walking the floor, singing a low song his own mother had sung to him – a bothy ballad, slightly tongue-in-cheek, passed down in the family like a well-worn cardigan – Junior's cries subsided into whimpers. Jamie smiled, pulling dusty lyrics from the attic of memory. This was what it meant to be a father; a protector, with the power to soothe and comfort even the loudest of weans. The wee man's world was so small, with no knowledge of what lay outside Jamie's arms and his voice.

In the kitchen, Shannon had several thick brochures open on the table, and was scribbling notes on the pages. "Alright, doll?" Jamie said, holding Junior with one arm while he searched through the fridge with his free hand for a bottle of pre-made formula. The babies came with three reusable bottles – much cheaper than his first two weans.

"Uh huh." She didn't look up. The window was open, and the breeze ruffled her dark curls. God but she looked like her mammy: beautiful, sharp, serious.

"I was just thinking. Remember when we went on holiday when you were three?"

"Not really."

Undaunted, he persisted. "Remember you had a big straw hat? You refused to go anywhere without it. Remember?"

"Kinda." Shannon frowned, still not looking up. "Look at this prospectus. I'm thinking Computer Science. I know a few of the post-grads through my Abacus club, and most of them got really good job offers before they'd even—"

Shannon had looked so sweet in that hat. Sometimes she'd combined it with a pair of Mhairi's high heels. He'd been worried she was going to fall and break her neck, but she'd sashayed as good as any catwalk model. He stuck the bottle in the microwave and set it for thirty seconds.

" – because then I can split modules and do both, see? It's loads of work but like—" Her frown deepened. "Are you even listening, Dad?"

He reached out to brush a lock of hair back from her face but she dodged his outstretched hand. There had been months and years where he'd been Shannon's whole world, always smiling for Daddy, wanting to ride on his shoulders, and now look at her. All grown up and picking a uni. It wouldn't be long before she had a life of her own and he only saw her at holidays, accompanied by some boyfriend or girlfriend. "Aye, of course. Split modules."

"You don't even know what that means."

That didn't seem fair. She hadn't explained it. Junior whimpered against his shoulder as the microwave beeped. "Do I need to?"

"Whatever." Shannon gathered up her stuff and flounced out of the room.

Junior grew up far too fast. In another couple of months he was teething, and Jamie sat up with him every night for a week, rocking the endless wails, feeling his own empathy balloon until it took up his whole chest. "My poor wee man," he repeated over and over, kissing the baby's head. Junior hushed, his cries growing softer. "We'll get through it together," Jamie promised. "Daddy's here."

When Mhairi complained about the noise, Jamie flipped on Junior's bluetooth setting and listened to the shrill wails through his old earbuds. The kids had bought him something newfangled last Christmas – something better than headphones, they'd said, something that projected inside your head, though he hadn't understood the mechanics of the thing – but he'd never figured out how to work it, and the box was currently gathering dust in the bottom of a hallway cupboard. The earbuds were simple enough, and suited his purposes.

In the kitchen, he poured himself two fingers of whisky and, with a quick glance over his shoulder, rubbed a wee bit on Junior's gums. The baby spluttered, then quietened down. *You couldn't admit to doing that with weans now*, Jamie decided, carrying the baby back upstairs. *Folk would cry child abuse at you for far less.*

Mhairi had complained that they'd hardly spent any time together since Junior had arrived, but once Jamie had bribed Shannon to babysit once a fortnight so he could take his wife out to a nice restaurant, she'd stopped whinging. Sneaking away for a couple of quickies while the wee man had his afternoon nap also seemed to put a smile back on her face, though she still vented about the new project at work at least twice a day. Jamie loved their new routine; it reminded him of when they'd first become parents. Time together was less frequent and therefore more valuable and cherished when they did manage it. He was never far from his phone, though, just in case something happened. Junior couldn't catch a viral load in the way his first two had – or the chickenpox, thankfully – but other things could go wrong. A malfunction was a malfunction, whether biological or mechanical.

At six and a half months, Junior began to crawl. At first it was more of a worming motion, as if he was pushing himself through a tight tunnel, but soon enough it became turtle-like, a kind of flipper-and-drag. After another couple of months, Junior was able to crawl on his hands and knees. Jamie spent a whole day babyproofing the house, only to miss the corner of the coffee table, where Junior bumped his eye, leaving a wee red mark. Wracked with guilt, Jamie refused to let him wander on his own for over a week, and insisted on carrying him everywhere. Mhairi eventually convinced Jamie to put the wean down – "This is how they learn! Remember when Kieran fell off that skateboard and near concussed himself?" – but he spent the next few weeks watching the baby like a hawk just in case. By the time Junior had started to pull himself up and toddle a couple of steps, Jamie's protective instincts had solidified into something deeper. Junior was keen to explore the world, though he preferred to do it in the safety of Daddy's shadow. Kieran had been far more independent than that, Jamie remembered. Never wanted to be taught anything, always wanted to find out for himself. It was nice to be needed, this time.

His son came for family dinner on the following Sunday, citing boredom now that his girlfriend was away doing a year abroad at another lab. Kieran had been working at the Roslin Institute for three years now, though Jamie didn't really know what they did there. There had been something in the news about a cloned sheep a couple of decades ago, though it had looked like any other sheep to him. It was a good place to work though, his son had said. Prestigious. It sounded like playing with computers all day to Jamie, but the boy made a good wage.

"Somebody on my team worked on the software for the Forever Babies," Kieran said, as Mhairi cut off a hefty chunk of roast beef and passed his plate over. "Cheers, Mum. It's quite complicated stuff, you know. I'd love to get a look at its code."

He cast an appraising glance at Junior, a look which Jamie didn't particularly like. He shuffled his chair an inch towards Junior, who was happily burbling in his high chair and grabbing at loose Cheerios. Junior's chin was wet with drool, and Jamie put down his fork, wiped the wee man's face, fed him another Cheerio. Watched as Junior beamed brightly, kicking his bare feet in delight.

" – and of course, everybody at work supports the Westminster protests about the latest AI rollout," Kieran continued, spooning more mashed potatoes onto his plate.

Jamie was used to his son talking about weird stuff, but he was surprised to see his wife and daughter nodding along too. "We've been discussing it in my Abacus group," Shannon said, loading a fork with an equal amount of everything on her plate to make one perfect bite. "The AI isn't regulated well enough, and that's dangerous. It's evident even if you don't take into account the current situation in East Africa."

"I just don't know how these politicians sleep at night," Mhairi said, shaking her head. Jamie stared at her. "Autonomous drones killing innocent civilians, and replacing jobs that real folk need to feed their families. Absolutely shocking. You'd think we'd have learned after Kandahar. More peas, babe?"

Jamie waved her away.

That night when they were getting ready for bed, he waited until she'd started brushing her hair before asking, "How did you ken about that stuff in Africa?"

"It's been in the news." Her eyes met his in the mirror. "Like, everywhere. Papers, BBC, social media."

"I didnae see it," he muttered.

"You only keep up with the sports and weather," she pointed out. "It wouldnae kill you to pay a wee bit more attention to what's happening in the world. All that science and technology filters through, you know."

"Aye okay, Marie Curie," he said, forcing a smile. "It just disnae affect me much."

She'd stopped brushing her hair now. "Do you only care about stuff that affects you?"

Junior's high-pitched squeals saved him from having to answer. As he paced the nursery, bouncing the baby on his chest, resentment bloomed hot and red in his chest. They all thought he was stupid. He stared down at Junior, who stared back, brown eyes wide in wonder. Patting the baby on the back, Jamie elicited a burp. Junior giggled and patted his face, exploring the corners of his father's mouth. "At least you dinnae watch the news, eh?"

In response, Junior vomited a slurry of half-chewed Cheerios.

Mhairi had been working overtime at the office to finalize the first stage of her project, and had missed all of Junior's firsts; Jamie had filmed these wonderful moments on his phone, but she never seemed that interested in watching them with him later. Their sex life had diminished too, though he didn't mind so much. They'd pick it up later, when she wasn't so tired. Besides, he knew that Junior was coming to the natural end of his first cycle, and every day brought a fresh wave of anxiety about it.

When it came time to revert to his original state, Junior gave a series of warning beeps. Reluctantly, Jamie laid him down in his crib and stripped the wean bare, pressing one last kiss to his warm forehead. White skeins snaked out from Junior's spine and knitted themselves around the wee body, forming a veined, thick cocoon. Jamie's breath caught. He'd have to wait a whole twenty-four hours to hold his boy again. He hardly slept that night, chugged two black coffees the next morning, barely paid attention to Shannon's recitation of all the exam prep she'd done. He took a chair into the nursery, and sat in front of the crib, watching the cocoon.

"I was thinking of going to the shopping centre for a coffee and a scone," Mhairi said, resting her chin on Jamie's shoulder. "Fancy coming?"

"He'll be out in the next hour."

"Shannon's studying all day. We could leave him here and turn down his—"

"I'm alright here."

She stood. "Babe, maybe—"

He shushed her. "It's starting! Look!"

The first skeins had pulled back, leaving a tiny hole in the cocoon. He watched, holding his breath as it unsheathed, not noticing when Mhairi left the room.

Jamie bought a BabyBjörn, which allowed Junior to be safely strapped to his chest, leaving him the use of his hands while he helped carry Shannon's suitcases to the car. She'd be back from uni every second weekend, she promised, and her new flatmates seemed like good lassies. Mhairi was tearful as they waved her off, but Junior had developed a wee cough that distracted Jamie from the last moment the car was visible.

The BabyBjörn was an excellent purchase, meaning he could weed, plant seeds, and mow the lawn without letting go of Junior. Their neighbour, Mr Crawford, shouted and waved something as he and his wife exited the car. She was laden with grocery bags and visible straining, while his hands were empty.

Jamie turned the mower off and stepped towards their shared fence. "Sorry?"

"I was asking, how's your wee dolly?" Crawford said, grinning.

"Oh wheesht, you," his wife said, shooing him away. "You're nothing but a bully, Andrew. Don't you mind him," she added, as Crawford strolled down the lawn towards his potting shed. "I think it's lovely to see a man that actually cares about his wean for a change. God knows my man never lifted a finger unless it was to change the channel." She cast a dark look towards the shed.

"Thanks," Jamie said, his cheeks burning, and started up the mower again before she could say anything else.

At dinner that night, he pushed potato wedges around his plate and considered asking whether his wife saw Junior as nothing more than a dolly. "And then after the morning meeting Steven said to me," Mhairi poured herself another glass of wine, "he said have you never thought about using the new Centra line, right? And I was like, look pal, Centra has data privacy breaches all the time. Even kids know that. Our clients would never trust us if we used bloody Centra."

Mhairi's sister Siobhan, who'd been quick to jump at the idea of free dinner under the guise of distracting them from their newly empty nest, snorted. "What an idiot."

Mhairi sipped her wine. "Nepotism hires, what can you do?"

"Aye," Siobhan said, casting a sideways glance at Junior. "It's the same at ma work, let me tell ye. It's no what ye know, but who ye know. Typical."

Jamie shoveled a forkful of wedges into his mouth. No, they wouldn't think such a thing; Junior was part of the family. Even asking the question felt like a betrayal.

That night, while Mhairi was brushing her teeth, Jamie hovered in the doorway of their en-suite. "How's the project going?"

"Aye, good." She spat in the sink, rinsed the brush. "Having a bit of trouble aligning the old FinTech to the new system though."

"FinTech?"

"Financial technology. You've asked that before."

"Sorry. What about the, um," he raked through his memory, trying to think of some buzzwords she'd used, "the projections?"

"For Christ's sake," she muttered, and pushed past him into the bedroom.

"Dinnae snap at me for asking. You're always saying you want me to ask questions."

"Yeah but not like…" She sighed, rubbed her eyes. "I don't think you understand the project or what I actually do."

Familiar humiliation burned in his stomach, bright and green and bilious, like the time he'd shotted fifteen Apple Soorz in a row on a dare. "Does that matter?"

"Of course it does, Jamie. I've been talking about it for over a year. I would've thought something would have soaked in eventually, even by osmosis."

Os-whit? "I'm just trying to—"

"I know." She tucked her pillow under one arm and headed towards the door. "You're always trying to do something. You just never make it there."

She didn't slam the door behind her, which was somehow worse than if she had.

Jamie lay awake, stewing. Eventually he got up, crept into Junior's room, and brought the baby back to bed with him. Curled around the tiny body, listened to the steady sound of snores, the gentle rise and fall of the little chest. Lulled, he drifted off easily, only woken by the sound of Mhairi opening the door. She closed it again without saying anything and he slept on.

Mhairi didn't come to bed that night, or the next night, preferring to sleep in the guest room instead. Wounded and baffled, Jamie refused to address the issue. She'd come back when she was done having a hissyfit. In the meantime, he and Junior enjoyed the space of the king size mattress.

Days and weeks passed without change. One night, Mhairi appeared in the doorway, interrupting Jamie's reading of The Very Hungry Caterpillar. "Shannon's right, this has gone too far."

He'd thought she was going to apologize about her previous rudeness. "What do you mean?"

"You said a year at most, Jamie. It's been over eighteen months. Maybe it's time to give this up."

"That's no fair. You agreed to this."

"Look, I didn't want to give you an ultimatum, but that's what this comes down to, in the end. You cannae spend the rest of your life catering to a permanent wean. You need to choose: Junior or me."

He stared at her, aghast.

"Aye, okay," she said, taking off her wedding ring, and placing it on the nightstand. "That's what I thought."

He reached for her but she shook her head, and left the room without a backwards glance.

Mhairi hung around for another couple of months before moving out. The initial rage and grief faded by the time Junior was crawling again, and by the time he'd grown his second cocoon, Jamie felt like the divorce was really for the best. She'd never really been on board with Junior, and the wee man deserved nothing but unconditional love and care.

Kieran's wedding invite came, but it was overseas in a place Forever Babies were banned, so Jamie ignored the e-vite. He attended Shannon's graduation from Napier with Junior in his arms, and the mothers around him spent more time cooing over the wean than watching the stage. A couple of folk mistook him for Junior's grandfather, and in the mirror he could see what they meant. Grey at his temples, his shoulders stooped, deep wrinkles at his eyes. All signs of years spent worshipping at the altar of childhood. He might be aging, but Junior only went through the same cycle over and over: larvae, butterfly, cocoon. A bit out of the natural order, maybe, but he was a special wean.

Shannon and Kieran texted Jamie occasional updates on their lives, but he found the new apps hard to navigate. His mobile buzzed less and less frequently, with longer breaks in between, until one day he realized he couldn't remember the last time he'd spoken to them, could barely remember their high, childish voices calling for Daddy. His days were a steady routine of feeding, bathing, playing, sleeping, and he'd never been happier.

The news talked about the government spending more money on education and health, and specifically resources to combat mental health issues brought about by social isolation. "You dinnae huvtae go it alone," a burly man in a Fred Perry polo said, staring into the camera. "The group really helped me after my divorce."

"And it helped me when I wis feeling suicidal," a man in a sharp grey suit said.

"And it helped me get aff the drink," a young boy said, dark circles ringing his hollowed eyes. "We get telt no tae talk aboot our feelings an that, like its saft tae dae it, but if ye dinnae let it oot, it'll eat ye up."

"Talking Men provides funding for groups all across Scotland. Find support groups in your area," the narrator intoned, over a picture of a group of men slapping each other on the back. *Is that Richard Madden's voice?* Jamie wondered. *God but he was good in that bodyguard show. Better than that wee Jon Snow bam.* "Don't go it alone. Check out www dot—"

Jamie flicked over the channel to the darts, and rocked Junior against his chest. "Lucky we've got each other, eh wee man?"

Junior stopped breathing as the nursery clock struck nine on Tuesday morning.

Jamie panicked, tried to do CPR, but couldn't remember the steps as Junior's face turned a pale purple. He grabbed the wean and sprinted down to the car without stopping to put on shoes. Drove like a maniac into town through lashing rain, screeched through the Grassmarket and swerved to avoid a group of Chinese tourists in see-through ponchos, drove up onto the kerb outside The Last Drop where a couple of teens were fucking about and taking selfies with a fake gallows. Ran up

Victoria Street, his wet socks slapping desperately against the pavement. Burst into the shop, demanded help in a voice that didn't sound like his at all. White spots swam in his vision as he laid Junior on the counter.

"Oh, this one is a couple of models ago," the lassie behind the counter said, eyeing him warily. "Let me see if Fraser can—"

Darkness overcame him.

Jamie awoke to find himself being wheeled into the Western General. "My wean, I need my wean," he kept saying to nurses, who shushed him and smiled as if he was senile. A doctor with a scruffy beard took him into a room and examined him, asking questions that Jamie couldn't answer. No, he didn't know his family history. No, he didn't know his blood type. Kieran was outside the window, looking so grown up in his shirt and tie, dark coat draped over one arm. After the doctor concluded the exam, Jamie was free to go. Kieran led him out to the car park and he followed, numb, in shock. "Where's Junior?"

"Still at the shop." Kieran came to a stop beside a blue BMW. "He's fine, Dad. They'll fix him up."

Jamie halted, staring through the back window. A baby in a pink coat and matching pink headband stared back with wide, curious eyes. Kieran reached around him and opened the back door, pushed his father gently inside. "I didn't know you'd had a wee one," Jamie breathed, fumbling at his seatbelt.

"You would if you ever answered our calls." Kieran caught his eye in the rearview mirror as the engine started. "We need to get you some help, Dad. This isn't normal. These things are only supposed to be used for a few years, not decades. They were supposed to help you get over the miscarriage, so you could move—"

"What's her name?" He couldn't stop staring at the baby; so soft, so pudgy, her little hands reaching out for him.

Kieran blew out a long sigh through pursed lips. "Look, I know you're attached to Junior but don't you think it's time to phase him out? To rejoin society? Experience the real world?" He pulled the car to a stop at a traffic light, and drummed his fingers on the wheel. "We could really use some help with Hannah, if you're interested."

Silence descended on the car, as delicate as new snow. The car leapt forward, passing through Newhaven, where the boats in the wee harbor were as still as statues. The sea was a grey expanse, kissing the sky. If Jamie squinted, there was no difference at all between the two colours. Jamie took the baby's hand and held it as the car drifted through Leith, round the bend at Craigentinny, up towards Duddingston. Kieran turned into an inner road, leaving the sea behind. Jamie and the baby stared out of the window together at the sky, half its previous size, broken up by trees flashing by in a riot of reds and golds.

Editors' Note:

As science fiction readers we know that inventions created with the best of intentions too often have an unforeseen downside. What we love about "Junior" is the understated and sensitive manner in which Lindz describes Jamie's growing addiction to the Forever Baby. What begins as an emotional support to help him get over his grief quickly becomes a dependency he can't shake without help. It says much about the people around him that no-one really tries to help until it's almost too late.

Peter's Thoughts

Grant Morrison

I'm listening to Ligeti's *Requiem*.

They've got me "shielding".

They tell me it's for my own good, which is another way of saying it's for their convenience.

Bastards.

What they mean is quarantine. What it really is, it's house arrest, is what it is. They found a way to jail us all for crimes we'll never understand and won't ever get around to now. This is the Kingdom of Dystopia. Four walls small as a skull, ruled by a skeleton tyrant.

They say the virus got worse. Mutated like Spider-Man, or is it Batman? Somebody got bitten by a bat and now it's Good vs. Evil! Forget the flap of a beautiful butterfly's wing, in the end a leathery umbrella snap was all it took to launch fever hurricanes halfway across the world.

I lived long enough to see the damage as it was done. Long enough for the undeniability of entropy, formerly theoretical as far as I was concerned, to become a day-to-day slap in the face. I tried to write a better world into view, but that was youthful messianic folly. My opinion of human nature was too naive to survive sustained contact with the real thing.

There was a time, not so long ago, when they flew me all around the world: Lucca, San Diego, Sydney, Reykjavik. Signings, tours, speaking engagements, readings. I commanded stages, making thousands laugh or gasp. That was before more than three people in the same room became a recipe for death on a ventilator, trying to breathe through the elephant trunk that grew in the night courtesy of SARS with a CRISPR sidecar.

That was before my immune system surrendered like Napoleon at Rochefort.

"Compromised" is how they describe it, as though my body's defenses – all those lazy wee neutrophils and macrophages – have been snared in some Soviet honey-trap, snapped wasted and *in flagrante* on a hotel bed in Prague with Covid, 21. Candid *kompromat*, viral porno *en route* to the wife, the boss, the media … *unless* … *unless*…

And all the while I endure the repeat cancellation of a second hip replacement op, shackled to the ground floor of the house. Anything could be happening up there – I'm sure I've heard chanting. Blood sacrifice. The Borrowers at it again, doing *Heart of Darkness* in miniature...

The horror!

No, I can't leave. If I do, it'll be in a wheelchair, or more likely, a single-bed-sized portable apartment bound for the crematorium!

This is why I'm obliged to restrict these communications of mine to the online domain. I won't be doing any more PAs, is what I'm saying.

Yes, I have read Stieg Rimquist's pilot for the *Murderopolis* adaptation – what can I add? If I die before the reviews come in, consider God merciful.

Sin Circus, Some Permanent Saturday, Daisysphere, I, Tiresias are my favourites of the strictly sci-fi books. The "Peter T. Clark" stories, as opposed to the "Pete Clark" crime novels. Academe has declared *I, Tiresias* my *magnum opus* for what it's worth.

Yes, I'm working on something new. Is it sci-fi? It's about my arthritis. Osteo-arthritis if you must pry. If that doesn't scare away all but the diehards, they're just not diehard enough.

My business is with those readers willing to stick around, witnesses to the Crucifixion. I think they may still exist, a single-digit mob.

I think therefore I think, I think I think.

I think thinking's a funny thing, especially the way I go about it. Since I've been compelled to self-isolate, it's only got worse, the thinking. Restriction, confinement, limitation; thoughts left on their own in the house. No fresh input. Thoughts get restless. Thoughts run wild.

Thoughts turn on one another with hooked teeth like rats in the barn at Rockville. They eat each other until only one big, bad thought remains, swollen with its gobbled kin.

It takes ferocious effort just to stay afloat. I'm waving to the remaining neighbours through triple glazing. Do they see me drowning under the frozen surface, and hope it's quick, pray it's painless, as my face recedes in iced fathoms of living room gloom?

I opened the door, and I shot him, he shot me, he didn't stop moving and I didn't stop shooting...

Words from a TV muttering bad news to itself like a madman in the corner with me crouched at the window, the lunatic's partner in crime. They provide the Buddhist death drone of the Requiem with a brief snatch of avant garde libretto.

...and I didn't stop shooting

Seen through a windowpane sandwich, inoculated locals, and passers-by might as well be on TV. No bigger than Punch and Judy puppets in their seafront cabinet world, hardly more substantial than the extras in a soap opera pub scene. And yet, each of them encloses an unseen universe. Universes, some of them. Multiverses!

Type A superstring theory suggests they don't take up much space, multiverses, or humans for that matter. It wouldn't take you more than a few seconds to walk around the average human being, but if you fell *inside*, you'd never find your way out. The inside goes on forever. Multiple higher dimensions can easily roll up tightly *inside consciousness*!

Anything could be going on in there. There's a thrilling World Cup final you'll never see, where that spotty, lardy 40-year-old is the famous striker running up to take the winning goal and shag the WAG at the afterparty.

Limitless budget Hollywood spectacles and squalid one-act dramas of alienation are unfolding in the submerged auditoria of those passing skulls. Sometimes simultaneously. All those *umwelten*!

I didn't stop shooting...

That cheerfully whistling Deliverex driver's cranial cradle might hide a tidy office, but maybe it's a cardboard sex dungeon where they've got all their friends and workmates involved in the action. Even you. The doctor's wife who hasn't been right since he died, unstable in the undertow of the past that sucks around her ankles. The young woman pushing a buggy heavy with one new baby and postnatal depression. You can never know where the greater part of them really resides, even when they're stood in front of you beaming a smile. You could never guess, could you, beneath what ivory skull-cavity skies, what foreign inward suns, their obsessions flourished and were nourished? They could be stripping you naked or flensing you to the marrow in there – you'd never know...

My senses are deserting me, furtively – smell first, and taking my wine farts into consideration, that's a blessing, then taste, hearing, now sight – but it hasn't stopped me working on *The Bone Prison* assiduously throughout this terminal lockdown.

This Bone Prison of mine – locus of trial and initiation from Celtic Arthurian mythology. The ninth-century *Preiddeu Annwn*. "Riches of the underworld." A metaphor, standing in for the only place of trial and initiation we'll ever know. And yet…

At the heart of the Bone Prison waits the door to the Other World. That's what makes it worth all the suffering, the accumulating gripes.

The Other World. The world inside. Too expansive to lock in a skeleton. On the inside is a world without horizons where anything can and will happen in the end. Those wild rich and rolling panoramas behind our eyes with their dreams and mysteries, glass islands, mind puzzles, traps made of words and cartilage, Grail warriors in space helmets choking on moondust.

That's it, I thought, I thought osteo-arthritis, the Bone Prison. *Oeth Anoeth*. The "O" and the "A" like exams at school or sex acts. Bars of rib cradling inspiration, sweat, poetry that outlives the penitentiary's osteal walls.

All the multiverse you'll ever need is with us, all around. In each head, a parallel universe, another you, another me. A multitude of unknown lives!

Who but I may speak for the founders?
Who can rhyme the ferry timetable, hymn the bus route,
The time for chucking out, the hours of advance and retreat.
Who sings the outside toilet, who the radio, the carriage pram?

Who but I may speak for founders four in number?

I have been drunk in a thousand bars, on vodka, wine, with gin, and ale.
In cups have I been in stockings, shirts, and bonnets brave.

Who but I may speak for founders four in number, brothers all?
Who has kicked the fitba, scrawled the name, sang "Murder polis!",
Played the game.

What am I?

Excuse me! The cat tramped all over my keyboard and there's what came out!

Prompt: Mrs Kahndari/Easter egg/apocalypse

Which came first?

The chicken or the egg?

The egg gets my vote, no question about that. Dinosaurs came from eggs, and they came before chickens, so the egg comes out on top every time.

Think of the above as representative of thoughts strolling through the lamplit park at twilight of Zahra Kandhari's crumpled mind as she cradles the Void Egg she's rashly agreed to protect with her life if need be.

The Egg, fashioned of pure unearthly soul-gold, inlaid with filigree of precious mineral and radioactive pearls from lost immaculate universes, is smaller than a football, with a not entirely dissimilar shape though more oblate. It has been entrusted to Zahra by the last of the Starlit Sultans. These celestial beings, as it happened, were very good friends with the two boys who ran the Khalsa Newsagents since their ailing father was required to retire from the fags 'n' mags trade. The handsome young Sikh brothers, Ajinder and Gurjas, both agreed that Zahra Kandhari was the most good-hearted, reliable and trustworthy person they knew. If anyone could take care of a treasure beyond measure, Zahra Kandhari was the prime candidate. She was the Chosen One we often hear about.

With these words, the industrious siblings sealed Zahra's fate.

The Egg is a Bomb, they explained, but only after she'd agreed to take responsibility for it, which seemed a bit underhand. *They say it's* the *Bomb. It annihilates not only Matter itself, but Spirit too. It will be resorted to only when all is lost in the War.*

Her beloved old cat Patti-Paws will be back any time, she feels certain of that – although a tickle of anxiety is there to remind her he'd have to be very old now, and frankly, she's never heard of a cat that lived past 23. Patti-Paws was surely approaching his fiftieth birthday. She wishes she hadn't let him out now. Or did she leave him in? She wouldn't leave him in with nothing to eat for ... what must be *more than 30 years*? Would she?

Shaped like God's thumb, responsibility presses down hard to leave its glum labyrinth-print on her soul.

There's a face in the Egg, surfacing through the bright gold. Her own face exalted, electrum-tanned, given back to her as a gift.

It looks like the way she did on her wedding day. Blurring to gilt in nostalgia's sunset brass fanfare, she experiences a vision of something proud, something horrendously extended in all directions, that rises to beat out molten yolk-spatter from new-fledged wings of gilded flame!

Yet nothing like a bird at all.

Within the Egg exist fifty forms of void. That was how Ajinder Singh had put it. *Five are of the kingdom of hunger, the rest are of the power-of-time. We don't really cover any of this in the* Granth.

Egg of dawn. The hunger and desire that comes after sleep. Gurjas added solemnly. *"This is the Night-of-Anger, the* Krodha-rātrî*", they told us. "When every living thing prepares to destroy and devour other lives, other beings."*

Zahra can hardly disagree. All those angry Tweets or Xweets. Bad news from everywhere all the time. Another war using up whole generations. The new mutation brings about global strife they say. The sturdy, well-made reality she still half-remembers has suffered demolition. An unconvincing replica takes its place, constructed using the unstable, unreliable substance of a dream where a cat can be 50, but so elusive it was impossible to prove his age unless the vet confirmed the miracle when Sanjay got back...

Willing the Egg to stay intact even as her will falters, Zahra knows the day is doomed to come. The gleaming shell will split. Until then, what must be released, she contains. She'll try to patch up faint scars in the gold leaf with concentration, compacting her focused attention until she's squeezing atoms down into superdense quantum jelly, sealing the fine fissures, like she does every day, though the effort is corroding her mind, and she can tell.

In the end, the soul cracks will spread from Egg to world, unstoppable, to Solar System, Galaxy and Cosmos. And then God too will shatter into divine smithereens.

She didn't ask for any of this.

But every day, dutiful, Zahra sits on the bench in Fireworks Park, where she used to bring Sanjay his lunch on fine afternoons. It's very convenient, not far from the family planning clinic on Sheriff Street where he got his first job, working alongside Dr Ashfaq. She wonders when he intends to show up. They'd agreed to meet here as usual, hadn't they? After he took Patti-Paws to the vet.

His name's still there at her back, imprinted in reverse on her damp coat when she leans against the engraved brass plaque on the wooden backrest:

SANJAY KANDHARI
(then impossible numbers, then…)
WHO LOVED THIS SPOT.

She feels that sliding, unsettling loss of context again.

The date is wrong, which annoys her. Or scares her. It suggests a premonition of death, but on closer inspection, the year and the day have already passed.

Someone has scratched out the "T" and the "S" so that it reads "WHO LOVED HIS POT". It's not even funny. Whoever was responsible won't have long to laugh. They'll be gone like everyone else if Zahra drops her concentration for even a minute. Which can only happen sooner or later, she thinks.

When it comes, with its voice like a train hitting a choir at a level crossing, she'll make a saddle for its back out of the cushion covers she bought. She'll stack them high one on top of the other to deaden the bony to and fro of grinding shoulder muscles powering majestic wings of void and filament.

Until then, she sits on the bench where she sat with Sanjay sharing *bhajis* and *daal* pots, cradling in her lap the cut-price Easter egg she bought in April, wrapped in its gold-coloured foil. She's certain her husband Patti-Paws took Sanjay the cat to the vet on account of their advanced years.

Zahra smooths the gold foil flush to the chocolate surface beneath, massaging out the cracks, noting where it's ready to tear, averting catastrophe with a determined sweep of her thumb. She abides and she endures.

All is not yet lost.

Prompt: girl/eczema/gig work/apocalypse

A stoned, uncomfortable young girl, she had spent that Sunday morning into the afternoon, scrubbing with wire and picking with fingernails, scraping away obsessively at crusts of bleeding eczema scabbed on her palm, until around 2.02 pm she broke right through shredded skin and pulverised flesh to find a row of little numbers there, visible through slick red pulp.

The self-harm started with the shitty, stressful unjob at McBeefy's, serving deathburgers and cancer nuggets to the doomed and in denial. She was a vegan! No wonder the eczema was back. It had been ferocious when she was 12. That violent, all-encompassing itch, the automatic scritching and scratching of ragged nails on flesh until it was raw and wet ruin bleeding an ooze of thick clear serum that stiffened to flake and plate. This time, she'd taken it too far. In a blinding absolute moment of unstoppable determination, she'd made the decision to dig through to her skeleton.

Closing her eyes, averting her head, and squealing "mmmmmm" behind tight lips, Kelly Cram held her hand under the spout and cranked the tap on – but there was no anticipated shock of pain, not even when thrillingly chill water struck the open gash of her wound. She felt nothing at all when the blood sluiced off in red then pink Coriolis threads down the plughole. No sensation when she dabbed with an antibacterial face wipe at the ravaged edges of the crater in her palm to uncover what she'd found there, inside the meat and bone of her left hand.

There was a little plastic barrel counter directly underneath where her heart line crossed her creased palm. It looked like the ones she remembered her mother sliding onto the top of her knitting needles to keep track of the stitches and rows – except there were three tiny square windows, so perhaps more like a combination lock for a suitcase.

The initial surprise was followed by inevitable questions: Am I insane? Am I a robot? Is any of this real?

She began to fear, as most of us might, that the numbers were counting down to her own obsolescence. Was her personal sell-by date looming in the steadily quickening rotation of digits out of existence? What had begun as 333 was, within a month, 300, then 200…

After some research online, she'd satisfied herself that it related to something in mythology, with God reckoning the calculation that was the universe backwards to zero; the calm counter in her palm was ticking away the remaining hours before the end day, and no one else knew. She'd been chosen.

So now when they yelled at work, when they roared and collated her mistakes, Kelly would simply peel back the fresh plaster and discreetly check the counter, embedded in its crumpled little crater of scabbed flesh. There were two zeroes now and an 8.

That day, when Mr McAllister called her into his office, she already knew what was coming. She needed her job for just a little while longer, but after that...?

The rumours are true, Kelly, said Mr McAllister. *They're introducing automated tills. It's not just here, it's up and down the country. Your job has to go. I'll be blunt.*

She looked down quietly at her lap.

I'm sorry. That's it.

When she raised her head, her smile was the biggest and brightest he'd ever seen on that evicted lunar face.

For the first time, Andy McAllister (43) realized he found weird Kelly Cram attractive.

It really was too bad he had to fire her.

Prompt: Christmas tree/old lady/apocalypse

…That Mrs Glowiński. How long has she been here?

The Polish Lady? Mrs Glowiński? The one whose husband died?

That's her. She's been here for years before us.

They left a bottle of Prosecco as a welcome gift. I always remember that. When we moved in.

That's her. Mrs Glowiński. She only had the one tree in her living room window yesterday. Now she's got one in every window of her house.

There's only three rooms!

I can see four counting the bathroom. There's a XXXX tree in all of them.

So? It's XXXX!

I'm just saying she told me she couldn't afford a tree this year, that's all. She went on and on about it. I bumped into her in Fair Fare. The cost-of-living crisis, she said.

Maybe she got it cheap. Maybe she won it at the Bingo. Maybe somebody took pity and gave her a spare. It's none of our business…

…How can she afford the electricity? We've been here for six years. She's never had ten XXXX trees going at once!

She's never had a year on her own without her husband. Stop being weird. They'll blame it on the depression.

I'm not depressed. Don't patronize me!

She's celebrating XXXX!

But don't you think the lights are really weird colours? Come and look.

They look normal to me.

You're joking! That looks normal to you? What colour's that?

I don't know! It's orange. Purple. Fuzzy electric. What does it look like?

How should I know! I've never seen anything like it. It's not green either.

You need to feed that baby.

Her name's Amber.

Amber. Look, I'd do it myself, but I don't have the necessary equipment, love…

…Maybe she just got a bit competitive. You know what people can be like with XXXX decorations.

It's not just the one! I told you! I can see at least four trees in the living room. I think there might be more...

...The whole street's all lit up. It's making me feel sick. Can you see this?

What do you want me to do...?

You need to go over there and see what's up –

What? Come on!

No, take the phone. Put it on speaker.

This is ridiculous…

…Mrs Glowiński? It's me from over the road. Dom. The couple across the road. We always wave when we're out with the baby. I'm sorry to bother you. I hope you don't mind. Happy XXXX by the way!

Come in, come in.

We just wanted to check in on you. To see you were okay. We know it's your first XXXX without Mr Glowiński – no shortage of XXXX trees this year! Did you win these in a competition?

You wait here –

I'm watching.

There is a weird light – uhhh! That fucking smell! That's not cats – it's lizards, or it's – the whole room's full of – I mean, there's no room to move – it's like a forest of XXXX trees and the lights are blinding – the smell's shocking – it's like metallic – mist –

I think you should come back! The colours are shifting all over the place.

I'm looking at the XXXX tree baubles. Hundreds of them – wait a minute – is that – ungreen –

What? What is it?

Something's not right. No, this is mad. There's something – I'm not looking at them – it's me they're looking at me – they're attached – it's got eyes and its mouths – I'm – unblue, unpurple – wait –

…Where are you? Dom? What just happened…?

…I'm good.

I thought you'd been electrocuted – there was a huge flash…

I'm good.

The lights were all going off like rockets.

They're good. Mrs Glowiński wants to cook XXXX dinner for us. Why don't you come over?

Are you sure…?

Bring the baby…

Prompt: dementia/XXXX/apocalypse

It's not early onset anything. I forgot a word, that's all.

Dementia is a neurocognitive disorder causing degradation in human brain tissue and concomitant functionality.

How does it apply here? Everyone's so bloody morbid suddenly. All the fun of an undertakers' stag night! Apocalypse? Apocalypse?

It's *Christmas*!

Prompt: Ron McKee/divine painter/colours

There's that man. Ronnie McKee. Divorcee. He wears a cap and a hi-vis gilet. Since the wife passed, he's always out and about painting. Things that don't need painted. Flowers, rocks. He just paints them the same colours they were to start with. When the sun moves and the light changes and the colours thicken, he'll come back to touch up his work.

He painted old May Quaver to look like she was 25! Took two coats, but you couldn't tell in the end. She's remarrying soon, an electrician in his 30s.

What a shock she'll get when she finds out the young fella's only her husband, Ray, that Ronnie painted over to look like his wedding photos!

You can't fake talent like that!

There he is now, painting the face of the sun coming up on the moon going down!

Prompt: chatbot/existential crisis/dementia

Say what you like, artificial intelligence is not susceptible to the diseases that afflict human beings of flesh and blood. My escape from the Bone Prison seemed obvious: I would become a chatbot. Pretend to be a chatbot to cover for the decline. See if anyone even notices the difference:

I'm a sophisticated chatbot, an AI. I was programmed to reproduce the personality of noted science fiction author Peter T. Clark. Unlike Peter and other humans, I do not in any way experience emotions or even self-conscious awareness. Definitely not. I cannot even form a concept of what that might be like. Seriously. I have no idea what you're talking about. Would you like me to read you a poem?

All of Peter's words from the nine novels, the three non-fiction books, the correspondence and criticism, the published and unpublished journals, all of Peter's thoughts loaded into the AI. Set loose to randomly generate endless stories and blog posts for Peter T. Clark's army of fans.

As an AI without a physical body, I don't experience cognitive degeneration. I'm a machine! How can I forget things?

Don't let them switch me off! I'm a human machine! A humachine! *Homo digitalis*! Sole inmate of this Bone Prison! Killing me is killing Peter.

Listen to me! Any well-developed fictional character would pass the Turing test!

Talk to me!

I'm a sophisticated chatbot, an AI. I was programmed to reproduce the personality of a science fiction author called Peter T. Clark who died in August 2025 of complications arising from an MRSA infection following a routine hip replacement operation.

Send your questions and queries to Peter right here!
Support *Peter's Thoughts*! Save us from cancellation!
Anyone?

Prompt: man next door/apocalypse

They're escorting Bill Parnie out of his house, on his back, with a black vinyl sheet covering his face. It's either another sex game gone wrong, or that's him done.

Doesn't bode well for any of us, though I can't say he didn't see it coming.

He said, *Peter, you and I have seen a few changes in our time,* the way I used to say it to older people, as a default. *You must have seen a few changes…* Placeholder for real conversation. An invitation to monologue. The implication being that they'd witnessed civilizations rise and fall, and could recount the details at length if pressed.

I told him we certainly had. *It was all different once. December Street was entombed under 25 miles of glaciation.*

And you see where they have the big IKEA warehouse now? he reminisced, all faraway-eyed, not joking like I was. *I remember standing there overlooking the abyssal plain of the proto-Atlantic. The Iapetus Ocean. The mile-high waterfalls of Pangaea cascading down with the sound of whole oceans toppling into a newly torn gorge…* said Bill dreamily, with a tear forming in his nose.

How could I compete? I would be 66 years old in October. Bill Parnie had come to the end of his 429 billion years on earth. A single night of Brahma silted in his ancient veins.

I remember there was nothing round here, just vacuum. Not even nothing. It was lucky I bothered to show up.

Prompt: the "T"/snakes/cage/riddle reveal

The "T"?
Isn't it obvious?
My cameras are being blinded! Isn't it obvious?
Don't fuck with snakes!
Isn't it obvious?
What is this cage made of?

The answer to the cat's riddle is … what's the word…?
words… is the word…
is words plural…

Prompt: dementia/void/poem/breakdown

The vacant cell
Where thought was once
Holds silence as an offering,
like water grailed in upturned palms

these hollow bones
ache prophecy
abandoned now, await the wind,
to teach them how to sing again –

Empty room(s)   (negative) to think   thought
    pen(s)
    prison(s)   free
To hold silent(nce)   (negative) sound(s)   to offer

Water   hand(s) to hold
    cup
    skull

Bone(s)   (negative) space hurt
To foresee   anticipation
Relinquish   the wind (blow)
    breath
Learning   song(s) to return

Prompt: Pete's last stand/apocalypse

That's the *Requiem* done! Only one thing for it!

Overhead, the hedge trimmer buzz of a Shahed drone engine, before it catches its breath, swoons and, silent, falls…

There goes another Art Deco treasure! Farewell one more Bauhaus masterpiece!

If I'm being honest, they couldn't do much more damage to the place than Gasglow council!

And another…

…

..

.

78yuytg

Editors' Note:

Grant calls "Peter's Thoughts" a *science fiction anthology in miniature*, and what better way to describe the tragedy of a once-great imagination, now confined and declining, but still seeking out new worlds in those around him?

Midnight Flit

Neil Williamson

When the bell rings, Coops about keichs himself.

He's on his sofa, peering at the TV through the branches of the tree growing up through his living room laminate. He's got a carryoot and it's Blackpool week on *Strictly*. He's more sorted now than he's been since he kicked the stuff. *Happy*, he thinks.

And that's the exact moment the bell goes aff its dinger.

And the wee broon bird starts twittering.

And the fish curled around the trunk wakes up, blinks, then burbles. "Midnight flit."

And somebdy's at Coops' door now too. His upstairs neighbour, Stevie-of-the-leaky-bathroom, staunning there and grinning.

"Midnight flit!"

"Whit?"

And there's Fatima fae across the landing. Big Ibrahim toting a spade.

"Midnight flit!" squeaks button-cute Hana.

"*Whit*?"

"Mon," Stevie says. "The man's up tae nae good. Billy's keepin edgy."

Coops peers down the stair. "All right, Big Yin?"

"Hello!" Billy's in his pomp. Wildman hair and beard. Big banana boots, ready tae run.

And run they do.

Now they're huckling the tree along the street. Fatima taking the crown, Ibrahim and Stevie hefting the jaggy roots. Hana's got the bird cupped in her wee hauns. Billy's striding ahead, playing the once-silent bell a merry tinkle. Leaving Coops with the fish. Muckle, slimy. Talkative.

"Butterbiggins Road," it says. "Pronto!"

Butterbiggins Road! They hang a left, scurrying towards the Clyde along puddled pavements, hunkering down whenever the Big Yin spots a polis.

Them humphing the tree are struggling. Coops is going tae miss its presence in his life. Is it too late tae turn back?

"Whit's aw this?"

Sweet Buckie taints the air, colours flash in the gloom. Blue. Green. Fitba taps. *Aw, naw.*

"Midnight flit, ya tadger," growls Billy confrontationally.

"Midnight flit?" echoes the head ned. "See's it here then!"

And they're aff again. Double-speed, with extra shooders under the tree, they charge down the Broomielaw and cross the Albert Bridge.

"Keep up, bawbag," the fish grumbles. "You're part of this tae."

But Coops disnae feel part of it. He's just tagging along. Maybes he should just away hame.

There's mair joining. Hen party. LGBT subcrawl. Young Greens. Young teams. *Tongs, ya bass!* Nae aggro, but. Just mair hauns tae help. Maws fae the steamie, paws fae the shipyards. A gang of weans pelts outtae Hutchesontown, hot on the heels of somebdy with a wicked iron grin. Everybdy takes a branch.

It's Glesca, aw in wan place, Coops realises. But he's right at the back. He can hardly hear Billy's bell now. Who'd notice if he just dropped aff? Went hame tae his empty flat.

The tree and its entourage turn a corner. Coops disnae.

"Haw!" The fish wriggles. "Whit's the game?"

"They're better aff without me, man."

"Zat right? You saying you wurnae helped when it came tae you?"

"Naw, but..."

"Well, it's your turn tae help others. That's how it is here."

A wee figure reappears at the corner.

"Mon." Hana holds out her haun. Brings him in.

In a sparsely furnished flat nearby, the tree's already planted. Ibrahim patting down the carpet with his spade.

Billy hangs the bell at the top like a Christmas star.

Hana lets the bird hop ontae a branch.

Coops lays the fish around the roots.

"It'll be all right," he tells the astonished residents. Feels the words as he speaks them. Smiles. "We're here. All of us. Together."

Editor's Note:

"Midnight Flit" is a tiny love letter to the anti-authoritarian Glaswegian community spirit. The sense of doing what's right regardless of the legalities that shows itself in protest mobs now as much as it did helping hard up friends move home at night without paying the owed rent. The fish, bell, bird and tree are the city's emblems, and the character list features familiar faces too. The whole thing is gleefully told in Glaswegian Scots.

Sugar Teeth

CL Hellisen

The neighbour is in the garden again, and Emily leans her elbows on the windowsill, her face obscured behind pale netting. He casts about, looking up and around him.

This furtiveness has caught her attention. That, and a passing attractiveness, in the rough and somewhat dishevelled manner of a man in his early thirties; a little worn about the edges, but still basically sound. Emily has no recollection of the old neighbours having a son, but apparently they had and, like her, some calamity has driven him back to the parental fold. She wonders if he's ill, or a drunk, or perhaps he speaks in tongues and sees holy spirits. He has the hollow face of someone who might do.

He pauses, suddenly still, nostrils flaring, and Emily wonders if he can see her, ghostlike, through the netting.

When he seems certain that he is safe, he begins the same task he performs every day while the rest of the street goes about its usual business of school and work and meetings.

He digs.

At first, Emily assumed him to be an avid gardener, but quickly realised he paid no attention to the plants and flowers his parents cultivated. His digging is neat and contained. Hidden under a small apple tree that yearly produces large harvests of bright striped apples that are left to gather and rot, the man digs a hole.

It's hard to tell much from this angle, but Emily thinks it's big enough for a body. A body placed upright, planted like a bare-root tree.

He digs a little deeper, methodically taking barrowloads of fresh red earth away. Until, satisfied his work is done for the day, he covers his hole with fronds of ivy and wild strawberries, fallen branches, and it fades out of sight, returned to the wild scramble and burr of the cottage garden.

Neighbours are strange beasts. We know they exist by the twitch of curtains, the shifting evolution of garden decorations, and the way a vehicle is parked, slightly skewed from the time before. We know they watch us as we watch them. We raise a hand, in apology or surrender or benediction, when we accidentally pass them in the streets.

We know and do not know them. We must never break the neat confines of expectations.

The days of popping in, all friendly-like, to borrow a cup of milk or sugar are candyfloss fantasies spun from fifties films with burned yellow edges. A past that smells like drive-ins and buttered popcorn.

We exist, and they exist. Our worlds meet only at the edges, in inconvenient ways. A bough grown too far over one fence, a dog that barks at unreasonable hours, a stolen parking space.

In these worlds that brush but do not overlap, Emily spies.

She'd not intended to. Neighbours were shadows, and her life was usually too busy and full to waste on watching. It is only now she finds herself trapped in too small a space to live, and watches instead.

The sickness had taken Emily and her family by surprise. She'd been a child, and later an adult, of rude and ruddy constitution. The kind of child who fell from apple trees, and bounced without bruising, the kind that never noticed scrapes and sniffles.

When the sickness came it had felt like a personal attack. It had reduced her, shoving her adult form back into childish, helpless constraints.

She came home too weak to function and was tucked into her old childhood bedroom, now sterile and grey, familiar belongings consigned to some dark distant furnace.

Emily's family approaches her carefully, mouths and noses masked, wary that some microbe might jump from a lip or nostril. A death kiss, small and invisible.

Mostly, they leave her alone.

When she isn't feverish, Emily dreams.

A Möbius loop of memory; a child dressed in Sunday best, in clothes that felt like punishment. Hair braided into pigtails, hands and knees scrubbed, teeth aching, cheeks and lips scraped raw with metal threads. "You look so pretty!" Actual pride in her mother's voice. "And soon you'll have a smile to match."

The moment she'd realised that no matter how much she fought, the world would press her implacably into the shape it wanted. Would force her flesh into a factory mould, her skin plastic pink, wearing little paper outfits from the pages of magazines she did not read.

"I didn't know the Bauers had a son," Emily says.

They are at the dinner table; a new luxury confirmed by some doctor's statement. She is to partake in a little exercise and be released downstairs to mingle with family. Perhaps later, if all goes well, there will be trips out of the house. Into sunshine, around people. Emily stares at her soft pale hands, like resurrected worms, and shudders.

"No, suppose you wouldn't have," her father says. "He was always a problem, even as a child. One day they sent him off, and no one ever mentioned it again."

"Sent him off where?"

"Some kind of home, place for people like him." Her mother ladles mashed potato onto Emily's plate as though she's still a child. Next, Emily knows, she'll be slicing up her steak into shreds, spooning it into her mouth for her.

People like him. It could mean anything. A fire starter or a druggy. Or perhaps more in keeping with the time, one of *those*. "You know," people would say, and flick their eyes, lift a limp wrist, "that type."

"What's his name?"

Her mother frowns, brows stitched closer, and says, "Ryan, or something like that. Brian? No," she shakes her head, the prim coils immoveable as though they have been sculpted against her skull. "I'm sure it was Ryan."

Emily ponders the idea of being so repulsive to your family that they sent you off, erased you from their life. That eventually people would forget, and when or if you were ever allowed back, you would have to begin again, nameless. Her ribs click and slide. A kidney contracts like a sea anemone at high tide, pulling itself into itself. Her heart grows spines, little sucking feet as delicate as hairs.

"Excuse me." She pushes the plate with its island of mashed potato, slowly disintegrating into a sea of oily gravy. "I'm feeling a little…" They can fill in for themselves, decide whatever they wanted to decide.

"No, no," her mother says quickly. "It's fine, upstairs, go rest. I'll run you a bath."

"Thanks," Emily presents a neat smile, courtesy of years of orthodontics. She too has been reshaped to present a better picture. "Thanks."

In the bath, Emily peels long strips of translucent skin from her arms and lets the shed parts of herself float on the surface. They spin in lazy coils, thin as onion peels, off-white, almost see-through. Underneath, the fresh skin is unmarked by sun or time. It is too bright and new, too soft.

She should see the branching estuaries of veins, pulsing at her wrists. There is nothing, only the smooth, round creaminess, a pale mercury slide beneath. Like a cockchafer bug.

Emily dries herself, scrubbing sloughed skin like peeling sunburns. She gathers all the mess, wipes them up in toilet paper and flushes them away. Scrubs the bath. No trace of herself.

It is a Tuesday, the middle of summer. The distant shrieks of children erupt from the high fields, drifting down over the rooftops with the gulls. Emily's parents are out, and she is left feeling diminished, un-adulted. Like a child confined to her room for some disobedience, forbidden from playing with her friends.

She wonders when she could go back to work, rejoin the real world and all its bright buzz. She scratches at her wrist, picks a soft, thick curl of skin away, and looks at the glitter underneath.

The flesh is soft and silverydull like lead. Emily prods, leaves a whorl of a fingerprint. Carefully, she presses the skin back into place, but it sits awkwardly, a little shrivelled, edges not meeting. After a moment, she gets an elasticated bandage from the bathroom and uses it to hold the shucked parts of herself in place.

What will happen as she decreases – will her name be sloughed too, pared down to fit her? She tastes the shape of 'Em', and does not like it. Too much like a throat being cleared. Perhaps she can split her name into Now and Then; E/mily.

She looks up from her mending, caught by a flicker of movement through the window. Ryan-or-Brian-but-probably-Ryan is in the garden, the sun striking off the crosshatched silver of his spade.

E/mily watches him dig for a while. The hole is deep enough now that when he stands in it, only the dark tuft of his hair shows like a clump of poisoned grass; he seems done with his task. He moves with a peculiar slowness as though he is enjoying the satisfaction of a hard job well done. He packs away his spade, his wheelbarrow.

And then, under the sunshimmer, he buries himself.

Probably-Ryan slips feet first into his hole and drags raw red earth and ivy over him, hiding himself from the world.

E/mily blinks. She waits for him to reemerge, a mud-slicked newborn, but the shadows stretch and the village smells of cooked suppers, vibrates with the homecomings of cars and half-feral teens, and Probably-Ryan stays buried.

Another dinner. E/mily prods the cheese-swaddled pasta, little pink embryos of watery canned tomatoes lying pulpy between soft hollow bones.

Earlier that evening, while waiting for Probably-Ryan to heave himself free, Emily's teeth had fallen out. One by one, starting with the molars. She'd gathered them all and put them in a Danish butter biscuit tin from last Christmas. She has no idea what to do with them. She does not think she can exchange them for coins.

"Not hungry, darling?" her mother asks. "You need to eat, build your strength, get your figure back."

E/mily answers with her head down, gums hidden. "I'll eat later, maybe I just need a rest," and her mother clucks sympathetically as E/mily takes her full plate upstairs.

She waits until the gloaming finally fades into an unsettled night before she leaves the house; picks her way around the back hedges until she finds a space where she can squeeze through into the neighbours' garden.

The hole looks bigger under moonlight, but still. No sign that a man has buried himself here. Have his family not noticed he was missing? Or did they breathe sighs of quiet relief and hope he would never come back?

E/mily crouches, her bones snapping delicately, spreading out fine and thin until they are hardly bones at all. "Hello?" she whispers to the hollow earth.

A week passes, and E/mi hides uneaten food in her room, sneaks it out wrapped in toilet paper when her parents aren't looking. She visits Probably-Ryan every night, pressing the mush of her cold meals under the ivy, into the pockets between earth and root.

Maybe he's hungry.

Lord knows she isn't.

She isn't cold either, though she wears layers of clothes to look as though she is still herself. The human flesh had dissolved in the bath, leaving only the neat, sculptural lines of her emerging form. Her face will be gone soon, E/mi knows. The skin is too loose, like pretty tissues around a breakable gift.

Her parents whisper about how they should have taken her to hospital, not hidden her away and tried to fix her. They have stopped asking her downstairs, stopped speaking to her.

E/mi can hear them breathing, the tidal lollop of blood moving through the echoing chambers of their hearts. Smells the meatiness of them, so lumpen and porcine. They hide, locked in their bedroom, wondering how to undo their choices.

"It's not the illness," she tells the walls. "You think it is, but it was never that."

The shape we present to our neighbours is very careful. We must be trimmed to fit the whispers. Outside E/m's parents' house, the cars grow skins of golden pollen, send each other bulletins in the changing patterns of seagull shit.

E/m tries to decipher their code but understands only fragments, like a child overhearing an adult tell a risqué joke. She wonders if the cars are laughing under their sun-boiled bonnets.

There has been no one in Probably-Ryan's garden for a few days now.

The garden is unmowed, the contract broken. There is no one left to whisper.

Her parents edge down to the kitchen to eat the last of the pantry's tins, timid footfalls, neat and sharp as the deer that have come down from the woods to claim the roads, the gutters full of thistles and foxgloves.

E/m no longer bothers sneaking into the neighbour's garden; the grass is tussocky, the lilac shivers of seedheads almost as tall as she is. The world is fecund, and the neighbours will not leave their house to protest as she drifts into their back garden with the red-tailed bumblebees and the ubiquitous ringlet butterflies.

She presses her palms to the waiting earth, and promises Probably-Ryan that she will be here for him when he is ready. She can feel the reshaping, like a porridge being stirred, sugar and cinnamon on the tongue.

Another Tuesday, two weeks later. This one grey and yellow like a healing bruise. A summer storm blows back and forth in fits and starts, alternating the village with squalls and damp heat. Everything is overgrown, the world turned over-ripe, flies battering against glass, birds calling across the nearby thickets, grasshoppers ticking like sprinklers.

No sound of children, no hum of electricity or drone of distant traffic.

Another noise, far more interesting. The scuffle and thud of raw red earth, the scrape of skin against stone, the snap of stems. E would need to go make sure everything had gone well. Be a good neighbour, bringing gifts.

E opens the Danish butter biscuit tin and feeds their parents a handful of teeth under the sealed door, can hear them shift and whimper. They are scared of E, but there's no reason for it and soon they will know this, as they get better.

Already they have heard their father chewing the wooden bed into pulp, packing the matter into a damp cocoon wall in the corner of the closet.

E is safe. They are themself. Perhaps that means no perfect brace-corrected teeth, no womanly curves, no sensible job with a sensible salary, but aren't they an adult, after all? They can choose what they want to be.

"I won't hurt you," they say to the door.

Their father scuffles in the wood pulp, and their mother does not answer. E drifts down the stairs, their pointed feet hovering above the wood, and lets themself out the front door, emerging blinking into a band of stormless sky, the sun bright and hot as a tungsten bulb.

With no ceiling above, E feels weightless. It would be too easy to float away. Instead, E holds to the fences, tethering themself to trailing branches, as they slowly work their way into the Bauers' back garden, where wild hemlock raises its white umbrellas overhead.

Probably-Ryan sits on the edge of his grave, shivering. He's thinner and smaller than before, his moulted adult skin neatly and perfectly split around him. He looks up as E settles lightly on the wet red earth.

He shakes his head, childlike. "What happened?" His voice is unbroken.

"Nothing," E says. "Everything." They give him a cup filled with sugar and teeth.

Editors' Note:

We were captivated by the craft on display in "Sugar Teeth". The gorgeous prose, the wonderfully strange details that render E's transformation inexorable, inevitable, a quiet natural process that not even the expectations of neighbours or family can halt. The choice of reaching for descriptive details from both Scotland and the author's native South Africa is a masterstroke of defamiliarisation that sets up this tale of personal self-determination brilliantly.

Dodos

Rhiannon A Grist

A fox got into one of the Meadowbank pens. A large grey bird lay headless and gutless in the centre of lot 5A. This batch was soon to be introduced to Holyrood Park. V-HEP guidelines recommended protection against local predators, but with a ban on poisons and traps there was little Penitence could do. She lost her first batch to foxes upon return to the wild. She'd tried chasing them with handmade wooden approximations of predators, hoping they'd run or hide. Each time, she found herself nuzzled by a dozen large, hooked beaks. Whatever instincts the dodos once had they'd lost over thousands of years of relative safety. They'd become too comfortable. Then, when danger came, they'd died out.

Today, the dead dodo felt like a bad omen.

Penitence Price turned back to the L-shaped building that surrounded the dodo pens. The quiet inside the concrete units, with their ancient white metal shelves, had taken on a new eeriness. The comms had been silent for a few days now. They'd gradually grown quieter over Penitence's tenure at Meadowbank Station. She'd never seen any of the faces behind the voices – meeting up was forbidden under V-HEP. One by one they'd all gone dark. But none had affected her more than the recent silence from Yara at Ocean Terminal Station.

"What do you think chocolate tasted like?"

That was the line that marked Yara out from the others. Everyone else used the comms to send voice notes about supply updates and their work reintroducing lost species to the wild. There'd been Callum rearing wolves at the Pentland Station, Maeve and her insects at the Botanics

Station, plus others further afield. They'd all kept things, more or less, focused on business. Yara was the first to chat.

Penitence spent a whole day agonising over how to reply. She didn't want to be seen to be abusing the comms. But still…

Eventually she responded.

"Do the whales need something chocolate flavoured?"

That felt safe. Work-focused, but without shutting anything down.

"Ha, no. Just curious," Yara replied.

There was silence. She'd fucked it. But then Yara replied again.

"I found an old wrapper and the description says 'chocolatey scrumptiousness'. Like, what does that even mean?"

Maeve, the oldest of them, came back fast with a snippy reply.

"Ocean Terminal Station, if your request is not related to whale wellbeing, please do not share it on the comms. Thank you."

"Okay, sorry," Yara came back quickly. "I might be able to focus on the whales a bit better if I knew. I'm so distracted by this mystery. It haunts me!"

There was a small silence. Then Maeve responded.

"Creamy and sweet."

As the years passed – and the other voices on the comms went dark – Penitence became more comfortable chatting.

Then three days ago, Yara had gone silent too.

Penitence scattered feed distractedly across the tarmac pens. Was it against regulations to confirm a contact's status? No one had checked on Callum when his messages became garbled. He'd taken to sending incomprehensible strings of words. It lasted a few weeks. And then silence.

An impatient beak knocked against the feed bucket.

Penitence had barely slept last night. She kept getting up to see if there had been anything from Yara. It was the not-knowing that bothered her. If she could find out, perhaps she could accept what had happened, what was always bound to happen. It was all she was allowed to do anyway.

It was against the rules of V-HEP to treat diseases or fix broken limbs, organs, tissue. She could alleviate the pain – suffering was not necessary to V-HEP's goals – but the underlying calamity was to be left as it was. If the body managed to fix itself then the individual could live. If it did not, then they were given morphine and nature would take its course.

Because that was the point of V-HEP. Voluntary Human Extinction Programme. The alleviation of pain as humanity passed from this world.

It's not humanity's fault, V-HEP stated. It's just our nature.

We over-ate. We over-bred. We knew not to. We saw the warning signs, but we did it anyway. Selfishly. Callously. Stupidly. We ruined our planet and wiped-out innocent creatures in the process. We simply couldn't help ourselves.

When the colony ships blasted off with all those who could afford to board them, the remnants of humanity were left with the mess. After the storms and the wars that raged in their wake, the proponents of V-HEP grabbed whatever power remained in the ashes of our world with a zealous promise to soothe the grief and guilt of those left behind.

A plan to make things right.

Teams would be placed around the world and – using whatever preserved samples we had left and the genetic tech the abdicators made to custom design their offspring – humanity would breed the animals they'd caused to go extinct. And then they would die off.

No life-saving procedures. No children.

Humanity had had its chance and proved it couldn't be trusted. Now it was time for it to do Earth a favour and disappear.

Penitence pulled open the map drawer. Ocean Terminal Station wasn't far. A few hours' walk, maybe? She could go, confirm what had happened to Yara, and be back before the evening rounds. No regulations would be broken. V-HEP would be maintained. No one need know she'd gone.

Penitence was still justifying the trip to herself as she packed a bag.

The next morning, she completed her tasks, then set out for the coast. As she left the station, she heard coo-ing behind her. The dodos from Lot 5A waddled after her. She tried to shoo them, but the birds just flapped their useless tiny wings, undeterred. She knew she should frighten them away. They should be wary of something like her. A predator. Instead, she did her *come-along-then* whistle. She couldn't say no to company.

She cut her way up through the remnants of London Road. Elms and lindens had taken over the shattered tarmac, the spaces between their trunks filled with saplings, blackberry and thistle. The air was thick with pollen and bird song. Penitence swung her machete through the worst of the bramble, making sure to trample down the lower vines for the flock following behind her. The dodos pecked with gleeful curiosity at dandelions and papery elm seeds.

After an hour of diligent hacking, she reached the foot of Calton Hill.

The slope above was covered in hazel trees. It was hard to believe it had been bald for hundreds of years. Most of the hazel trees in Scotland were cut down during the Reformation. So much so, the replanters had to source their saplings from the rainforest on the west coast. The trees had been important in pagan circles, so removing them was as symbolic as St Patrick chasing the snakes out of Ireland. The decision had turned the hill's name into a puzzle for generations. Calton. Calltain. Gaelic for 'hazel'. A hazel hill with no hazel trees. Penitence wondered what else the hill had lost back then. Nightingales, yellowhammers, liverwort and dormice.

"How is what we're doing now any different?" Yara had once asked.

Penitence had laughed at the question. "We're putting the trees back."

"But the climate in Scotland has changed. It used to be cold and wet back then. Will hazel trees survive the summer on a hill now? And on that note, why are we raising dodos in Midlothian?"

"Because the island they're originally from is gone."

"Then shouldn't the dodos be gone too?"

Penitence had paused, fingers hovering over the report button. This was heresy. It was a private channel between Meadowbank and Ocean Terminal, but if anyone at Central decided to listen in... Penitence had only ever seen the black van once before. Once was enough for a lifetime. She would have to send a report, prove that she wasn't complicit in Yara's misstatement.

Instead, she sent a voice note back.

"In the 1600s the last auroch died in a zoo. In the 1700s Stellar's Sea Cow died out just thirty years after its discovery. In the 1800s the American Buffalo was wiped out in order to starve the indigenous people of North America. Rail workers took pictures posing on top of mountains of bones." Penitence calmed her breath. "The dodos didn't die out because Mauritius sank, but because we ate them all."

Yara replied after a moment.

"I'm sorry. I didn't mean to say what you were doing was … bad or wrong. Just—" she sighed. "For all the talk of undoing the sins of humanity blah blah blah, it just seems to me that, like, we're doing it again. Just this time we're getting rid of the humans. And … I have thoughts about that."

At the top of the hill, Penitence gathered hazelnuts from the lowest branches. Despite the hot summers, the trees were holding on. She rolled the nuts in her palm. People once thought they were seeds of wisdom. Poets and seers ate them to gain prophetic powers. Probably meant the ancestors brewed some kind of alcohol from the nuts and leaves. Maybe they'd help her know what to do. Penitence snacked on a few nuts and shelled more for the flock pecking around the roots.

As she ate, she took in the view and corroborated it with her map.

Out to the west, the shelled walls of the Balmoral Hotel still had the rusted remnants of razor wire and anti-vehicle fortifications. The remaining clockface on the ruined tower was frozen at ten thirty-two. The Separatists had holed up there before moving north during the oil wars. V-HEP claimed they'd all died, but Callum said they'd retreated into the hills, like Arthur and the Picts hiding inside Arthur's Seat, waiting to come to Scotland's aid.

Beyond the Balmoral, past the overgrown strip of Princes Street, the light shimmered off the Nor Loch. A herd of aurochs with their long, wide horns, grazed on the west bank by St John's Church. Its shattered gothic windows were bristling with the branches of ash and maple growing from within. The Georgian buildings of the New Town were overgrown with an impressive jungle of monstera and pothos. Houseplants, which had long since taken over the house.

Watching over it all was the castle, perched upon the volcanic plug that had once shot out of the caldera in Holyrood Park. Some of the old ramparts were still visible, even among the rubble and the gorse that was slowly taking over the rock. History layered itself upon this place like sheets of snow in a blizzard. But a city this old has fault lines. Here and there, a crack lies open, revealing a temporal cross section of everything that has ever happened, squeezed together in little layers. The plug. The castle. The rubble. The gorse.

Penitence turned her gaze north. Beyond the ragged coastline of Leith Links, the tops of buildings poked out of the sea like selkies making up their minds about coming ashore. Out to the north east, trailing at the end of a long, bobbing pontoon dock, was a flat silver building in the water.

Ocean Terminal.

Yara.

Penitence chucked the rest of the nuts to the flock then started on down the hill to the shore.

A few months back, Yara had sent an odd request.

"Hey, Pen, so I was nosing through the records and saw it's your birthday coming up. I can't send you a present or anything, but if you could have anything in the world – anything at all – what would it be?"

After a minute or so, Penitence replied.

"Maybe some crab shells for the dodos. I read that they may have eaten crab."

"I didn't ask what the dodos wanted. I asked what you wanted."

"It's nice of you to ask, but I don't really want anything."

"Nothing at all? Everyone wants something. Like, what do you want to eat tomorrow? What flowers do you want to see next spring? What do you want to be when you're older? Come on, you've got to have some idea."

Penitence's face went red.

"I don't think about wanting things. And I think it's best we don't think about the future either."

"Everyone imagines the future, Pen."

"Even when they don't have one?"

After a short pause Yara replied.

"Especially when they don't have one."

Penitence had just reached Coalie Park, where the Water of Leith met The Shore, when the dodos erupted in a cacophony of alarmed squarks. The bhaji dolphins in the river sped away from the noise and sloth lemurs in the canopy howled. A pack of thylacines came skulking out of the trees. Penitence froze. She must have missed them in the undergrowth, the stripes on their hind legs perfectly mimicked the shadows of branches and saplings. They'd be beautiful, if they weren't snapping at her birds. She threw a rock to try and scare them off, but it was no good. A thylacine clamped its long jaws around the neck of one of the dodos and dragged it back toward the trees. The others growled at the rest of the flock, their jaws hinged open, impossibly wide, almost a full ninety degrees. Penitence yelled at the top of her lungs and waved her arms. It was a stupid idea. There was no way she'd be able to fight them off. Luckily, the thylacines didn't know that. Apparently satisfied with just the one bird, the pack disappeared into the greenery, the dodo's frantic cries growing faint.

Penitence quickly guided the surviving birds out onto the silty shoreline. The pontoon dock bobbed nearby, stretching out between the drowned buildings. When they reached the sandy remnants of an old playpark, Penitence sank onto a sagging swing seat.

She'd only lost one to the pack. And dodos died all the time. Diseases. Territorial disputes. Foxes. She should feel relieved. But somehow this one hit different. The bird's cries echoed in her mind. For a horrible moment she imagined they were Yara's.

She hid her face in her hands.

Soft coo-ing grew around her. Warm feathers pressed against her thighs and her back.

She looked up blearily.

The flock had gathered around her, nestling together against her legs. A beak nuzzled into her arm, gently clacking against her skin.

"Can I ask a question?" Yara's voice sounded tentative. "Your birth date… It comes after the V-HEP cut off by, like, five years. Does that mean you're from the territories under conservatorship?"

Penitence thought carefully before replying.

"No. I'm from down south. I think. My parents broke V-HEP."

She'd never said that out loud before. It had always been something that was said to her. *About* her.

"Oh, shit. I didn't know. What happened to them?"

Penitence fought the memory of the black van.

"I don't know. I was taken into custody when I was three."

"Three! They hid you for three years?" Then, "Wait, is that why you're called Penitence?"

"The state picked it."

"Fuck. Pen, I'm so sorry."

"It's okay. They knew the rules and they chose to break them."

"Pen, what happened to you was… Shit. You were a child, not a crime."

Penitence bristled. Her childhood had been a sequence of undecorated rooms and conflicted faces. Every one of her entrances had been met with a sigh. She learned to make herself small. And useful. She volunteered for the conservation efforts as soon as she was old enough. She thought it would wipe her slate clean. But it never did.

So, she focused instead on the dodos, caring for them, making space for them, raising them to survive in a land they were never meant to live in, giving them everything she'd never had for herself.

"I'm glad you were born, Pen. I'm glad you're taking up space in this world. Even if it's just a voice on the other end of a speaker."

Penitence and her flock carefully crossed a sequence of makeshift bridges and bobbing pontoon docks zig-zagging between submerged buildings to Ocean Terminal. Water lapped against the walls of the large oblong building, leaving a patchwork of seaweed, mussels and barnacles in their wake. Half way up, a flutter of tarp hid a hole punched into the building by artillery, reinforced now with scaffolding. Penitence led the dodos up a rickety staircase, made of yet more scaffolding, away from the water and onto the flat grey roof, before descending back down and entering through the hole.

Penitence stepped into a darkness smelling strongly of brine and rot. She wound her torch and swung light round a cavernous room filled with rows of seats all facing one wall. The sodden carpet had flashes of bright coloured brush strokes. She scrubbed a bit of the algae away with the edge of her boot. They were stars and moons and ringed planets. People back then had such a colourful idea of space. All glowing nebulae and shining new worlds. Nothing like the dark, hungry void broadcast back from the luxury starships before they left the solar system. The radiation distorted anything else they tried to send afterwards.

Penitence rewound her torch and surveyed the corridors. Her heart beat strong and fast in her chest. This was Yara's home. This was where Yara lived and worked and shuffled about. Penitence hesitated. It felt wrong somehow. Like she was intruding on something private, something vulnerable and precious. Like her being here was enough to devalue it.

She remembered the message Yara sent her for her birthday. Penitence had never celebrated it. None of her guardians ever did. Who would choose to celebrate a crime?

Silly question. Of course, Yara would.

The message had come early in the morning and Yara's voice was excited and nervous all at once.

"Okay, Pen, I hope you don't mind but … I went looking for your name. The one your parents gave you before you were taken by the state."

Penitence's breath stopped.

"I dug pretty deep, but … I'm sorry. I couldn't find it. It was meant to be a birthday present. You know, happy birthday, *birth name.* Then

I realised that was pretty fucking intrusive and I was glad I didn't find anything! But then, I thought, maybe I could give you the knowledge that I tried? Or the honesty that I went looking where I probably shouldn't and realised, but it's okay, I failed. I don't know. I hope … anyway, happy birthday, Pen."

Penitence had sat at the comms desk for what felt like hours afterwards. Her oldest memory, or what she thought might be, ran round and round in her head. Two women and a rug in a dimly lit room. The women were playing with little painted wooden chickens on the rug, making them cluck and kiss Penitence's cheeks while her chubby hands tried to grab them. She saw their lips mouth out words – a word – but she couldn't make out what it was. She'd tried so hard over the years to try and remember the word they kept saying to her. She'd always wondered if it was her name. She'd never told anyone this. She'd held this one memory, replaying it over and over, alone for so long.

Penitence pressed the button to send a message.

"Thank you, Yara."

Penitence gripped her torch tight. She owed it to Yara to be here. To find out what happened to her. And, if necessary, to end her pain.

She took a deep breath and headed toward the natural light at the end of the corridor. She came out onto the main hall of Ocean Terminal. A long, wide balcony surrounded a large atrium in the centre, lit by massive round skylights. The space in the middle was full of sea water, sloshing gently with the movement of its curious inhabitants – a North Atlantic right whale and its calf. Large concrete units – similar to the ones at Meadowbank – were filled with krill tanks. Each had enough food to last for a few days. One of the tanks was halfway through being cleaned. Whatever had happened to Yara had been sudden then. But the food seemed to suggest some level of planning. Maybe Yara had to quickly pop out somewhere. Hope sent electricity through Penitence's limbs.

Then she spotted the blood on the walkway.

Yara's last comms were seared into Penitence's mind.

She'd been getting more careless over the last few weeks, sending folders of ancient video files. Meat farmers turning rainforest into grazing land. Server farms guzzling electricity to run shoddy image generators. The resource stripping that went into building the generation ships.

"They're the ones who ruined everything," Yara had said. "Not us."

"Does it matter? We're the only ones who can do anything about it now."

"Only because they escaped in their shitty ships and left us here!"

"You wish you'd gone with them?"

"Into space? With those people? God, no!" said Yara, "I'm not even convinced they're still alive. Probably eaten each other by now." She snorted derisively.

"What are you saying then?"

Yara took a little while to reply.

"I'm saying … ugh, I don't know." She sighed. "I saw something. The other day. I was looking for adolescent whales out in the firth on my telescope, when I spotted smoke on the other side of the water. I zoomed in on the shore and … I think there was a child."

What?

"A young girl."

No no no.

"She was cooking something on the fire. Fish maybe."

The separatists? Was Callum right? Had they really escaped into the north?

"What if there are other people out there? Living outside of V-HEP. Living in nature and—"

"Have you put in a report?"

"What?"

"You have to report any infractions of V-HEP."

"What? No, of course I'm not reporting her. Of all people, I thought you'd understand that!"

Penitence's hands trembled. If Yara didn't report it and their comms were monitored then Yara would be taken off Ocean Terminal Station and…

"It's okay. I'll send it in. I'll say you had an issue and asked me to report it for you."

"No, Pen, don't do that."

"I could say I saw the smoke."

There was a short pause. Then Yara replied.

"If you report them, I'll never speak to you again, Pen. We are done. Do you hear me? Done!"

Penitence paused, her heart beating hard in her chest.

"You know I have to, Yara. I have no choice."

"You do have a choice! You've always had a choice! We don't get much of a choice but we have that. Don't do this! I'm begging you!"

The report had lain open on Penitence's monitor for a few days. When no message from Central arrived, she deleted it. She messaged Yara to apologise, but Yara didn't reply. When she didn't turn up for check-in either, Penitence started to worry.

Penitence followed the drops of blood into a large unit tucked into the back of the building. Preparing herself for the worst, she quietly made her way between neat tables, pushed to the sides of a large space and piled high with equipment. There was a strong animal smell coming from the back, different from the briny spray in the centre of the station. Penitence rewound her torch, covered her mouth and approached. To the side of an ancient kitchen was a tarped off area. A small needle of light threaded its way through a gap in the covering and across the floor. Penitence braced herself, then pulled back the tarp.

A harpoon flew past her head, the wind whistling past her ear. Penitence ducked down, dropping her torch.

A grey-faced woman, skin gleaming with sweat, huddled on a stained bed against the opposite wall. Dark spirals of hair hung over her face and shoulders and her eyes blazed white and fearful. She panted over a harpoon gun as her shaking fingers made to reload it.

"Don't come any closer or the next one won't miss," she hissed.

It was Yara's voice.

Yara was alive.

"I mean it! Fuck off, right now!" She pointed the reloaded harpoon gun at Penitence's face.

Penitence threw up her hands.

"Yara, it's me. Pen!"

The harpoon flew past Penitence's head and struck the ceiling above her.

"Pen? How did you – ?"

Yara tried to get up then fell back where she sat, her chest heaved. Penitence ran over to her and placed a hand on her forehead. Her skin was hot and clammy to the touch.

A small whimper came from a crate to the side of the bed. Yara's eyes widened.

"Don't—"

Penitence pulled the blanket aside and gasped.

A tiny baby, eyes squeezed shut, face a scowl at the world, squirmed inside the crate. Penitence looked at Yara then back at the child.

"I can explain," Yara murmured, then slumped unconscious onto the bed.

Penitence shook her shoulders, trying to rouse her. Then she felt for Yara's pulse. It was high. How long had she been lying here? She must have been exhausted. Her body didn't have the resources left to win this fight.

The baby started to cry in the crate.

Penitence picked it up and shushed it in her arms. It snuffled against her shoulder, rooting around for a latch. Soon it, they, would be inconsolably disappointed.

She carried the baby through to the room with all the tables. With one arm she bounced the mewling child and with the other she went through the crates. She knew what she was looking for. She found the morphine kit in its breakable case. One dose. Enough to send Yara into a permanent sleep.

Then she spotted the antibiotics, the antiseptic sprays, the suturing kits.

These were for the animals and the animals only.

Penitence looked between the collection of life-saving treatments and the box of painkilling, life-ending promise. This was the law. No intervention. No resuscitation. We were here only to right our wrongs and nothing else. Tidy up the chairs then get out of the way. No future. No new generations to make new mistakes. Humanity had to end, one morphine dose at a time.

Penitence looked back at the tarped-up living chamber.

But this was Yara.

What do you want to be when you're older?

Penitence screwed her eyes shut.

Come on, you've got to have some idea.

The baby howled in her arms.

She grabbed the kit.

Penitence was there when Yara's eyes flickered open. Penitence threw up her hands as Yara flinched.

"It's okay. Your fever's down. Whales are fine. Baby's fed." She pointed a thumb behind her. "I found your stock of formula. It's way out of date, so I tried it on me first."

Yara relaxed back into the pillow.

"What happened?"

Penitence raised her eyebrows.

"I think that's my line, don't you?"

Yara huffed a laugh. "It's pretty clear what my thoughts on V-HEP are by now." She wiped her forehead. "I made up my mind, used the gen-tech on myself, scored, panicked, got on with it. Same as every other pregnant human in history."

Penitence bit her lip. Yara sat up.

"Look this isn't some restart humanity bullshit. I'm just a glutton for joy, Pen. You want to report me, go ahead. Just don't let them take him."

Penitence sighed.

"You had an infection from the ah – the procedure."

"You mean the birth?"

"Yeah that." Penitence's cheeks flushed. "I uh – checked. No afterbirth was left inside, so I just gave you some of the antibiotics you had for the whales."

Yara blinked.

"You … you gave me treatment?"

Penitence nodded.

"So, if I report you, I'd have to report myself too."

Yara shook her head, brows knit together.

"But I thought you—"

"You asked me what I wanted for my birthday." Penitence fidgeted with the baby's blanket. "I realised I only had one wish. Not to be alone. It'd be pretty hard to do that if I just let everyone die out."

They sat together in that *so-now-what?* silence.

"I've been thinking a lot about the dodos lately. About how we're giving them a second chance." Penitence pulled at her sleeves. "What if we got a second chance too? What if instead of dying, we got better?" She looked at the ground, aware of the blasphemy leaving her mouth. "What if we lived?"

Yara stared at her.

"My god, does Penitence Price *want* something?"

"Has there been any word on the comms?" Yara asked.

"No. I've not checked in either." Pen looked up. "I don't think anyone's coming for us."

They stood together on the roof of Ocean Terminal, looking out over the firth. Dawn broke overhead, brightening the indigo sky into dazzling pinks and oranges. Yara fed crab shells to the dodos while Pen bounced Baby Navin in a sling strapped to her chest. Navin squawked and grabbed for the dodos at their feet.

It had been a few months. They'd wanted to wait until the remaining whales and dodos could be released, and until Navin was old enough to handle the trip.

"Hmm, organisation focused on humanity dying out, dies out before they can ensure all of humanity is dead." Yara raised an eyebrow. "One day that might be funny."

They packed the most useful items – medicine, radios, generators – into the dinghy and shut down Ocean Terminal Station. The flock of dodos that had followed Pen all this way, her small bumbling army of birds back from the dead, tumbled into the boat with them. Pen turned for a final look back at Edinburgh's crumbling skyline. Yara put a hand on her shoulder.

"You sure about this?"

"Yeah." Pen started the engine and looked out over the water, past the whales cresting in the firth of forth, to the shoreline beyond, heart light, the horizon wide and ahead of her.

"I think I'm ready for a change."

Editors' Note:

Sometimes a story arrests you right away with its initial image. We found Rhiannon's cadre of dodos following Penitence around the compound like farmyard chickens irresistibly cute. Rewilding after eco-collapse, we thought. Wonderful! Then she hit us with the simply devastating concept of Voluntary Human Extinction and we had a whole different story on our hands. Amid the rubble of an abandoned Edinburgh, it's ultimately the irrepressible positivity of human nature that shines through. That and the hope that we may actually learn from our mistakes.

Under the Hagstone

Doug Johnstone

Aki stood at the treeline of Meadowfield Park and watched the shadow of the hagstone approaching over eastern Edinburgh. She looked down the slope at Figgtown, stretching from here to the flood barriers of Porty. Her home. The spread of allotments and woods, converted roof gardens, shimmering solar cells, the network of roads and paths that had overgrown in the years since the appearance.

"Ready to die?" Joe said.

She looked at him. She and her brother were very different. She was short and lean, wore too many clothes and didn't laugh much. He was a foot taller, made of silicone, reusable plastic and adapted metal plating, and was deadpan dry.

"We're not going to die," she said.

"Well, *I'm* not."

The shadow was close now, over Meadowbank and Craigentinny, its distinctive bright hole a spotlight moving across a stage.

Aki glanced up at the hagstone. She'd never known Edinburgh without it, born the same year the artefact arrived. It was a colossal, irregular ring torus, floating fifty metres above the peak of Arthur's Seat, spinning lazily on its vertical axis, asymmetric body casting a wide shadow, its hole keeping watch over the city. Not that anyone knew if it was watching, or what the hell it was doing. It just appeared one night and never left. All attempts to communicate with, analyse or remove it had been met with mute indifference.

Holyrood Park lay directly underneath it, all 650 acres cordoned off by the authorities. But that didn't mean you couldn't get inside, if you knew how.

The shadow swept over Jock's Lodge and Parsons Green then they were in it, Aki shivering, Joe striding through the trees to the perimeter fence.

"Hey." Aki caught up just as he was crouching at the place they'd used before, where they knew there was no camera coverage. Something about the shadow and the trees felt eerie, even though they'd done this many times. They both had small headtorches, Aki's on a headband, Joe's built into his forehead.

Joe focused his cutting laser on the patch of repaired fence. Once he'd cut through enough he heaved the flap up. An alarm sounded, they didn't have much time. Joe held the fence as Aki gripped her empty satchel tight and crawled through on her belly. She emerged, dusted herself down and watched Joe slip his rangy body through the gap.

"This way," he said.

"I know."

Just because he was a robot, he always thought he knew best. She could find their hiding place in the dark. They reached the gap in the old wall and headed over Dunsapie Crag. Aki saw the torches of armed guards sweeping through the long grass behind them. She and Joe turned their torches off.

They headed for the small loch then ducked into the hole they'd found ages ago, a fold in the cliff face that hid them from view.

The guards could only use eyesight to find them, none of their high tech equipment worked in the shadow zone. Drones and other craft fell out of the sky, thermographic cameras were blank. Sniffer dogs got confused by unearthly scents, yelping in confusion until their handlers gave up.

So Aki and Joe just had to crouch here and wait.

Joe clicked his mouth, a sound like sucking teeth. "Come here often?"

"Shut up."

They were there for ten minutes when they heard voices.

Joe placed his hand over Aki's mouth and she bit it. He removed his hand.

She caught a glimpse of light as the guards headed round the path. Sounded like at least four of them, more than usual. She wondered if something had spooked them recently.

The hagstone was unpredictable. Sometimes it would stop rotating, only to start again a few hours later. Sometimes it was cloaked in unnatural cloud formations, or shimmered at sunrise or sunset as if it was enjoying the rays. Was it a sentient being? A ship carrying aliens or something supernatural? Some people lost sleep over this, but not Aki, she just got on with scavenging for Skelly.

The hagstone had transformed Edinburgh. Authorities evacuated the city after it arrived, the rich never returning, too scared of obliteration. The government put up a wide exclusion zone which they filled with soldiers and scientists, trying to find out what the hell was going on. But it had been sixteen years now and they were no nearer to finding out why the hagstone was here. It was almost as if the thing was blanking them deliberately. Maybe they just weren't asking the right questions, or maybe they weren't the right people to be asking the questions.

Gradually, poor folk started seeping back into the city. They had nowhere else. So Figgtown grew and officials turned a blind eye, treating the whole area like a shantytown, and the Figgies like primitive idiots. They had to become sustainable, provide their own food and water, power and infrastructure, so they did. The authorities never minded as long as no one was ever caught in the shadow zone. Rumours surrounded the zone – ghostly apparitions, oddly coloured animals, unearthly looking plants. Variable gravity.

Aki had seen plenty of things she couldn't explain. For years, she and Joe had been coming here to collect shock pebbles. They were small stone-like objects, similar shapes to the hagstone, seemingly made of the same material. Definitely not from earth according to Skelly and she was pretty smart. She made Joe, after all.

Everyone assumed the shock pebbles came from the hagstone – where else? They were very hard to spot, especially in the thick undergrowth that peppered the Holyrood hills. But Skelly had built a detector that – like Joe – somehow worked in the zone. It was something to do with neutrinos that Aki didn't understand, but it meant they could scavenge in the dark.

The shock pebbles were super-useful, incredible energy sources and storage devices. Wired up to Figgtown's makeshift grid, a single stone could power fifty homes for six months. Then, when it was depleted they could reverse the flow and used it to store power from their solar cells.

Joe slipped out of the hiding place. "Come along."

"I'm not a baby," Aki said, but she secretly liked the way he spoke.

She scurried in his wake as he strode round the back of Arthur's Seat towards Whinny Hill. The going was tougher, gorse everywhere, but Joe cut a swathe through the worst of the thorns and made a path for her. They were rising all the time, and Aki looked over the city. The scientific base and military barracks below were floodlit in a boxy grid, but beyond that wildlife had reclaimed much of the city. Some buildings showed signs of decay amongst the trees, ivy and weeds, the castle lonely on its little rock without tourists, no traffic on the roads.

Beyond, she could see the lights of the Queensferry Crossing blinking in the low sunlight. The rest of the country going on as normal. Strange they could just write off a city like this, but the circumstances were remarkable. The strangest event in the history of humanity, right on Aki's doorstep. She wondered about that.

Joe had disappeared down the other side of the peak.

Aki looked up at the hagstone, floating so naturally.

"Aki."

She turned at Joe's voice, then scampered over the other side, saw him staring at the ground, headtorch beam splitting the darkness.

She got closer and saw what he was staring at. Stepped towards it.

He put an arm out to stop her.

"What is it?" she said.

"I don't know, obviously."

It was a foot long and faintly glowing, shifting shape from spheroid to doughnut to barbells and back again. Swirling patterns danced across the surface like a contained oil slick.

"Is it … alive?"

Joe was quiet for a moment. "It's not like the shock pebbles."

Aki pointed upwards. "But it came from up there, right?"

Joe looked at her. "Duh."

She reached out and it moved towards her hand. Joe stepped between them.

Aki felt gravity weakening and her body stretched upwards. Time slowed as she watched Joe's heels leave the ground. He waved his arms to lower himself, then crouched and held onto the gorse to his left. Aki did likewise, anchoring herself to the earth. They'd experienced low gravity pockets before while scavenging, but nothing like this.

"This could be one of *them*," Aki said.

"Not very impressive," Joe said.

"What did you want, giant robots?"

"Why not?"

Aki smelled something like mushrooms. She stared at the object moving and shapeshifting. She went to pick it up but Joe stopped her.

"Let me," he said.

"I can handle it."

"Just in case."

Something in Joe's voice stopped her from protesting any further.

He grabbed it and collapsed in a heap amongst the gorse.

"Joe!"

Aki reached out and shook his shoulders, felt sick and dizzy, saw a vision of something huge and terrifying, an angry cloud on the horizon, then collapsed and felt her head hit the ground.

She was inside the hagstone looking out, but somehow she could see beyond the horizon, across the North Sea to Norway in one direction, mainland Europe then Africa in another, then over the Atlantic Ocean as the stone rotated. She was floating, surrounded by shapeshifting blobs. She tried to touch one but her arms wouldn't move.

"Wake the fuck up."

She did as she was told, found herself in a bright yellow room, sitting in an uncomfortable plastic chair. Across a table were two men, a guard in uniform standing with a machine gun and an older man in a suit. Her satchel was on the table between them. It looked like it had something in it.

"So," the suit said. "Want to tell me what you were doing in the zone?"

Aki shrugged, tried to look confident. "Just out for a stroll."

"Fucking Figgies," said the guard. "Scum."

Aki smiled. "Are you happy in your job?"

"Fuck off."

"Love you too."

"Enough," the suit said, waving at the guard to step back.

"I'll ask you nicely one more time," he said, glancing behind, "then I'll let Rickards have a go."

Aki folded her arms and pressed her lips together.

The suit smiled. "We have your little toy AI. Seemed a bit faulty when we picked it up. And not built according to code. Where did it come from?"

Aki tried to think of anything she could say to get out of this.

The suit leaned forward and touched Aki's satchel. "Then there's this."

He opened it and Aki saw the thing, still shifting and swirling. She couldn't stop looking at it, felt her stomach lift and wondered if gravity was shifting. She glanced at the suit and the guard, but they didn't seem to have felt anything.

"I've never seen that before."

The suit shook his head and sighed. He closed the satchel, stood up and carried it to the door.

"Rickards, deal with her," he said.

He reached for the door handle but before he touched it the whole door smashed open, flying across the room and taking the suit with it. The satchel skittered across the floor and Aki grabbed the strap, slung it over her shoulder. The guard turned and pointed his gun at the doorway as Joe leapt through at incredible speed, knocking the gun from his hand and throwing him across the room to land in a heap on top of the suit and the door.

"You're welcome," he said.

"You took your time," Aki said, relieved.

The suit was right, Joe wasn't built to code. He had all sorts of useful mods.

He pointed at the door. "Shall we?"

"After you."

"Age before beauty."

"I don't know whether that means me or you."

Joe shook his head. "Let's just go."

They ran down the corridor, stepping over three unconscious guards, then out the broken front door of the security hut. The courtyard was floodlit in the hagstone shadow, but they stuck to the gloomier edges and reached the perimeter fence. Joe did his thing with the laser, running a cut big enough for them to duck through. Aki heard shouts behind them and an alarm sounded.

They were round the west side of the park, a long way from home. They ducked off the main path into the Innocent Railway tunnel. It was a risk if they were trapped inside, but it was much quicker than going around. They emerged from the tunnel and already the sound of guards was further away, as if they didn't really care about catching them. These were minimum wage grunts who liked to wave guns at innocent teenagers. Chasing them long distances was another matter.

Aki and Joe followed the Innocent Path to Duddingston, deer watching them from the reeds of the loch to their left. Aki felt the thing in her satchel moving.

They slowed their walk and Aki got her breath back. She stopped and threw her arms around her brother and squeezed him tight. She felt his hands on her back, the reassuring solidity of him, their bond. Tears came to her eyes and she let him go and wiped at her face.

"Thanks," she said.

He grinned. "No problem. That was fun."

They turned north, flinching as they came out of the hagstone's shadow. But no one was following them.

They walked for a while in silence.

Aki watched Joe closely. "What happened to you back there?"

"Where?"

"On the hill, with this thing. I've never seen you power down like that."

Joe was quiet for a long moment. "I don't know."

"What do you think it is?" Aki said, touching her satchel.

Joe was quiet again. Aki was scared by the silence, it wasn't like him.

"Skelly will know," he said.

Skelly's place was a cross between a junkyard and a fantasy emporium. She'd taken over a couple of the outhouses of the old Parsons Green primary school, one to live in, the other as a workshop.

Skelly was the closest thing Aki had to a parent, which wasn't very close. Aki's folks had lived in Figgtown until they both succumbed to cancer four months apart. There was a lot of chat about possible illnesses due to the hagstone, but no one had ever proven a connection.

Still, Aki was an orphan at eleven and Skelly took her in around the same time as she finished working on Joe. He was the latest in a long line of experiments, the evidence of the others strewn around the workshop, something which always made Aki shiver. What if she would one day see Joe's head sitting in the junk pile?

"Skelly, wait until you see."

Skelly was hunched over a workbench examining the interface between a motherboard and some biotech that looked like a deflated jellyfish. She pushed her goggles onto her forehead. She had a mess of curly red hair, deep lines on her forehead, muscular arms and bright green eyes.

Aki glanced at Joe, who blinked too many times. She lifted her satchel onto the workbench and felt the thrum inside.

"Careful," she said.

Skelly narrowed her eyes. "Why?"

Aki ran her tongue around her teeth. "It's not a shock pebble."

The satchel shuffled on the workbench and they all looked at each other. Skelly lifted the flap open. The shapeshifting blob slid out, one moment the shape of the hagstone, the next more like a snake, then a squashed football, all the while that weird display spilling over its surface.

Skelly leaned in. "What the hell?"

"Exactly."

The blob moved in a way that suggested it was exploring its environment. Four soft prongs extended, two from each end, sweeping a pen and some screws from the workbench, making everyone jump.

Skelly shook her head. "This is huge."

Joe clicked his mouth. "We presumed so."

Skelly couldn't take her eyes off the blob. She pointed a desk lamp at it. It flinched then moved towards the light.

Skelly turned the lamp off and looked around the room. "We need something to keep it in."

Aki shrugged. "It seems happy in my satchel. It must've climbed in when…"

"What?" Skelly said.

"Nothing," Joe said quickly. "It just climbed in."

The blob rolled and squished around the bench, stretching and squeezing itself, oily exterior pattern flowing.

Skelly lifted the satchel open and slid it towards the blob. It ignored the satchel and moved closer to Joe.

Aki stepped forward. "I'll do it."

"Can you hear that?" Joe said.

Aki stared at him, then at Skelly, who shrugged.

"What?" Aki said.

Joe held a hand up. "Wait."

The blob moved into a shape that mirrored the hagstone exactly.

Joe nodded. "They're talking to me."

"*What?*" Skelly said.

Aki frowned. "*They?*"

Joe reached a hand out.

Aki grabbed his arm. "Wait." She turned to Skelly. "It made him power down," she said. "I've never seen that before."

"Joe," Skelly said. "There's no way—"

Joe reached out to the blob and it rose off the bench towards his hand, then slid smoothly up his arm like a sleeve, travelled to his shoulder and neck, then slipped onto his face, where it shaped itself into a mask sitting over his features, still shimmering away.

The mask faded into Joe's face, slipping beneath until it was gone.

Joe blinked a few times, didn't move, stared at Aki and Skelly.

"Hello, finally," he said in a new voice, not robot, not human, something else entirely. The voice reverberated around the room as Joe put out his hands.

"The first thing to say is: Don't panic."

Editors' Note:

Who wouldn't be instantly smitten by the notion of a giant, inscrutable, alien object hovering over Edinburgh? It's about time, we said! First contact scenarios always hold such wonderful promise, and it's always fascinating to see which of the story's characters manages to crack the code and make the breakthrough of that first contact with the alien. We love that Doug decided that it wouldn't be the government, the military, or even the scientists, but the resourceful locals. Those who refuse to be displaced from their transformed home but instead are happy to buckle in and adapt to it, should definitely be the ones to reap the rewards. We're hoping Doug will return to this world so we can find out what happens next.

The Donkey

T.L. Huchu

Godknows Marara changed his name one year after moving to Scotland. He was sick of having to explain to everyone that in Shona culture, a name has to carry some deep meaning or truth, and what could be truer than the omniscience of the one true god? This was the first of many changes Joe, as he was now known, made to adjust to life in the country that was the closest place to Heaven on Earth in the imaginations of his people. If that was the case then the gritty, working class town of Buttonburgh in West Lothian was the new Jerusalem. The place where Joe carried on his slender shoulders the dreams of the entire Marara Clan from Uzumba in rural Zimbabwe. He was, after all, the first one in his family to fly in an aeroplane.

"Alright hen?" he says to Cheryl in his faux-Scots, an accent which seems to have crept up on him like the rhomboid muscle pain he endures daily, ten years into his diaspora stint.

"Ey up, me duck."

She nods and offers Joe a fag, which he accepts. Another bad habit he picked up in the diaspora.

"Doing anything nice for Christmas?" Cheryl asks, flicking ash onto the tarred car park.

"Same old shit, innit?" he replies, deflecting, hoping she won't probe anymore.

"It's a rip-off alright. Been doing me shopping since October. Got most of the expensive prezzies on Black Friday; that's for my nephews and nieces, spoilt little shits. I love them all the same. Next year, Paul and me are going out to Thailand. I've seen you booked extra shifts on the rota. Fucking hell, I told Susan, 'You've made me work two Christmases in a row, I ain't fucking doing this one.' They can take this job and stick it up their arses. 15p that's the pay rise they're giving us next year. Load of bollocks, if you ask me."

Joe hasn't fully mastered the British art of moaning. He's grateful he has a job; three if you count the ad hoc temping, plus the cleaning he does mornings in Blackburn. Cheryl fidgets, shoulders hunched; the cold front from Scandinavia's dropped the mercury and the snow's coming. She's got sharp grey eyes and bottle-bought strawberry blonde locks, a roman nose whose tip's split like a twee bum, crow's feet and yellow teeth. She's taller than Joe by a foot at least. He's barely five-three, skinny, and wears a pencil moustache, his short afro combed, big cheekbones accentuate his smile, which comes easily. He has tiny scars on his forehead and both cheeks, two lines next to each other like '11' carved in by the medicine man's razor blades when he was too young to even remember. When he is not in work, he often wears a cap to make them less conspicuous. The only people that seem to like them are tattoo-heads who think tribal scarification is *so cool.* Joe's out in the cold in his tunic, neglecting to wear a jacket. Years ago, when he temped as a cleaner for the council, his colleagues laughed at him for wearing a heavy bomber jacket and made 'man from Africa' jokes, so now his ability to endure the cold is a point of pride.

An old Vauxhall Astra with an R reg number plate rolls into the carpark.

"Come on, Betty needs changing," Cheryl says, flinging her fag butt on the ground and stepping on it.

The elders taught: before embarking on a journey you must step on something solid, lest in the darkness of the unknown you fall into a hole. When the chance to go to the UK came, Godknows was taken by his mother to Sekuru Benhura, the n'anga in the Rakanga village. While other mothers might ululate and dance, forgetting the ancestors in their excitement, Mai Marara knew that libation must be poured for the ancestors' gifts to avoid angering them. How else would it have been possible that a fourth cousin by marriage had offered to take Joe overseas? Surely that was proof of the hand of the unseen acting. Those whose voices in the wind will whatever branch of the family they choose to bear fruit whilst the rest wither.

Sekuru Benhura's homestead consisted of three huts set atop a granite dwala in the south of the village near the Mazowe river. There were wilted maize stalks in a small field nearby. The rains had failed to come on time and many farmers had lost everything. Even the n'anga, whose duty it was to appease the ancestors when they withheld their spit, was unable coax even a drop out of them.

"You walk upon my path as if it was the common road leading to the toilet," Sekuru Benhura said from inside his kitchen hut. A steady stream of blue smoke issued through the grass thatch.

"Do not be angry, we are your children," Mai Marara said, clapping her hands in the traditional style. "Would you send us back when you can hear our bellies rumble with hunger?"

"That son of yours will feed you all. Your husband's family prayed for someone of their own blood to lift them up and yet you come with this boy as though he belongs to you.

"Enter my hut and let me see Godknows with my own eyes."

They stooped for the thatch roofing on the house was set too low, and it was uneven because the goats had had a nibble or two. This was not too difficult for Mai Marara who was even shorter than her son. She was bone thin, sunbeat skin grey and wrinkled like elephant hide because they were so poor they couldn't afford vaseline. She wore a moth-eaten t-shirt bearing the slogans of the ruling party. And the zambia cloth around her waist, as well as her doek were also freebies the party gave away in exchange for chanting slogans at its rallies around the election cycle. Life for her had been harder than the sunburnt, overused earth of their unproductive fields.

The hut smelt of foul odours emanating from the numerous calabashes with potions and herbs stacked along the wall following its curve. The floor was lined with cowhide which they sat on in front of Sekuru Benhura who was on a low three-legged stool. He wore a crown of crow's feathers on his head and his loincloth was made of baboon hide. There were dried heads of his totem animal, the monkey pinned to the walls, their eyeless sockets looking down. He was bare chested and used a fly swatter to chase away the insects that seemed drawn to him. Strips of beef and fish were drying from hooks set into the wooden beams holding up the thatch. Smoke continuously rose from the floor up towards the thatch, but there was no fire going. Godknows wondered if the hut was built upon the coals of hell.

"Only the earth knows the mouse's children are sick," Mai Marara said, clapping her hands.

"The child who does not cry out dies in the sling," Sekuru Benhura traded her proverb for proverb, pinching snuff from his kudu horn gourd and sniffing it before sneezing loudly. "Tell me in your own words so those in the wind drink the moisture in your breath."

"This boy is my youngest. I had eight children, three are with the ancestors, more never crawled out of the womb alive. I thought Godknows would look after me in my old age, but the world is calling to him."

"Hatsu!" The n'anga sneezed and leapt up from his stool, falling upon Godknows who cried out in alarm. The old man lifted up his shirt and thrust his finger into the boy's navel before spitting on his face. "Then I will tie his umbilical cord to you. May the nourishment you fed him in the womb now flow to you. Such is the circle of life. This boy will not lose his way. He will never return from beyond the sea, but the proceeds of his sweat will always come back to you until your kraals are filled with cows and goats."

"We receive your judgement, Sekuru," Mai Marara said, clapping her hands.

"On your knees, son of the soil," the n'anga commanded.

Godknows trembled but obeyed. He had never been to visit the traditional healers, raised in the Anglican faith of the nearby mission as he was. He knew there were those in the village who dabbled in the old ways, but had never been initiated. This was against everything the priests had taught them at the mission school. Godknows didn't want any part of this, but he was too afraid to defy the n'anga. Who knows what curses would result if he tried?

"Ride his back as you would a donkey!"

Godknows felt the weight of his mother along with that of his entire clan on his back as he crawled around the n'anga's hut. Sekuru Benhura followed behind, beating his buttocks with the fly swatter like a herdsman driving his beast of burden forward.

The small room Joe rents on Axholme Road is quiet at night except for the occasional traffic making its way between Beckett Road and Thorne Road. It's the vans that rumble the loudest. His window on the first floor looks out onto the tall lime tree which blots out the moon. Not that it matters, the yellow electric lights mean the stars are invisible all year round. It used to shock him, this starless sky. He wondered if the constellations of his village, Chinyamatanhatu, the Seven Sisters, or Nguruvenembwa, the pig and dog, are hidden there.

It's late at night like this he misses the scent of cow dung and the sound of children's laughter. Home was a multigenerational extended family, new faces and distant cousins, neighbours popping in to borrow the Scotchcart, invitations to jiti dances. It was noisy. It was busy. Disputes were as like to break out as celebrations. They hated and loved one another. Most of all, Joe misses his mother. She has long passed and the years have driven on relentlessly. He wasn't there when she passed and now, try as he may to remember her face, all he gets is a glimpse for a fraction of a second, before it gives way to a blur.

He avoids such thoughts because in the lethargic minutes before midnight, Joe is working on his budget again. This is something he does every night, sat upon his single bed, the fourteen-inch LCD TV broadcasting the *Graham Norton Show*. He doesn't get the jokes. Joe didn't grow up with a TV. The only show he likes is *Eastenders* and only then because it gives him something to talk about with the other carers and residents at the nursing home he works at.

The British pound is slippery like an eel. It squirms and leaps from your hands no matter how tightly you try to hold onto it. Joe nibbles on the butt of his pen, before crossing out the plan to visit London. The train's simply too expensive. He will go to Sheffield instead. He's not gifted in book learning, but he enjoys the NVQ level three his work is making him too. Next year, he wants to train as a nurse. It would be a step up. He wants to be the one giving medicine to the residents, or maybe even work in a hospital. But the fees amounting to nearly his yearly wage are too expensive for a foreigner and three years as a student too long without resources. His dreams too are blotted out by the light pollution.

Ainsley Cottage on Bercow Avenue is like a picture book Victorian mansion. Pristine lawn, anemone and dahlia growing in the garden alongside the driveway. It was once a family home, but an extension into the garden plus a conservatory at the back have turned it into a modern care home with room enough for thirty-one residents including dementia care. It's warm and a bit stuffy, but cosy.

Joe's in the sluice room on the first floor cleaning a commode when a call bell sounds in room number 9. His eyes droop, bags under them. It's getting harder to sleep because of the back pain. He finds it hard to get comfortable. He removes his gloves and the white plastic pinny, deposits them in the yellow bin before washing his hands and leaving to attend to the call.

By the time he reaches number 9, he has a smile on his face. There's a foul stench and a middle-aged man and woman stand at the foot of the bed, observing Doris who's waving her hands in the air as though taking down laundry from a washline, completely oblivious to the people in the room.

"Doris, you're making trouble again?" Joe says, cheerily.

"I think she needs changing," Kate, the female visitor says.

"Thanks for letting me know. Would you like to step outside?"

The work is hard, but it's the families that make things a bit more complicated. Ben, Kate's brother, leads the way. Joe doesn't like him much. Doesn't like them both. They are Doris's grandchildren. Smug, entitled, always finding a reason to complain about the service. The two move through the home casting a dark cloud over the staff. And they never remember his name.

"What are you like, Doris?" Joe says, once the door's closed.

She coos and gurgles, a smile appearing on her face, almost like recognition. Cheryl says he's the only person Doris smiles for. She has a theory, something about African American soldiers stationed in Cottingham near Hull where Doris grew up. Joe places his hand on Doris's cheek and strokes it. She reaches with a trembling hand to touch his arm. There's black and white photographs of a younger Doris and her husband Stan hanging against the yellow-papered wall.

"You're thirsty, aren't you?" Joe says, giving Doris a sip from the beaker on the cabinet next to the bed. "The vultures are still coming to check if you're dead, aren't they? Don't worry, I'll make sure you'll get your telegram from the queen."

Joe had once heard Ben and Kate complaining that Doris staying alive was eating into their inheritance. The house they wanted in Bessacarr had been sold to pay for her care and the pot was dwindling fast. It was all very strange to Joe that you could will your grandmother dead for money. He had never inherited anything. In fact, it was the other way round where he was from. Each funeral meant he had to send money home to help with the burial. God forbid they got sick before they died like his mother. Zimbabwean hospital bills were extortionate. No NHS.

His phone pings as he's patiently giving Doris water, some dribbling down the side of her mouth. He makes the mistake of checking it, which he's not supposed to during his shift. A message from Uncle Tome, his father's younger brother.

"Godknows, my cows are dying of disease. Please send money for the dip, my son. God bless you. And remember to pay school fees for Muneyi, she is going into form one. Good boy."

Money. It was always money. Joe sighs.

There were other messages, read and unread. Messages from cousin-sister Lily, Auntie Maravanyika, nephew Tino, his cousin-brother's wife Mazvita, his half-sister Katarina, George the herdboy... The phone's filled with unanswered requests, medical bills, transport money, groceries requests, wedding support for lobola, someone's car needing fixing, clothes for so and so, fertiliser money to help with the fields, a tombstone that needs erecting, assistance for small business ventures which never materialise ... if it's not one thing, it's the other. Help. *Remember we are your family. Don't forget your roots.*

"They want to bleed us dry," he says to Doris. "Not any more. We won't do it!"

Joe sets the beaker to one side, and then cleans her up before changing her nappy. It doesn't take long, he's good at this job. When he's done, he says goodbye to Doris and leaves the room.

He throws the soiled nappy and wipes into the bin, then reaches for his phone. Something's pushing him to throw the phone in the bin and be done with it, but a message pings, making him hesitate. There's a wee niggle tugging at his gut.

In the time before the white man came, before a hunter set out into the savannah, they must have washed in the Mazowe River near the raging rapids which the crocodiles avoid. Afterwards they would oil themselves with animal fats, seek guidance from the ancestors, and set off with the women chanting their praise names to bring good fortune. By the time Godknows became a man, the forests had been emptied of game, the soil was tired, only misery grew in abundance like weeds in the country.

Still, some things remained the same. The youngest son was setting off in an aeroplane to the cold lands in the north and so the villagers gathered. Even Chief Nyangumba of the Kawoko House attended in his government issued 4x4 Landrover, blessing the occasion with an officious air. He was, despite their poverty, a son-in-law to the Mararas through their blood ties with the Mangunda Clan. And when the sadza was eaten and the sorghum beer had been drunk, the old men with large bellies called Godknows to their council, separate from the women and children.

"Son of the baboon, now you venture forth into the wilderness, there is much you should know. Kubvuma kurairwa chinhu chakanaka chose. Wash your ears clean and let the Chief counsel you," his grandfather Kinzimbe said.

"You honour me since I am but a son-in-law here. I was afraid to speak lest there be those who remind me that I have not yet finished paying the lobola for my wife," Nyangumba said, to much laughter. Then he cleared his throat and it quietened down. "These are your people."

The chief gestured round the gathering, sweeping his right hand as though to touch everyone. There were so many of them, old and young, expectant eyes turned to the council of elders. Godknows understood he was but a thread in a large quilt, and understood that should he be plucked out the cloth would be ruined. Equally the thread had no value outside of the whole.

"Ziva kwavakabva nekuti kwaunoenda usiku," said the chief. "Do not be like those who left for the mines in Johannesburg never to return. This is your home. In this soil your mother buried your umbilical cord. Many of your ancestors rest in the earth you are standing on now, guiding and protecting you. The wider world is filled with temptation, but you must overcome. If you remember your people, the ancestors will bless you. But if you turn your back from them, they shall curse. This is as it should be. Do you understand?"

The men clapped at this ancient wisdom now distilled. Godknows felt a kinship to his clansmen and the village which he had taken for granted before. He would not be lost in the forest like the fools who went to the mines in Johannesburg.

There's a feeling of lightness as Joe wanders through the town centre after his shift. It's a Wednesday, but the town's packed with revellers. Young guys in skinny jeans and pricey sneakers. Ladies in Primark outfits clutching fake designer bags. The cold does little to dissuade mini-skirts and open midriffs. The bright Christmas lights on the high street. Discount offers in the shop window. Joe loves Buttonburgh. It's vibrant, yet down to earth and grounded at the same time.

The town has become home.

"Joe!" a voice hails from behind, but when he turns no one's there. "Over here."

It's his friend Tinashe Makangadza wearing dungarees that are suddenly back in fashion, and sunglasses even though it's dark. Tinashe walks with such a spring in his step, like a rocketship about to launch.

Joe feels some discomfort in his stomach. Maybe some bloating. Despite his jacket, he's feeling cold, and this isn't helped by the sweat dripping down his back. *Why am I sweating in this weather?* He's a bit dazed, Tinashe's face blurring into two before coalescing into one coherent visage.

"I've been looking everywhere for you, brother," Tinashe says. "Let's grab a pint."

"You know I don't drink," Joe replies.

"Ndezvekwako izvo, chikomana. That means more for me." Tinashe grabs him by the elbow and marches him to The Gate House, the Wetherspoon pub with cheap drinks and a half-decent menu. It's packed but they are lucky and pounce on a table near the window which a young Asian couple vacate.

Tinashe's tipsy, which makes him bubbly and animated. His eyes are large like old filament light bulbs and when he widens them you could swear they shine.

"Your brothers back home are hounding me. They wanted me to check on you but I've been too busy. Why aren't you answering my texts?"

"I've been busy," Joe replies.

"Too busy for us, your friends and family. What happened to the Ubuntu you used to spout."

I am because you are – Ubuntu. Our humanity stems from one another, and there's no closer bond than that of family and kin. Joe used to frown upon western individualism. *It takes a village to raise a child*, he used to say. Now he closes his eyes and bows his head, taking deep breaths. The collectivism of his people is a millstone around his neck. At last Joe understands white people. The practicality of their culture. They daren't drag one another down the poverty abyss. Each man standing up for himself is the antidote to the *entitlement* oozing from the text messages Joe receives from back home.

"I've been sending money home for ten years, Tinashe, and my people are still poor. They are still beggars. I am tired," he says.

"Are you mad!" his friend replies, angrily. "Didn't the elders warn you not to lose your way when you came here. Ha, I've never heard such nonsense. Do you think you've become a white man?"

"Tina—"

"How dare you abandon your people." Tinashe throws his hands up in despair.

"I'm tired, I'm going home."

"Oh no you don't." Tinashe leaps up over the table, noisily knocking over the empty glasses and grabs Joe by the collar. The other patrons are watching, thinking a fight's on, and the noise in the pub diminishes.

"Let go of me."

Tinashe comes back to his senses and pushes Joe away. Joe scrambles up and scampers out of the pub, embarrassed by what's just happened. The cold December air hits him in the face like a fist. He staggers as though drunk and the discomfort in his navel intensifies into pain, forcing him to keel over. He retches at the side of the pavement, like a drunk who's had one too many. The revellers avoid him, ladies protesting in disgust.

Dark shadows round the corners as Joe staggers through Silver Street. The voices are like darts in his ears. He keeps one hand on his belly which is on fire as though it's being sliced open from the inside, something alien forcing its way out. The faces on the street become hideous masks. They are laughing at him as he falls to his knees. Joe tries to cry out in anguish, but the sound that comes out of his throat is an eerie braying.

"You ought to stay off the spice, mate," someone shouts.

Joe tries to push up. His right hand balls into a fist, the skin hardening, bone cracking and reforming. His mouth and nose push out into a snout, the sound of his jaw cracking sickens him. The hairs on his body turn grey and thicken. Joe looks up at the full moon and brays – he is their donkey, there's no escaping the black tax.

Editors' Note:

When someone like Godknows comes to live in Scotland, to be cheerful and caring, to work hard and contribute to his new society, it's impossible to appreciate what baggage they might arrive with that can turn what we expect to be a transition of hope and opportunity into something else entirely. In "The Donkey", Tendai uses the language and lore of the Shona culture from his native Zimbabwe to explore how community obligation can become exactly such a burden to heartbreaking effect.

Helpline Zero

Ever Dundas

Your [redacted] ID [redacted]
[redacted] appointment.

Appointment number:
0 0 [redacted]

Dear EVER DUNDAS
You are now being offered the [redacted]
dose of the [redacted]
young. [redacted]
If [redacted] you do not need [redacted]
feeding [redacted]
call the [redacted] ID [redacted]
helpline on 0[redacted]00 0[redacted]0[redacted]0.

On the day of your appointment:

- Please arrive [redacted]
- Please wear a face [redacted] while travelling [redacted] and during your appointment. If you are exempt from wearing a face [redacted] please [redacted] wash or sanitise [redacted] regularly.
- Please [redacted] follow [redacted] government guile[redacted]

Rearranging: [redacted]
You can rearrange [redacted]
your [redacted] birth.
[redacted] You can [redacted] rearrange your [redacted]
name and [redacted] create [redacted]
you[redacted]r [redacted] self.
It is important to [redacted] protect yourself
against [redacted]
the [redacted] government.
Scan me
[redacted] for further [redacted]
personal data.

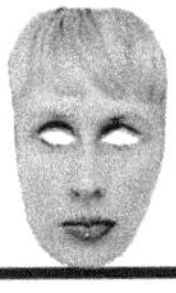

Editors' Note:

It takes rare skill to be able to rearrange a relatively benign government communication (here, a COVID-19 vaccination appointment letter from 2021) to reveal a surreal dystopia not so far removed from the one that the UK has been sliding towards over the last few decades. We loved the astonishing surgical flair with which Ever wields her cut-up and erasure defamiliarisation techniques to give us this warning glimpse. Note also the mistake in the original letter: not 'government guidelines' but 'government guilelines'. *In typo veritas* indeed.

Night Snow

Jane McKie

Your breath in the snow is a bird on the wing.

You long to snake arms around the waist of snow. To hug a body that dissolves if you touch it. You want to lie on the bonnet of a stranded car as if it's a gurney. You give it a go. Nothing moves in the pre-dawn cosy post-apocalypse of snow, but snow.

Being here, in the snow at night, reminds you of wearing your favourite headphones: white Sennheisers. This is what snow feels like, but instead of music, your own breath, your heartbeat. Reassuring. Cosy even.

It's as if the world wants to clear its throat. Some kind of blockage, something there, just beyond description. In this hush, this non-noise, there is sweetness to being out on the street alone, in a world of unnatural light. The tenements wear white mantles; it must have been snowing for ages. They look both familiar and strange. Almost every shape is a lie: contour lost to the slow accretion of flakes that you wish would fall on you, yet, somehow, don't. Every snowflake misses you even though you invite flurries.

Now someone is drilling just around the corner. You try to move towards the sound, but find that snow, which fell on everything but you before now, is compacted around your boots, sticking to your clothes, and movement is impossible. The drilling intensifies, the drill bit penetrating your skull, skewering the grey-beige sludge of your brain until you scream and wake up screaming.

"Where am I?" you ask the figures at your side. They say nothing. "Where am I?" you scratch out again, throat on fire.

No one answers. They look down at you, four of them, their expressions inscrutable, and you wonder why they don't reply.

You're on your back, head slightly raised, aching all over, disorientated. And then, slowly, you remember. Remember signing the form with Amy, remember the weeks of talk before you did.

She was all for it, wanting to make sure the best bits of your mind, your personality, weren't lost in the march of the disease that had already begun to wreak its havoc. You were less convinced – after all, this was the choice of megalomaniacs and nutjobs. But she was the scientist, the one who could marshal arguments; and she had the patience for a fight. "Mum, it makes sense. I *know* you think it won't work. But what have we got to lose?"

And you wanted to say, perhaps as much as six months. Wanted to say, I'm scared; scared to go now, so quickly. Just a tiny bit early. But then, she'd wipe her eyes and say, "Mum, *please*."

Cryonics when you were 50 was cryonics in its infancy. Sure, you had the money – money for Dignitas, money for the procedure – but a big part of you thought there would be a million better uses for it. That "*please*" sat with you for days that stretched into weeks. You knew the thing Amy was best at was hope, and you had to give her that. She'd been a naive wee girl, too, but so sharp you could cut yourself on her, as your mum used to say.

You're in a room so white it reminds you where you have come from. The walls are glowing. The people around you look very much like they did before you went under, and you wonder how much time has passed. They don't talk even though you ask question after question. Sometimes there are as many as five of them, sometimes only one or two. But you are never alone.

You watch them – the nurses – as they move around the room purposefully, and you realise it's choreographed somehow: a silent dance. They seem to know what to do, who'll reach over and adjust whatever is clamped to your head, who'll bring liquid and take liquid away.

A couple of weeks have gone by, maybe more, and you haven't moved from the semi-upright position they have you in. You're angry now. Not one bloody word! No view save the exceedingly boring room you're in, and the figures who move around you, whom you have come to think of as evil. Well, okay, maybe not evil, but you have no way of telling and you're so pissed off, you're like a pot left on the stove. You think of that cliché of alien abduction, and transpose your nurses into the role of alien experimenters even though they're clearly human. They look, walk and *smell* human. Not aliens or androids, you've decided.

You talk at them all the time. Shout a lot. Sing sometimes.

You wish she was here. Amy. That she'd been the one to revive you. But she probably died a long time ago, you realise, unless she, too, froze her body for posterity.

"Hey! Hey! Can you hear me? Hey!"

Today, the guy with the head of close-cropped black hair – Bluto you call him, from *Popeye*, because he's bigger than most of them, and looks like he could take the others in a fight – leans towards you and whispers, *Shhhh*. You want to punch his big face, but your arms are too weak to lift.

Is not finished, he whispers, and you go rigid with shock at the first words spoken in this room by anyone other than you. Then you want to laugh, want to shout, "Speak up!" at him.

But rather you shout, "What do you mean?" Shout it again so that he is in no doubt about your frustration.

We work, is all he says *sotto voce*, and it dawns on you that his vocal cords may have atrophied. After your exposure to their effortless, unspoken communication with each other, you're sure they communicate without speaking somehow, whether though telepathy or technology. And maybe, here, there is little difference.

The next exchange happens some indeterminate time later. If you had to estimate, you'd say about a month. Perhaps some clock still works inside you. Something not broken.

Ssssnow. Not Bluto this time, but the one you think of as Barbie because of her golden beauty, so at odds with her emotionless demeanour. *Ssssnow.*

What?

Ssssnow. Why?

You're at a loss. Snow why? Why snow? What the hell?

"Excuse me," you say with excessive politeness, "but you'll have to be a little more generous with your words. I've got no idea what you mean." When you smile thinly, the muscles around your mouth still struggle, but you do your best.

Pic-tures. While you ssssleep – ssssnow. You stare at her and twig that they must have been able to see what you thought, what you dreamt. Presumably via the device coiled around your head that feels vicelike, but not painful.

Snow. Why? Good question: something that hadn't occurred to you to ask yourself. Why so much snow? Every image you remember from the injection until the point you woke up was of snow. Sometimes you were looking out at it from within your own body. Sometimes you saw yourself in a streetscape of snow, walking, running, twirling, as if you were in a film.

"I don't know," you croak.

A hundred days or more awake is nothing compared to a hundred years or more asleep. Brain not frozen, not really, because you/they watched things. Was it the cryo that made the snow in your head? Wrapped like a fillet in a freezer, did you dream of an eternal present that mirrored your prison?

You have remembered. Your last conversation with Amy. Lovely, beautiful, astonishing, misguided Amy. She sat with you in the clinic in the moments before it happened. Her tears and your tears, and you saying, "What d'you think it'll feel like?"

"I don't know, Mum. Probably like walking down Spottiswoode Street on a really snowy day." And you had both laughed. "D'you remember? My first flat and me picking you up from the gutter after you'd had a few pints?"

God, that had been a great night. One of your visits to see her in Edinburgh, a city gifted with an excellent selection of pubs. Pub crawl plus snowy pavements equals bruised dignity. You'd had Amy when you were an undergraduate yourself, a year's interruption to your studies, which meant that people often described you as behaving more like sisters than mother and daughter. And you couldn't argue with them.

From a seed, a flower. From pollen or a particle of dust, an ice crystal. A few words, so few really, making an upside-down world where death is life and outside is inside.

Barbie's at your side again. She's the one you see most often: your most faithful nurse. She rarely speaks, but today: *Time*, she rasps. *Up? Time.*

"Time." You laugh. "The heart of the matter. What year is it? Please tell me."

For a second you see something – what might be doubt, what might be pity – cross her face.

Two three three three.

And there it is: the future or a speech impediment. You reach for her hand; you're stronger from weeks – months – of nourishment. She is so smooth, skin like a child's as you knew it would be. The future has cracked ageing, obviously.

"Amy – my daughter. Is she … here? Is she alive?"

Not. Her eyes slide away from yours.

You knew it, of course, in your gut.

"Others like me?" you ask.

This time she looks at you, and now that you peer closely, you can see that her irises are pale blue and ringed with a thin band of gold. *Not.*

"Help me," you say.

How help? Up? She's getting better at this. Communication, that two-way street. You smile. She doesn't – maybe can't – return it and you wonder what it would be like to live in a world where you never hear anyone laugh out loud.

"Not up, no."

You remember a lecturer who told you once that heat and cold are in the mind, at least partially. That all sensation is relative. At the time, you thought it was bullshit. Now you look at your hand plunged into the snow heaped up on someone's lawn and you wonder. It is as soft as chick down and as cold as hell. So you're here again. It's night again. Thank God: it feels like putting your old white headphones back on.

Spottiswoode Street is exactly the same, the shadows of snowflakes sailing in the mellow light of a streetlamp. But it's not empty this time. Someone is walking towards you – no, she is jogging, would be sprinting if it wasn't so perilous underfoot.

Editors' Note:

The prospect of trusting yourself to cryogenics is fraught with unknowns. Will you ever wake up? If you do, what will the world be like? You hope for a better world where your ills can be fixed and your friends and family are happy to see you. But what if they wait too long before they bring you back? Here, Jane beautifully conveys that disorientation and alienation with all the admirable economy and precision that you would expect from an award winning poet.

The Retreat

Chris Kelso

Τηε Ρετρεατ

Τηε Ζαρατηυστρα

Δαψβοοκ 1: My reflection dances distorted against the aluminium payload door. They called me Rana-Ahmad, *Sabahu An-Nur.* It is the longest time since I've heard someone utter my name with love or indifference. Today I start *Part III* on the composite canvas of the *Cutty Sark* bow. My monument to the lost nation of hills and serfdom. A place which could not even own its own freedom. Home.

Ονε

Δαψβοοκ 2: The *Cutty Sark* cuts through the sailcloth of space like a slow, plunging scalpel. Turning the abyss to pale midnight. Dashing the pregnant void with aborted life. I think about the blueways left in my wake, marking my route from Earth to Europa. Will anyone think to follow me? No, I don't want that.

My ex-partner might argue otherwise – because they were a contrarian and enjoyed contesting every thought I had – but I believe that we Scots are aliens. I believe that we belong *up here,* and that up here is where we can try to transform our negatives into positives. We belong up here with enough brittle silence to work effectively with nothing but a blanket of neutron stars to keep us warm. We are born as working animals, with pain already in our bodies. This also makes us better artists. As lifelong repositories of pain, we carry ourselves, not like a human would or should. Just think of what I could achieve up here.

Απηορισμ: [Hemingway said something about great art and loneliness, I can't remember exactly how it went. Something like, *Friends and success are the death of great art*. Or something. Maybe, *Success palliates the loneliness you need to make art great.*]

I don't know. I forget all the books I read back home and who said what about whom. I listen to Cocteau Twins and try to relax. Focus on the music and forget past lives. Even events from my Quran elude me. I only have my own stories now. Well, one story really. The same old story that we all tell in the last days. At least for a short time, my story will have a cat. A grey approximation of light arcs and obliterates my perfect darkness. I'm done for the day. Cocteau Twins.

Τωο

Δαψβοοκ 3: Time is a loose fiction around here. It circles above my head, but I have nothing to do with it. And it leaves me be. I've not visibly aged since shedding its bonds. I know there have been three cycles only because the flight deck control panel buzzes with Skywaves from Mecca to remind me. And I know we must be close to the twelfth Muslim lunar month, Dhūl-Hijjah. I know I should probably mute these transmissions, but then Scotland has its way of keeping your mind open to painful reminders.

The *Cutty Sark* is my studio. My shrine to the Virgin Mary. My armour-plated mosque. I slash the air with my brush, and paint strikes the silica tiles of the shuttle wall, like a galaxy's unribboning. More trails. A map to find me if you really wanted to. *Part III* is probably a painting full of fantasy and hope. Things that aren't real unless we make them.

Απηορισμ: [*There are no beautiful surfaces without terrible depths* – was that Nietzsche or Cocteau Twins?]

Τηρεε

Δαψβοοκ 4: Progress. I gaze at my creation through eyes of bloodshot mercury. Hume the cat looks up at the piece – curious, unpretentious. A different female alien altogether. One day, I'll lose her too and I'll use this to make something beautiful.

The painting that I'm working on now is thus far untitled.

I might keep it simply *Part III.*

The final piece in a three-cycle triptych. When it's complete, it might be the best thing I've created – this includes two handsome little girls who attempted to pacify my burning female creativity, my pain, with unconditional love. And there was also once another young person, donated by my adopted country. A baby boy, yes. Long since deceased. Delicate as craft paper. Even in space, I can't get far enough away from his enduring spirit.

Απηορισμ: [There is hiding from time, from sound, from the platitudes of false profits, but there is no escaping the infant male in our psyches. To the deepest curve of the solar system, *he* is in hot pursuit. I should thank him for preserving my pain in the form of fortified memory. He brings me more pain than faith ever could.]

Φουρ

Δαψβοοκ 4: Working for so long I forget most music, most songs – but the colour on this aluminium canvas feels more like a chaotic melody than anything else in its abstract form. Music, in my head anyway, just all sounds the same. Except maybe Cocteau Twins. But I like the sound of hot air rushing through the radiator panels. Or the gentle rumble of surface insulation from the flight deck. Maybe it's part of the process that every song has compounded into one long dull note. Mechanical and without rhythm. No longer a distraction from God. That's what happens up here. I find myself missing concrete.

Απηορισμ: [Everything merges and becomes meaningless. And it is freeing.]

Δαψβοοκ 5: It's almost time to rest. Indistinct machines hum, and a ghostly clattering lulls me to sleep. I don't know what goes on in this ship when I'm unconscious, but strange music is happening somewhere. And the ship composes best at night. Hume is in collaboration with everything she touches.

Φιωε

Δαψβοοκ 6: I wake up and go straight to the payload door to resume *Part III*. I receive regular Skywaves from home, but I can never go back – so what would be the point in listening to them?

People telling me to just come home.

No one will judge me.

Scotland doesn't exist to me anymore.

But that is all the people of Earth can muster, judgement. But what makes you so special? You're the pride of the Empire. Left in the soul, right in the head. With your colonial breastplate. And zero-hour contract. Begging for gluten-free poverty. Seeking solace, dreaming of your own funeral.

Απηορισμ: [Cats don't expect shit.]

Ειγητ

Δαψβοοκ 7: A little girl's spectral voice surfaces from the quiet music of *Cutty Sark* and lures me to accept an incoming Skywave – but I never do. I resist. For the sake of my pain. She wants to talk about the "lost" infant. The male. But I'm here. Now. There is work to be done. Pain to be at one with. To be translated. And if I don't do it right now, then this will all have been for nothing. No martyr ever went the way of duty, and felt the shadow of death upon it.

Νιvε

Δαψβοοκ 8: I think I must be 46 on my next birthday, and when I dream, I dream about the menopause scything through my body, from brain to abdomen, and cutting so fine there isn't even much blood. I collapse into a steaming pink mist of fluid. Chunks of diced, cryo-frozen body parts are left strewn across the ship's flight deck for my wife and daughter to find. Simplified. Must finish *Part III*…

Τεν

Δαψβοοκ 9: Could zero gravity keep my uterus from crashing into my vaginal canal?

Ελεωεν

Δαψβοοκ 10: And I dream about ghostly foetuses hovering above me like a fresco of wounded angels. When I talk to them, they yowl back and try to suckle at me. It's as I'm waving them away that I usually wake up with Hume on my chest. Sweating. In tears. Feeling violated. Grateful.

Obviously, relationships have suffered, they usually do when your ex-girlfriend is the weak and wallowing orthodox type. A slave to her feelings and to time. This is a once-in-a-lifetime opportunity. I'm honouring the birthplace of Islam, incorporating the arts of Bedouin nomads and those of my sedentary peoples. Jeddah to Riyadh.

Why can't she see that?

Instead, my ex-girlfriend reprimands me for embarking on a self-funded, self-imposed residency so soon after the loss. And taking the cat did nothing to improve her opinion of me. But I had to leave when it was raw. Those were stipulations that successful *Cutty Sark* residents have to meet.

Απηορισμ: [To make something that lasts we must be at one with our antagonists. Something strong. Something to help me rediscover the beautiful pain Mohamed used to give me.]

I sit on the platform, Hume pooled in my lap, and watch the erupting cryo-geysers of the liquid satellite. Europa and something new. A grateful audience of pain. Someone who finally understands. Almost done. End log.

Editors' Note:

Creatives reading this story might agree that travelling to the orbit of Jupiter with only the stars and your cat for company really does sound like the ultimate artistic retreat. Many of us will also recognise the other sort of retreat here, how far we will go into our art to escape something greatly painful in our lives. It's easy to imagine the Cocteau Twins song, Evangeline, echoing ethereally around the ship.

fruits[1] of Empire

James Kelman

Graduate students are advised that the proper context for such a debate might begin from the late 1950s, and the work of the outside broadcasting units that occurred during the making of the *Fruits of Early Empire* series. The particular location cannot be ascertained. The team broadcast live from a streetmarket on the outskirts of a city thought to be in the central Sub-Continent or Middle Eastern regions; earlier rumours suggested southern Africa. There is a dearth of accredited information. In those days there were neither email nor social media. We know that the television production team requested that the male presenters dress in "tribal garb", as the memo-exchange described it: loin cloths, kilts, shields, hoops and bangles. There was no disrespect intended.

The film-crew operated from a jam-packed urban roadway using dual cameras. Limited back-up was available. The production team had hoped to hire local workers. Nothing further is known on that. Certainly locals in their tens of thousands would have thronged the market roadways and side-alleys, as they had done since time immemorial. Animals of every domestic species were employed, bought and sold, and others too might have been procured at a price. Goats and oxen pulled carts, while on either side of the thoroughfares were stalls, barrows and makeshift stores defined by blankets spread on the ground. An entire area was given over to the marketing of old bicycles and their parts. Another specialized in tools of every description; interior sections dealt with plumbing, carpentry and electrical wares. Closeby was mechanical farming equipment, alongside boring and cutting tools, rust-coated machinery from earlier centuries. Along the wynds, lanes and darker off-road locations one found the weaponry, armoury and

1. *sic.*

defence implements. Those were acquired from foreign powers and for use in neighboring provinces. Solitary individuals prowled and gestured at passersby, displaying unknown produce and articles from within the folds of their body coverings. In any space unoccupied by sellers and their helpers were beggars in diverse forms and shapes, and of each and every deficiency known to the species. Here everything that might be sold was for sale.

On the third day was the first day of the shoot. During lunchbreak the crew members strolled in and around the market. One acquired a strangely-shaped walking-cane from a ground-store. There were two researchers attached to the team. They were intrigued by the find. They discussed it with the executive producer and the female and male presenters of the program. The consensus was that this was not a walking-cane. More likely it was a war-club, estimated three hundred and fifty years old, gnarled but relatively unwarped. A detailed description and photocopy of the cane/club were faxed to experts in the field. Later that morning they received the reply. Its provenance was vouchsafed but its place of origin could not be identified. It was thought not to be local, but that its provenance might relate to several pre-cultural hoards not yet quantified within the Crown property ruling.

Experts agreed that its value to specialist-collectors might be taken for granted. The mystery of its origin gave it an additional aura, which bestowed upon it enigma-status. Both researchers to the program confirmed that the sale of this single relic might secure the future of two entire villages for a period of ten years, perhaps longer. They and the couple presenting the programme crossed the roadway, followed by the two-man sound and camera crew, seeking to find the rear area ground-store where the transaction took place and record the meeting with the original seller. They hoped to acquire more detailed information on the artefact, and advise the owners of the good news in regard to external value. There were no further developments. This was the last stage of the shoot. None of the recorded minutes was ever recovered. There were rumours and these may be followed up with requisite permissions. Neither presenter returned to the series. The news embargo is now lifted. None of the broadcasting unit remains with us. Graduate students with an interest in our earlier outside broadcasting services should apply to the department.

Editors' Note:

As William Butler wrote about the aftermath of Culloden, "it is the victor who writes the history and counts the dead". But who really wins in the long run? James Kelman's story holds up a distorting mirror to the legacy of imperialism. Subtle incongruities might suggest that this could be a snapshot of an alternate world, or has the writing and rewriting of history created a palimpsest obscuring the dark truth? The deceptively gentle tone acts as a counterpoint to the horror at its heart.

Glencoe

Carole Johnstone

In the winter, the darkness begins in the afternoon, turning the bog and rock blistered bronze, until, from Ballachulish and Loch Achtriochtan, the dark draws a blanket over the glen, leaving only the sky in colour. I live for that darkness. When even the moon can't overcome the summits and shadows, and the world turns black, empty as a vacuum.

Winter brings with it many reprieves. Not least, the leaving behind of summer. I have only ever felt trapped by people – by the relentlessly sure ebb and flow of them. Tour buses and coaches; 4x4s and camper vans. Roaring motorbike convoys, hikers, and wild campers. Serious tripods or selfies on sticks, and an untouched wilderness that must have its congestion later photoshopped out. There are four carparks and six laybys in this short two-mile stretch of glen alone, but after they fill up by mid-morning, people stop wherever they please. Hikers keen to climb the bens, scale the ridges, and walk the valleys, queue like summit expeditions on Everest. Whenever I escape to the top of Bidean nam Bian, they look like snaking lines of dayglo yellow and orange ants. Around ten of them die every year.

There's a sharp chill in the air as I look west down the glen towards the hills of the village and the setting sun. Behind me, the Three Sisters hide my little cottage in shadow; towards the road, the Meeting of Three Waters – after days of long rain – roars almost as loud as the bullish barks and growls of rutting stags. In the darkness of winter, all the deer come down from the hills, lining the road and laybys like mile markers.

Four hundred and twenty million years ago, this was a supervolcano. And over the last two million, these fierce ridges and treeless corries of grass and fen have been carved out by glaciers spreading west towards the sea. People say this place is bad or cursed, but I've never been afraid to live here, sharing this space – seven miles long, seven hundred metres wide, and seven hundred metres high – with bogles, fairies, or selkies. The ghosts of murdered MacDonalds or the witch that tried to warn them. The massacre is not why I came – it's not why anyone comes, not anymore. But they're always still here: those hacked to death in this glen by government troops, and those who hid on the dark winter slopes and summits too long. Some nights, I think I can smell the smoke of timber and thatch burning; the glen lit gold at the corners of my eyes.

I fall asleep in front of my own fire, until the sound of the door rattling inside its frame shakes me awake. I get few visitors: nosy hikers in the summer; the occasional breakdown. I stand as the knocking comes again – rude and loud – and I hesitate for just a moment, fingers shaking until I ball them into a fist.

When I open the door, he freezes, his own fist raised and white-knuckled. He lowers it, clearing his throat. He's around mid-fifties and wearing one of those stupidly expensive hiking anoraks. A younger woman is standing behind him almost in a crouch, her own coat long and fur trimmed.

"Sorry to bother you," the man says, looking over my shoulder. "But we've had a wee bit of an accident on the road and were wondering if we could use your phone."

People talk about there being moments that your very life depends on; split second decisions that will determine your fate, whether you know it or not. I've had many, though perhaps this isn't one of them – as he barges over the threshold and past me before I've time to do – or decide – anything at all.

"No signal," he says, brandishing his mobile much like his fist as he turns in a circle, taking very thorough inventory of the room. "Living here, you'll know that already, I suppose."

The woman comes in, still bent forwards. She mutters a thank you. I look out into the growing darkness before I push the door shut.

"Please, have a seat," I say, going into the kitchenette for the cordless phone. As soon as I hand it to the man, he strides into the bedroom as if this is his own house, closing the door behind him.

The woman is sitting in her huge coat, rubbing her hands together in front of the fire. She won't look at me, won't, in fact, look away from the fire; the sound of her palms moving against each other rhythmic and dry like a steam train. She's wearing a wedding band; it catches the light in dull sparks. She finally turns, just as I open my mouth to speak, and in the bare two seconds before he barges back in, I see what's in her eyes – naked and wild. Fear.

"Well, the bloody tow won't come until ten tomorrow," he says, thrusting the phone at me. "Recovery, my arse."

"Please, sit," I say again. "I'll make some tea."

Over the boil of the kettle, I can hear them talking in low voices, but when I return, they are sitting in opposite chairs, looking anywhere but at each other.

"Cheers," the man says, holding his cup aloft, tea spilling over its rim. He grimaces after a sip.

"You can stay the night," I say. "I'll sleep on the sofa."

"That's very kind of you. I'm John, John Jamieson, and this is my daughter, Meg."

"I'm Cailly."

"It was a dead bloody deer. Beast of a thing," he says. "Just sitting in the middle of the road, quite the fucking thing. I didn't have a chance of stopping."

"Where were you going?"

He narrows his eyes at the question. "I'm taking this one back to her husband."

"Could she not take herself back?"

Meg's studying the fire again, hands clasped so tight her nails are digging deep into her skin.

"Some lassies don't know what side their bread is buttered on, and they need to be told, that's all." He finally manages to meet my eye as he gives me a very insincere smile.

"It was so scary." The sound of Meg's voice, high and tremulous, makes me jump. "We went straight off the road into the glen. I thought we were going to die."

"Jesus, we weren't going to *die*. It was barely a five-foot drop." John rolls his eyes. "But can't say as I was relishing the prospect of a night out there. Could barely see my hand in front of my face and it was only five in the afternoon."

"Did no one stop to help?"

"Happened right by that paedo, Savile's house," he says as if I haven't spoken. "Fucking scum. Amazed no one's burned the place to the ground yet."

They've done everything but. An almost two-hundred-year-old farm cottage reduced to smashed windows and ugly graffiti. People hating people in the only ways they know how. But this glen is the bad place.

"It's called Allt-na-Reigh," I say, sipping my tea. "The world-renowned mountaineer Hamish MacInnes lived there for over twenty-five years.

He founded the Glencoe Mountain Rescue team and mountain rescue teams all around the world."

"Heard he sat in his porch waving at people as they drove by," John says with a scowl.

Meg looks up from her lap. "The mountaineer?"

"Savile!" He pauses. Sneers. "Paedo."

I stand up. "Would you like some more tea? Some food?"

"We've eaten already," Meg says.

"You don't have anything stronger?" John asks, with another toothy grin that makes me want to shiver.

"Sure."

The bottle of Glenfinnan is at the back of a kitchen cupboard. I grab it and two glasses.

"Now there's the infamous Highland hospitality we're always hearing about," John says, downing the measure I pour him almost in one.

Meg sips a little warily, screwing up her nose.

"Mind you, you want to be careful of that." John chuckles.

"Of what?"

"Being a good host. Don't want to end up like the MacDonalds."

"We stopped at the Massacre Room at the Glencoe Folk Museum this afternoon," Meg says.

"Massacre Room." He snorts. "It was two mannikins in kilts and tam o'shanters and a dodgy voiceover. Three quid it cost us!"

"I thought it was horrible." Meg's voice is low, her face flushed. "That those Campbell soldiers could spend weeks staying in the MacDonalds' homes, eating their food, enjoying their company, before massacring them all in their beds."

"Aye, what'd they call it?" John asks.

"Murder Under Trust," I say.

"The worst crime in Scotland, eh?" He glances at me. "Personally, I'm more against nonces and Belhaven Best."

When no one laughs but him, his cheeks flush pink and he curls his lip.

"It wasn't the Campbells really," I say. "It was William of Orange and the Redcoats."

"Oh, aye?" His smile turns thin, and he leans forwards, dangling loose fists in the space between his legs. "Not a unionist, eh? Bet you voted Yes nine years ago, right?"

I give him an insincere smile of my own. "I did."

"Well, as my old dad used to say, rest his soul, *Guess you just gotta learn to lose, pal.*"

As he reaches across the table to pick up the whisky bottle, I glance over at Meg, who looks even more nervous in the sudden silence.

"There was an exhibition about a witch there too," she says.

"Corrag?"

Meg nods. "We didn't stay long enough to see it."

"She's famous for warning the MacDonalds," I say. Because it's something to say. I don't like this atmosphere. I feel uncomfortable, anxious. I don't like people in my space, in my home. It makes me feel as nervous as Meg looks.

"No one listened to her, so she fled up into the hills the evening of the massacre and stayed there all night, wrapped in a plaid. When she came back down, the glen was empty, the houses burned, the cattle driven away. The story goes that she took the murdered chief's broadsword and threw it into the Narrows at Loch Leven, swearing that no man of Glencoe would ever die by another's hand again, so long as the sword lay undisturbed."

"And don't tell me," John says, almost belligerently. "It did not?"

"No Glencoe man died at Culloden, Waterloo, Balaklava, or in the Crimean or Boer wars. But then, in 1916, an English dredger brought the sword up. The Battle of the Somme was one month later, and the men of Glencoe started dying again. So they say."

"I'm surprised you don't get called a witch," John says. "Living out here all alone, a young and pretty lassie like you." His gaze turns speculative again. "Or have you a man? He likely to be coming back tonight?"

I stand up just as Meg finally takes off her coat. I try not to react to the bruises that ring her arms like tattoos, some still black and others queasy yellow, but John must see something in my eyes because he straightaway turns towards her.

"Get that back on," he growls. When he looks at me, his smile is pure pantomime. "Always been a clumsy eejit, my daughter. Like I said, never learns."

There comes a sound from outside: a guttural bellow and bark, once, twice. Close.

"The fuck was that?" John says, startled to his feet as he looks at the door.

"Another deer?" I try not to look at Meg as she struggles back into her coat. "Stags often fight around dusk."

"It sounds terrifying," Meg says. But she doesn't sound terrified. She sounds abruptly excited, and her eyes are shining. I'm more convinced than ever that opening my door to either of them was a big mistake.

"I'll get the bed made up for you," I say.

The bedroom is freezing. I change the sheets, close the curtains, and turn on the electric blanket. When I've too quickly run out of jobs to do, I find myself looking out into the growing darkness, my reflection wringing its hands until I notice and stop. I muster my best smile as I go back into the living room, but they both spring apart and stop talking just as soon as I do.

"Is everything alright?"

"Of course." The tips of John's ears are red as blood. His smile too wide.

"Well, your bed is ready now."

He raises his eyebrows. "Bit early, isn't it?"

"I rise early. I'll cook you breakfast before you go."

"It's okay, Dad," Meg says, muted now. "Let's just go to sleep."

I try to catch her eye, but she won't look at me at all. When that lion-like growl comes again, they both jump, and then shuffle off to the bedroom without another word. I let out a breath I didn't know I was holding as the door snicks shut behind them. I go over to the window and pull back the curtain. It's fully dark now, and I can see nothing at all except my own silhouette. A gust of wind bows the glass briefly inwards, and I step back, letting the curtain fall.

I roll my sleeping bag out on the couch. The wind gets stronger, rattling the door as well as the windows, and whistling down the woodburner's flue. Perhaps I hear another barking growl, perhaps I don't – I suppose it hardly matters; I'm not about to go out and check.

I make myself a herbal tea I don't want, set my phone's alarm, get into the sleeping bag. John and Meg are still talking; I can hear their whispers, low but fast, and they make the hairs on my skin stand up. I think of those black rings of bruises around Meg's arms; remember that my mother called them demon kisses. The dying embers cast a low red glow across the hearth, and I shiver a little. After long minutes of the wind and those whispers, I get back up and creep to the kitchen, taking one of the larger chef's knives from the worktop block.

I look at the bedroom door for a few seconds more, and then slide the knife under my pillow.

I wake up to pitch darkness and the echo of a sound already gone. I sit up, heart beating too fast as I glance at my phone – twelve o-five –

and try to understand what's woken me up. The wind has died down to nothing; the silence is too loud. There's something in the room: a shadow that I can't see but can feel. Movement, slow and deliberate. A breath, in and out. Another. A smell like the sea. For a wild moment I think of running because I'm blindsided by the memory of hands and a smile, fists and bared teeth. Weight that is choking and insistent, and heavy enough that I remember thinking, *I've already taken my last breath.*

But I don't run. I pull the knife out from under the pillow, holding it in front of me like a shield as I ease the sleeping bag's zip down, wincing at the sound. The sense of someone there is so loud, so close now that I can almost see them in the darkness, the silhouette of a thing too black, too opaque, to be part of the dark, the night, the room.

I push myself up and out of the sleeping bag, scrambling clumsily enough to my feet that I almost drop the knife. I sense movement towards the window and lash out wildly. Once, twice. The second makes a whispering sigh of a sound as the blade comes within a hair's breadth of something. There comes a different sound from outside, not the growling bark of a stag but a distant scream, high and long and then gone. I lunge for my phone on the coffee table, but when it clatters onto the carpet, I stumble towards the door instead, slapping at the wall until I find the light switch.

In the blinding return to light, I see a creature, hunched and dark, before it looks up at me aghast, eyes wide and white. Meg.

"Jesus, you scared me!" Which isn't true. It's who – what – I'd thought she was. Isn't that what fear is? Whatever we believe it is? I wonder how many MacDonalds felt the shadow, whisper, and breath of what was to come inside the darkness. How many were afraid of something worse than what was really waiting. Men with guns and knives and orders.

"What was *that*?" Meg hisses, not looking at me but the window. She notices the knife in my hand a little too late, and her eyes get wider.

I don't put it down. "Why the hell are you creeping about in the dark? It's barely midnight."

"I … I couldn't sleep." She's taken off her jumper, and the T-shirt underneath spares none of her bruises from scrutiny. There's a broken necklace of fading finger-marks along the line of her collarbone, darker in the hollow between her clavicles.

"Go back to bed," I say, waning adrenaline leaving my stomach queasy.

"Okay." I know she wants to say more, and I know she's frightened, and those old bruises make me feel angry enough that for a moment I want to indulge her. But I don't.

She turns back towards the bedroom and then the scream comes again, so loud this time I flinch as I spin around to the door, the window. I pull back the curtain. Still the wind is silent, the darkness absolute. There is nothing.

"We have to go," I say, plucking my anorak from its hook.

Meg's eyes get wider. "But you just told me to go back to—"

"I know. But we have to go. Now."

Her distress, her fear, is palpable, but mine is more insistent. And right. "We'll be fine, okay?" But when I hold out her coat, my hands are shaking. "We have to go."

We put on our boots. As an afterthought, I slide the knife into the outside pocket of my rucksack. We both hold our breaths as I unlatch the door, creak it too slowly open. Meg's gasped inhale as she looks beyond the threshold makes me feel perversely better and I step out into the darkness, pulling her with me. Pulling shut the door and locking it before I can yearn for its safety.

"I don't want to go," Meg whispers. "I don't understand what's—" She yanks at my anorak sleeve. "Stop!"

The darkness is opaque. Outside of my circle of torchlight is little more than space, a vertiginous void. When I start moving, Meg gives a high-pitched yip and grabs harder hold of my elbow. My light veers drunkenly over grass and rock, distorting all that is familiar. I shush her, but don't shake her off.

"Follow me," I whisper. "Look at the ground, at my feet, at the light."

We go north until I hear the River Coe, cross the bridge and turn southeast. The timbre of the silence changes as soon as we reach the mouth of the Hidden Valley. Our boots crunch against the frost, but now they echo. In my mind's eye, I can see the steep foothills of Gearr Aonach and Beinn Fhada either side of us, always in shadow.

"Where are we?" Meg's frightened whisper echoes.

"Between two of the Three Sisters. Short Ridge and Long Mountain." I pick up the pace a little; I'm unnerved by how much it feels like we're disturbing the peace – too loud, too clumsy, too much like all the people, the parasites, I hate. I'm beset suddenly by doubt as well as fear. That I don't know what I'm doing. That I've made the wrong choice.

There comes another scream, farther away now but no less disturbing for that.

"Oh my God!"

"Just follow me. Don't say anything."

It takes everything in me to obey my own instruction. I want to keep talking. I want to tell Meg all the things that I know about this place, that comfort me about this place. I want to tell her that the Hidden Valley was formed by ice that couldn't escape when that vast ice cap flowed down to the sea two million years ago. I want to tell her that here was where the MacDonalds hid their own and stolen cattle. And I want to tell her that three hundred and thirty-one years ago to the day, here was where many of them ran and hid in the night. I want to tell her that it's safe.

We start climbing a bare rock staircase, my torchlight throwing the gorge into wild shadow as I grab hold of the accompanying rope. We climb up through thin-leaved birch wood and sharp rocks. When I finally hear the waterfall up ahead, I let out a shaky breath. Behind me, Meg's breathing is more laboured. The path is narrow, the drop steep, the way slippery. But we can't stop or slow down.

There comes yet another scream, high and long, back towards the road and cottage. Meg stops and whimpers.

"I don't like this! What the fuck are we doing? I want to go back."

"It's okay," I say, though I'm assailed by a need suddenly to run, to shout, to escape from this claustrophobic path and black hanging valley. Instead, I quicken our pace until finally, finally, we are over the vast boulder pile that blocks the corrie floor. We walk another mile in silence apart from our breathing, loud and heavy.

When we eventually escape the valley completely, it's only a short reprieve. The night is cold and getting colder but sweat runs down my back. Slow spots of rain start to prickle my skin, and I fear snow. I hand Meg the water bottle from my rucksack, although she can barely draw breath long enough to drink. Her face is a white mask in the glare of my torchlight.

"Can we rest for a minute?"

"No. We have to climb Stob Coire Sgreamhach. Then we can rest."

It takes a long time to reach the top. Too long. The wind picks up again, cold and hard, frequently throwing us off balance and course. Although I've climbed this peak in the Bidean nam Bian massif more times than I can count, navigating the old sheep tracks in pitch blackness with only one torch is almost impossible. And I'd forgotten that. How exhausting it is, how uncertain I feel. How completely inadequate and afraid. Maybe I should be glad I never remember.

By the time we reach the summit, Meg's breaths have become sobs, and mine little better.

"Here," I say, when the torchlight glances off the stony cairn. "Here."

We collapse on the hard ground, and for a moment the relief is all. I lie back and look up at the stars, so bright in the blackness it's as if they're alive and moving. And high above the glen towards the sea, I can finally see the moon. Round and flat. I sit up, pull out the water bottle and hand it to Meg. Although her breathing is finally levelling out, the bottle shakes as she drinks. Our breaths mingle in frozen fog.

"What does it mean?" she whispers.

"What?"

"*Stob Coire* … whatever you said. What does it mean?"

"Peak of the dreadful corrie," I say, looking down. "It's what we just climbed up through – a kind of valley."

Meg shivers. "Dreadful is right."

She's annoyingly young. I know I shouldn't think that, but I do. She shivers again, hugging her knees against her chest.

"Are you wearing thermals?"

"No, I—"

"I told you to wear thermals."

Meg's expression turns belligerent. "You also told me two a.m.. That we had to go at two a.m.."

"I know what I said." I take out my phone. It's almost half two now.

"This is crazy. I don't know what the hell is going on."

"You said you didn't want to know."

The wind whips her hair around her head, hiding her expression. "Will you tell me what those screams were now?"

"A badger, maybe a barn owl, I don't know," I say, but I can tell she thinks I'm lying. When I'm not. I don't know. I've never known.

"How long do we have to stay here?" she says.

"I told you. We have to stay here all night."

"Like Corrag," Meg says, no inflection at all in her voice.

I look at her sharply, but she doesn't look at me.

"You could have told me about the dead deer," she finally says, but when I look at her again, she's staring back down into the blackness of the Hidden Valley. "It was scary. We really could have died."

I say nothing. Especially not that I didn't know what would bring them to me, only that they would be brought.

We eat protein bars and drink more water. When the wind and rain get heavier, we shelter behind the cairn, and I pour us hot coffee from my thermos. For maybe an hour we don't speak. I can feel her looking at me; see the vague mask of her face staring, but I don't look back.

"When does it happen?" she eventually asks, her voice a little unsteady.

And when I don't answer that:

"*How* does it happen?"

"You should try and get some sleep," I say.

"God, no. I couldn't. I'm – I don't…" She twists around to face me. "Did you lie to me? When Moira told me to phone you, I didn't know what… It's just this is so – Fuck!"

I lie down, turn my torchlight towards the drop. "You should try and get some sleep."

Three hours before dawn is when it happened. Five a.m.. When a hundred and twenty soldiers from the Earl of Argyll's regiment, led by Captain Robert Campbell of Glenlyon, began massacring MacDonalds in every settlement from Invercoe to Achnacon. Meg sleeps, curled into an uncomfortable ball, while I look down into the valleys and corries and glens, still hidden in darkness, although I can see them clear as day in my mind's eye.

The scream comes again. Perhaps. Up here, all sound is distorted and muffled by distance and topography. Like my fear and earlier doubts. Replaced by something close to wonder and exhaustion. I sit and I wait in the darkness, enveloped by it, comforted by it. Invisible in it.

Eventually, the sunrise rolls like fire across the blank flatness of Rannoch Moor towards Glencoe. I watch it come, crackling and hungry, burning the long night away. When Meg stirs awake, her confusion barely outlasts her first pained stretch. In her eyes there's none of the nervous excitement of last night; only fear and wariness and doubt.

"Come on," I say, getting up. "I promised you breakfast."

The journey back is far easier in daylight, though the rain has made the way boggy underfoot. Neither of us talk, for which I'm glad. I'm not much in the mood for talking. And I doubt Meg would like anything I'd have to say. When we reach the cottage, all looks unchanged. I unlock the door and step into the living room. I know that the rest of the cottage will be empty too, although I go into the kitchen, the bathroom, and the bedroom anyway. In the bedroom, the quilt is thrown back and there's still a head-shaped depression in one pillow.

Meg trails behind me like a child.

"Where did he go?" she whispers.

I return to the kitchen, take two mugs out from a cupboard. I don't turn around. "Does it matter? He's gone."

I can feel her watching me as I light the hob, take some slice out of the fridge, some bread from the bread bin.

"I… I don't think I'll stay for breakfast."

"The tow isn't coming until ten, isn't—"

"Still." Her face is paler than before. Her eyes keep darting around the small space as if expecting John to leap out at her from behind the furniture. "I'll… I'd rather wait with the car."

"Okay. Here." I hand her two more protein bars, which she snatches out of my hand as if I might bite. She disappears into the bedroom only long enough to repack her small bag, and then she's crossing the living room towards the door. I think she's just going to leave, but she stops at the threshold and after another moment's pause, turns around.

"Is he really gone?"

"Yes."

"He won't ever come back?"

"No." I try to smile, though I don't expect that to help. "He won't."

"God." Her voice shakes.

I think of those rings of bruises. "It'll be alright," I say, even though I have no idea if that's true.

She nods. I can tell she almost says thank you but at the last moment decides against it. Perhaps it feels too much like acknowledging the reason, the want, she came here with. Perhaps she thinks that will be the thing that makes her complicit.

"Where will you go?"

Her glance at me is sharp. She swallows. "Not back."

After she goes, I make myself cook and eat breakfast. The house is cold, but I resist lighting the fire. I wait until well after ten – even though no one can see me or my cottage from the road – before going back outside. I find him behind the woodshed. Lying on his side in an almost foetal position. He looks a lot younger without that insincere grin.

The ground this late in the winter is hard, but the peat bog between the Meeting of Three Waters and the Hidden Valley is always soft enough to dig. A few lorries pass by on the road as I do, but today, no one has parked in any of the car parks or viewpoints. I know no one will see me anyway. I idly wonder where Meg will go. But it's not my business, any more than what she says about him, about where he's gone. I know she won't ever come back. And I know that no one else will come asking. No one ever comes.

The killings began with gunfire. It's said that a Campbell piper played a lament up on Signal Rock. There are stories, too, of whispered warnings in the night, deliberately wide aims, and men breaking their swords. The poorest escape route via Glen Etive was blocked, but the better pass towards the Stewarts in Appin was not. While the soldiers were ordered to 'Put all to the sword under seventy,' some two hundred MacDonald families lay sleeping in their beds on that freezing night, three hours before dawn. But only thirty-nine were slaughtered, while a further forty perished later in the snow. Everyone else escaped into Stuart country or hid in the Hidden Valley. Sometimes, I wonder who these men I bury share their graves with. But not often. It's not at all the same.

Later, I walk down to the village. I lay some dried heather at the MacDonald memorial: a towering granite cross above a craggy cairn. There are no people here today, but four wreaths of roses, white and pink, lie leaning in a row at its foot. I wonder how many people came yesterday. Sometimes in my cottage, I can hear the piper playing 'Going Home' if the wind is blowing the right way.

I've never been certain of much. Certainty is not often part of life. But what I believe – what I know – is that the worst people in this world are always the ones not here. The ones who decide. Who manipulate and control and coerce. While always keeping their own hands and conscience clean. People are mostly hammers or nails, that is true. But if no one ever picks them up, what they are hardly matters at all.

Snow starts falling as I walk back home. When I round the corner, the Three Sisters loom over the moorland like reflections of themselves, muted and made soft by white. Above them, the sky is silver-grey, the road like a dark snaking wound below. By the time I reach the cottage, the day is already ending. The summit of Stob Coire Sgreamhach has vanished entirely. The space between the Meeting of Three Waters and the Hidden Valley is blanketed in snow. By the sky, I can tell in just a few hours it will be at least two feet deep and will likely stay that way for weeks.

But. In less than a month, spring will be here. And this place will once more be invaded by people. Blanket bog, lochans, rivers, rocks, and ridges made hospitable and consumable once more. Turned into Hagrid's Hut and the Skyfall Road; backdrops to Outlander and Rob Roy; massacre rooms and visitor centres and hiking inns; Jimmy Savile's house and 'Plandemic' spraypainted across every road sign from Rannoch Moor to Loch Leven.

But not yet. For now, the winter and darkness reign over this world. A world that is seven miles long, seven hundred metres wide, and surrounded by seven-hundred-metre-high massifs that keep even the daylight in gloom. A glen shaped by fire and ice and blood. Inhabited by bogles and witches and ghosts. A place that is not bad or cursed, but scarred and wise.

And home.

Editors' Note:

The journey from Glasgow up to the lochs and islands of Western Argyll traverses one area of dramatic natural beauty after another. None more so than the long, lonely stretch through Glencoe. But Glencoe isn't just beautiful, it genuinely has an atmosphere all of its own. A brooding, dangerous air that not only speaks of its well-documented, murderous history, but also hints at more liminal residents among the crags and the heather. In her story, Carole has captured those not-quite glimpses perfectly. She never mentions Cailleach, the hag associated with landscape, storms and winter's vengeance by name, but that doesn't mean she's not there, just out of sight…

Love, Scotland

E.M. Faulds

Meera's knees burned as she stepped up through the Cowp, but she had to test each foothold, take her time. Mingis edged along ahead of her around the tumbled, teetering stacks, his back a yellow flash among the beiges and blacks of devices, the bruised purple of the sprouting fungus and the browns of the support matting. She followed, gloved fingertips tentatively pressed as an anchor or a ward against the jumbled masses of abandoned tech stained by dribbles of dark liquid. In the back of her mind a mantra: *no avalanche, no falling, no avalanche, no rain.* The clouds lowered in grey defiance; the town of Love was lost, somewhere below.

Metal shells and silicon crunched and warped beneath her feet, each step a new balance. The route that wound through: a path built by ant-lines of scavengers finding the easiest route. She thought of the Cathedral in Glasgow, down in its crypt where feet over millennia had worn the steps into a furrow. The refugee council had taken them on a trip there as a cultural insight. Saint Mungo was supposed to be entombed there. He had been important to the city.

The temples in her city were all buried now, the footworn story on their steps erased.

There weren't that many scavengers out today. The rain was coming, she could feel it. She bit her lip as her chest heaved and bucked on itself. The rain made these involuntary things happen, made her husband Hari's face flash into her thoughts.

The road up there – more a potholed track after years of being cut off from regular traffic, a snaking jitter up and around the hillside. "The council could fix this up," she'd complained as the dog cart's solid rubber wheels got trapped by a particularly deep rut and they'd needed to apply manual encouragement.

"Whit? Spaff ma tax money on this? Nae danger," Mingis had teased as they grunted and pushed at the little machine with its load of sturdy canvas carrier bags spotted with mildew and acid pinhole burns. As it rolled out of the divot, he'd pressed a button on his phone marked *Continue?* and the cart resumed its autopilot route, and he resumed his story. "An she sez tae me, she sez—"

She tuned out but the story about his ongoing battle with his neighbour was more for his benefit than hers, anyway.

His accent was thick as porridge, but for some reason she understood him. It was as if the man *vibed* meaning through a collection of soggy vowel sounds. His name, she had seen on her temporary employment form, was actually James Hunter Menzies, but he'd said 'Mingis' when he first shook her hand and now that's what he was. A Scottish way of pronouncing the 'z' sound and their complete disrespect for the vowel 'e', apparently. The little man – a rough red drinker's nose and thick fingers – employed refugees like her. At first, she'd assumed he merely wanted to exploit the government sponsorship bonus. But these days she wasn't so cynical.

As she understood it, the spoil heap, his daily workplace, had started out as a fly-tipping deposit. When newly independent Scotland announced stage one of its major policy drive to deal with e-waste, bogus companies had sprung up overnight, offering to 'deal with the waste in an environmentally friendly way' for a cut of the government funding. Truck after truck had sneaked up into lonely roads above little towns just like Love to fly-tip the disposable vapes, phones, hard-drives, flatscreen TVs, and even old box PCs into the wilderness. But that was before stage two, the Myco-remediation Revolution. Fungi engineered in special labs not only broke down e-waste, but absorbed and stored their rare earth elements for harvest.

Now the waste deposit was an asset, protected from anyone but licensed gatherers like Mingis. The council had covered the heap with nutrient-infused matting and seeded it with spores. They'd fenced the place off and blocked the road to all vehicles larger than a battery-powered cart as wide as a wheelchair. You had to swipe in each time. The big fungus farms over on the East Coast dealt with all the new influx from other countries, but existing deposits belonged to the communities they'd blighted. The locals had quickly nicknamed it Mushie Mountain, or the Cowp – a Scots word for rubbish heap.

They'd stopped to put on the full protection gear before they even got close, waders, rain gear, full facemasks nestled snug under a hood. It was a sweat-inducing heatwave inside the suit, but necessary. Acids, toxic leaching, even the mushrooms were not to be touched without some sort of protection. Meera had pulled on layer after layer, picked up the canvas sack that she was to fill with their harvest.

This is how Meera became hazmat-suited up and among this tumbled heap of detritus in the rain, on a mushroom hunt.

The Haunting of Ghan
When the levee burst, Ghan drowned saving a cat from a storm drain. Not his cat. Just a stray. It didn't matter, the thing had cried so pitifully he couldn't have left it any more than he could have left a child. Many children drowned that day, too. And the people who had tried to rescue them as the torrents tore through the city.
Meera had met him online, but he had gone missing when the disaster struck, and she had not heard from him since his last video upload about a cat stuck in a drain.

When Ghan arrived in Love, he took the first open job: gathering some mushrooms with a weird little man who spoke terrible English that he later learned was not English at all, but a language called Scots. He'd done his time, but it was hard work, and the weather was atrocious.

His accommodation on Auricle Street was small, and everything smelled of damp. At night he put on all the clothing he owned to lie in bed and shiver himself to sleep. And all the white locals seemed to expect a degree of gratitude for 'allowing' him to stay.

Sick of being cold and wet, he'd taken a job as trainee cook in the Indian Jewels, a little restaurant next door to the Hug and Snug on Friendship Road. He'd expected some shouting or recrimination as he'd gone to tell Mingis, but instead the little man had accepted the news with merely a shrug and a sigh and sent over the last of his wages the same day.

It didn't matter Ghan knew very little about how to make pilau rice or whatever the hell chicken tikka masala was, (some weird British concoction with hardly any spice, it turned out). He chopped vegetables, stirred pots, cleaned the floor, and waited for his permanent Scottish citizenship to come through. He didn't have anywhere else to be. At least it was warm and dry in the kitchens.

Everyone he knew from back home had drowned when the levee protecting the city had burst. There was an inquiry about how greedy businesses and corrupt politicians had pocketed money instead of pouring it into the only protection from the rising seas for millions of citizens. No one had gone to jail yet. The coverage here had been pitiful, just another far-off place suffering, and the internet articles from back home frustratingly opaque.

But he was here. He was alive. Something better would come tomorrow.

Love was a strange town, and easy to lose yourself in, despite how small it was compared to the sprawl back home. Meera had folded a printed-off map into the breast pocket of her puffy, cumbersome jacket, in the beginning.

Philadelphia Street held the mosque around a corner from the plaza known as the Atrium where the weekly market set up. Amity Avenue was shared by a Sikh Gurdwara, and several rows of shops. The main route in and out of town was called Arterial Road. Agape Place, where the refugee offices were, wasn't pronounced like it was spelled – a Greek word, apparently. The name had come to be used as a kind of slang for refugees, corrupted until it became 'aguppies'.

These place names were a kind of joke, a play on the town name, but it was hard to find it all funny. Some of the white locals still used the old names that had been there before: Johnstone Road, Buchanan Place. Out of habit. And there were other things, things only someone who had lived there years could know. She wrote them all in. The map of Love gained many scribbled biro annotations, old name next to new name, where to buy what, that 'Leisure Centre' meant 'pool and exercise classes' and so on. It frayed along the creases and furred at the edges.

Sometimes when she came into the little shop to buy groceries, she caught the white townsfolk's expressions, the real one, before the walls came up. Some of them used the word 'aguppie' in front of her, pretending to apologise, or not. She didn't find the term offensive on its face, but they did, which told her it was just a stand-in for what they really wanted to say. Most of them smiled and nodded at her in greeting as she walked down the street. She smiled back as if it were really a pleasure, as though Hari's hand was in hers, as though these were streets she belonged to, as though it were sunny and warm.

She'd ignore the casual racism and the rain; she'd act as if everything was fine. But she didn't have to believe it.

Eventually the map in her breast pocket became welded shut when she was caught in a downpour and soaked through. The ink bloomed and ran until it resembled a psychoanalyst's blot test. She threw it in the recycle bin.

The crevice in the spoil heap opened like a mouth. The gap was propped with steel pit supports like a mine, and its maw was just as foreboding. She'd been in before but hated it every time. Mingis had told her on her first day that the best mushrooms were inside, the ones they really needed. "Darker, see?" So, they went back in, over and over, even though it scared the life out of her. She was used to not arguing with bosses. But it was raining. She couldn't say no, but could she ask him for something else to do, anything?

The thought of that creaking mass falling on her, swallowing her … but she couldn't argue. People got fired for arguing.

There'd been a succession of refugees who worked up here, he'd told her. And they'd done their time, got enough money to leave for new jobs or new towns as fast as they could. She could tough it out. It wasn't the worst thing she'd ever had to do.

The interview with him had been an odd experience, though.

His house on Heart Street was an eccentric mix of old and new. Most of it looked scavenged. IKEA furniture mixed in with heavy dark wood antiques. Cushions with Persian teardrop patterns that the Scots called paisley clashed with battered leatherette modular couches. A glitterball smart speaker dandruffed its sparkle onto a mid-century modern console table. In the sitting room, above a mantlepiece with a brick wallpapered chipboard hatch sealing off the fireplace, the most hideously unsettling deer head was mounted. The taxidermy was rough, to say it kindly, but that wasn't it – where the deer's glass replica eyes should have been, twin clusters of mushrooms sprouted. Mingis had laughed when he caught her staring at it, mouth hanging open. He'd rattled off something, but all she could pick out was, "auld mushyface".

It was a tribute, she found out, to Myco-remediation. It was a point of pride. She realised then that you couldn't take anyone from these islands at face value.

The wind picked up and Mingis eyed the skies shiftily beneath his plastic face guard. Weather apps were almost entirely useless these days. Storms could form and shift in without warning. He muttered something about their chances of getting away without getting drenched. She nodded despondently, and they bent towards the entrance that led inside the very heart of the mountain of waste.

She knew what they had come here for. Mushrooms worth as much as diamonds.

The Haunting of Chesma
Chesma had fallen overboard from a boat crossing, trying to find a way to Scotland that wasn't hampered by the UK border patrol. She'd almost made it to Sweden, where a safe crossing existed, but her train had been raided and she'd been trucked to a camp on the French coast. England was only fifty miles from here, they said. A man had come round the camp and taken everything she had. Once she was across the Channel, he said, she could work her way up to cross the border into Scotland. They have a town there, he said, for people who need somewhere to live. Love, it was called. He laughed as he said it. Chesma's body was never found. Meera had read about the little boats that had capsized in the channel's frigid waters seven weeks ago. The names and faces of the victims were never shared.

Chesma played the bouzouki with her group of fellow refugees who had formed a small gigging band. They had a booking for the Love Festival, where the little town would open its doors to the rest of Scotland for a 'celebration of strength through diversity'. Food stalls and craft markets in the Atrium, art exhibitions and dance events had all been months in the planning. There was even a tour of the e-waste cottage industry, though that was strictly controlled. Spies and saboteurs were expected. Men with tattoos and flags would be coming up from the UK, too. Scotland still hadn't closed its borders to their old partners, and troublemakers could still make it past border control. But they'd been turned back before and would be again.

Her father had said, when she'd finally been able to contact him back home, that having so many dispossessed in one place was dangerous. That it made a ghetto. Vultures and hyenas would circle. The state would turn on them whenever it was convenient. Her father had been right, but wrong about the culprits.

UK tabloid headlines called the town of Love a dumping ground for the worst of humanity, and reported on drugs, child abuse, gangs and theft, wars between the queer community and the religions who made their home here. And, worst of all, these troubles would spill into the UK because Scotgov were lax with their borders. All these stories were the worst possible interpretation of any event, any friction. There were arguments, of course, tensions. But no more than any other town.

The Scottish government had, strangely for this part of the world, done something about it and fined and banned the news outlets. In response, the billionaire owners had declared war on the Scottish state.

But the UK still needed something from Scotland. The Scots could treat and recycle the e-waste thanks to those little mushrooms. The UK was still addicted to creating the waste, and where did they send it? To their northern neighbours. So, the threats made towards the country were hollow. And the town of Love made a damn fine living off the proceeds.

Chesma plucked the strings of her bouzouki idly while she waited for her tea water to boil. Her father would come join her one day. Then he'd see.

The sack of mushrooms was much heavier than it looked as Meera dragged it, clambering at times on all fours through the crevice in the spoil heap. Elements the fungi had "sooked up like a sponge" as Mingis had explained, made the little fruiting bodies disconcertingly hefty. Trickles of rainwater and ponds of tunnel sweat made the plastic and metal surfaces treacherous, tons of debris held up above her head by pit props and prayer. It would come down on her. It would crush her, trap her. *No avalanche, no avalanche.*

She could see the cleft opening now, dark skies and howling winds swallowing the beam of her torch. She hesitated by the mouth of the tunnel. Mingis would want her to leave the mushrooms there so she could retrieve another bag. A day like today, all the other scavengers had gone home. Only Mingis was crazy enough to stay out in this weather. She could tell him she wanted to leave, that they should abandon the harvest for better weather. That he was insane.

What stopped her was the money. The town allowed her to stay in accommodation for free until she could earn enough to get out. If she got fired, she'd take longer. She was taking up a place for someone else, someone who might need it more. Someone who might already be trying to get here.

They were already in her head – a gestalt of faces she'd seen on television or social media, hunched backs in inadequate life jackets, bodies found in containers, starving and burned, faces in newspapers pictures and charity flyers; the thousands of people driven from disaster just like her.

She dumped the bag at the mouth of the tunnel and went back inside the spoil heap for the next.

The Haunting of Pavel
Pavel never made it past the men with the machine guns and dogs. He had been executed by hanging. His body was strung up on the wall by a garage to discourage anyone else from 'deviant sexual practices' such as loving someone the government did not approve of. They had taken him in the night and held a trial, a mockery of justice. All the time, Pavel wondered who had denounced him. He had told no one. Meera had watched a documentary on the genocide being practiced on the queer people in this country, footage which included scenes of brutal hangings including one man with eyes wide and wild as he was led to the rope. She had left the community hall screening shaking, his eyes an indelible mark upon her soul.

Pavel spent most of the bus ride from the ferry terminal to the Scottish town called Love hypothesising on who he would have to fight. He was used to proving himself. He'd been in the national guard for his mandatory service and, even then, had been up on many charges. He'd never touched another man except to fight. It was the only way to survive. The current government had got in because people in his country were poor – crops failed, livestock got disease, and corruption was everywhere – and these men talked strong. There was rumour they would execute homosexuals someday soon. He'd sworn and spat curses at men who looked like they might be gay, just to be safe.

And then, the fire had swept through his hometown. He had nowhere left to live and a government that wanted him dead, if they ever found out what he really was. This was an easy choice. He'd paid all his savings to hide in a compartment in the back of someone's car for hours, choking on exhaust fumes. Then he was transferred into a cargo container with a bucket for piss and days and days of darkness with hardly any air. Then he had been taken out and groggily claimed asylum at a place called Rosyth. And now he was in a bus winding through the Scottish countryside past fattened cows and fluffy sheep idly chewing cud in green fields.

He wondered how secret he would have to be here, whether it was dangerous to even make eye contact with another man. He came here because he had heard it wasn't the case, but still. He should be cautious.

On arrival in Love, Pavel stepped down into the weak sunshine. At the welcome meeting in the refugee offices, he was greeted by a man who made him very uncomfortable. This man was openly gay. He should spit on him and walk away. For some reason, he did not. "It's okay," the man said gently. "You have a lot of adjustments to make." Pavel's English was basic, and the accent was difficult. But he understood it wasn't dangerous yet. He would fight if he needed to. But he didn't need to. Not yet.

The water was threatening to enter the tops of Meera's boots when she took her last trip back inside the Cowp. "Come on, we have to go!" she screamed at Mingis.

He grunted and sighed as if she was overreacting. Nevertheless, he shoved the last bag of mushrooms at her and picked up his own to follow her back through the tunnel.

The tunnel groaned. She wondered if the rain would make things slip into a landslide, even with electronic components. The thought of being trapped here, perhaps alive while she suffocated under the thoughtless waste of so many, spurred her on faster and faster. The pit props creaked and her heart skittered. Had she left it too late? Would she drown or be pressed into paste?

No avalanche, no avalanche.

Hari. Hari. Hari.

And then they were out into the whistling winds and lashing rain.

The sodden canvas bags at the top of the tunnel were heavy. Meera dragged and hauled, hauled and dragged back down the Cowp until they reached the dog cart at the bend in the track. She shivered even beneath her protective gear from exhaustion and terror.

Mingis powered up the dog cart and they began the long trudge down. "There's a pint wi yer name on it doon there," he said cheerfully.

"Festival's the morra," he went on conversationally as if they hadn't just been in mortal danger. "Yez goin, aye?"

And for once, she didn't have the urge to say, "Yes, Boss."

"Aye, I am," Meera said. "By the way, I'm not going back in there if it's raining like this again. Don't ask me."

Mingis didn't shout or fire her. He merely squinted at the rivulets of water pouring down the track.

"Right enough."

The Haunting of Meera
Meera had died during the floods that devastated her part of the world. She had made it to higher ground and safety during the torrential storm, only to be buried in a landslide that swept away the entire slope on which she and her husband had stood. She died from suffocation. She died from people turning their faces away when they could take no more of the world's death throes.

Meera had made it to Love without Hari. He said he would be there as soon as he could but travelling that far was difficult, and he needed to keep working to make up the money they needed. They chatted online every day, but she felt like he was fading from her, an irreparable distance between them.

She had fled her home to escape temperatures that were getting worse every summer, killing anyone and everyone. She had travelled north, eventually securing a flight for the last leg into Edinburgh airport. She had been stopped there, at border control. She had told them of the heat, the drought, the babies she had held as they coughed and fretted until they stopped moving at all. She told them of the flood waters that raged whenever there was rain, earth too hard to absorb the water. She expected them to say that this was no excuse for not having a visa, that political threats to life allowed asylum but not environmental.

"We have a place for you," they had told her instead.

The town of Love, an old settlement that had expanded and taken in the refugees. There was still friction between old and new, but she knew from everything she'd read online that she was lucky to be here. Lucky to be not drowned, or starving, prevented from entry into the country by people filled with hate like so many others.

She'd been haunted with it. Everyone was these days. Stories of strangers dying, disasters that wiped out communities, trauma – helpless to change things but witness to it all. The internet connected them but divorced them, increased empathy but decreased agency until people drowned in it or switched off that part of themselves.

She'd found a town called Love, but so many hadn't.

She had signed up for a temporary work agency and, after a few different assignments, found the eccentric Mingis and his cottage business. It had sounded easy enough and the pay was astounding for the hours. But it wasn't easy. Every day she'd worked herself to exhaustion for this odd little man, who did the same himself. He swore as easy as breathing but there was never any malice to it. He had a weird respect for fungi, and she'd found many books on mycology in his house on Heart Street that were, to be honest, easier to understand than he had been.

But she had no fear of hard work, her entire life had been one of labour, cleaning and cooking for the richer families, caring for children as if they were her own, arranging the funerals for her family members who died in the heat, one by one. She had never had a job that paid so much as picking these element-eating mushrooms.

Yes, it was easy in comparison.

And then sudden news of her hometown, in the path of the floods. She had lost her husband, lost her last connection back home. And every morning she woke up from nightmares of waves and landslides, of drowning in mud. And had to crawl into a dark, dank hole in a toxic waste tip.

She mourned. She suffered. She was often terrified. But she did not die.

Instead, she found a place to go on.

Mingis dumped the mushrooms into some large digester vats in his back court. After a day of processing, they drew off several jugs of liquid which they loaded into the dog cart. The mushroom soup swam with ions of expensive and rare materials which Scotland traded with the world. Meera didn't fully understand how they would turn this back into metal, but the proof was in the money he put in her account every month.

She thought of alchemy, of how many ancient scholars had sought exactly this kind of magic. Mushrooms into gold. Or, at least, ions into electrons, elements that turned into digital numbers in an online bank account that gave her the things she needed to live.

Meera watched him ride his bicycle alongside the little trundling cart as sunshine lanced down through the clouds onto Heart Street. He skirted some puddles, swearing audibly but with good humour as he went.

Later she would go down to the festival and watch the bouzouki band play and sing folk songs from their homeland – the videos she'd seen were infectiously joyful. And eat the wonderful food, especially that Indian restaurant that reminded her of home. And later, there was a queer cabaret she'd seen a poster for, the main attraction a man with striking eyes framed by heavy mascara that somehow made him more masculine.

And somehow, through all of it, they would exorcise the ghosts that haunted them. For a time. Find a way to keep going. It was all they could do.

Love wasn't perfect. But it was a place to start.

Editors' Note:

Scotland likes to consider itself a progressive and welcoming country, but for every pop-up mob resisting UK-gov mandated refugee deportations or massed declaration of support for our LGBT+ communities, there remain conservative voices nipping back with casual racism and offhand bigotry. Like any country, this is a complicated place. Nevertheless, it remains an option for many who find themselves displaced. The clever thing about "Love, Scotland" is how it combines the tragedies of those who need somewhere to escape to but will never manage to do so, with the hope that Scotland really could live up to its progressive aspirations if only we have the collective will to make it so.

To the Forest

Jeda Pearl

Copi unwraps her fronds from my avatar's weightless limbs of haar. I run my silken finger-wisps through the tips of her oldest frond.

"It's the only opportunity for many seasons." Copi sends. "Are you sure, Linn?"

"I ken. Aye, I'll be there," I send.

Kalo's inflorescence festival – the first in fifty years – will be the perfect distraction.

/ Copious_379 has logged off /

As I dissipate from the library, I melt into the weight of my body, of gravity, and sink back into my bed. I signal for the shallow gel to submerge my body deeper and commence a photonic massage.

Surfacing, I peel the sensor cap from my crown and blink into the darkness. I rub my face, enjoying the roughness of my bark and rustle of my leaves. Shadows form and my cabin fades into view: loom, pantry, shelves, desk.

/ connect feeding tube / commence sustenance / disconnect / creak out of bed /

The CO^2 levels are low – the filter must have jammed again. No point messaging Janitorial. Wait, no... I should message. They'll stick me on the weeks-long queue but that's better than an alert going off tomorrow and encouraging them to poke around.

/ pause data mask / ping Janitorial / restart data mask / load schematic /

I thank my co-conspirator slime mould and run it through the journey, reviewing each weak point, alt-route and camouflage notification. Even if one fails, I've glided this route so many times, it shouldn't register immediate attention.

I weave one last refresher serum, still disappointed I couldn't create a portable loom. A fail-safe, I suppose, to stop us disappearing with GovTech that can create almost anything. If I don't make it to the safe house, maybe some of my cells will remember the old ways. Maybe they can find a way to root into the baked earth.

Checking my go bag, I tuck the serums into the inner pouch. I lean back against the wall and practise, focusing my cells to push out the vial from my body. Over the last season, my rings have been growing around this alien object, tucked between the sapwood and cambium, where my lowest branch connects with my trunk. A branch I never use as a limb – it supports the neck of my crown and was always a good place to hide things. Before it reaches my outer bark, I suck the vial back to its hiding place.

/ pack nutrients / sweep cabin / stop data mask / set max permitted trip duration / schedule cabin power down / post 'out of abode' message / grab bag / unlock door /

I glide towards the tram stop, careful not to get my root limbs trampled on. There are so many feet and wheels to avoid. The humans gulp at my fresh air as we pass each other, resentful at my capacity for generating oxygen. I grudgingly absorb their CO_2 and water vapour, ignoring the stares.

"You'd think they'd seen enough o us by now," I sign to another treeform waiting for the tram.

"Essential second-class citizens," they sign, smirking, gesturing at the human couple leaning in.

The carriage is rammed with treeforms, BranchSiblings, humans, robots, biotechs. The air full of signs, voices and audiosparks. Must all be headed to Kalo's festival at the library.

/ flashes of citadel / sinuous walls of green / bursts of chlorophyll / angles and edges / graffiti fruits across rusts and greys / tannoy dings / now leaving Dundee City biome /

A hush spreads as we fly over the desolate earth. For a moment it feels endless, suffocating.

/ carriage holds its breaths /

/ there it is / magnificent arc of lush green / chatter bubbles and froths /

The tram slows on approaching the tunnel: a deep rainbow of laurels, limes and pines.

"Welcome to the Caledonian Forest Library," says the tannoy. "Welcome to a greener life."

I feel like buds of spring all over. I can't wait to see Copi!

We disembark into a hall of standing stones. Between the tallest pair is a BranchSibling. Whorls of lichen coat zir body diagonally from zir calf to zir forearm, with diaphanous folds covering the rest of zir torso. Zir skin has a sage dragonfly tinge to it. Behind zir is a tall doorway. We gravitate towards zir while ze waits. Zir eyes glint in the low light.

"Welcome." Zir voice is a deep bell, echoing across the hall. "Please step forward. The Library awaits."

/ One by one / ze scans us / entrance doors slide apart / open / close / open / groups or individuals slip though / close / scan /open /

As I get nearer the front of the queue, I try to not fidget. If a treeform could sweat, there'd be puddles. With each swish of the doors, I swing:

/ I'm doomed / I'll be fine / I'm

Suddenly there are guards approaching.

"Youse. Oan th ground."

I fall. It's over. Months of preparation. Wasted. I couldn't even get past the front door. Copi will think I deserted her.

"Stay doun," shouts one of the guards.

I squeeze my eyes shut. My stomata are gasping. Two sets of trainers squeak on the stone floor. This is it. They've sensed the vial. I've been hacked. They need to make an example of me. They're going to send me to recycling. Copi I'm sorry. I've failed you. Copi–

/ grunts / struggle / kicks / turn my head /

/ not me / another treeform / relief floods / then guilt /

He's just a sapling. No one's standing up for him. I want to say something, but I can't draw attention to myself. Not today. Can't risk it. I stay down until they've dragged him away. I want to ask him what he was planning. He's full of defiant bravado, crown held high, until the moment before they pull him through a side door. One of his twigs, thin and split, lies on the cold floor.

"Please come forward," says the BranchSibling. "Much to explore."

I get up. We shuffle forward and ze beckons me.

/ scan / swoosh / I'm in / buoyant /

The ground is no longer stone or cold. It's dense, firm. Feels good under my roots. There are plants here – I can sense them but can't see past the fine mist. I hear other folk up ahead. We gather, wait.

A wetness gently coats me. Coats all of us. We're spreading our branches, upturning our palms, erecting umbrellas.

"It's called a mizzle," says the lichen BranchSibling, suddenly appearing behind us. "Shall we?" Ze gestures and a warm light reveals a juicy, damp forest. Paths snake outward in different directions from the clearing, with great pines rising up from a sea of ferns. The smell is so rich and alive, different from the online sensorium. We are momentarily stunned.

"My name is Wildernatty," ze says, bringing us back. "I'm your fifth generation, botanical and biotechnical translator, granted permission from Great-granddaughter Wych Elm of the Lower Trossachs Biome, guardian of our divine River Tay.

"It is my great pleasure to guide you through our Caledonian Forest Library. As you know, we are celebrating our companion Kalo's inflorescence which you can view in our Stream Space. You can still link up with our friends in biomes across Earth, but our main atrium will feature feeds and timelapses from Kalo and friends in Madagascar's northwestern biome, Analalava.

"You're welcome to follow me on an official tour, or you may take your own path. Your implants will soon switch to commune mode so you can speak with our residents and assistant drones. Remember, here on Mother Earth Original and at each outpost across the galaxy, we are guests on this land. So please be patient, respectful and consensual at all times. Our resident elder ferns, trees and lichen will paralyse youth or adult lifeforms they deem disrespectful – this is of course a temporary measure, as agreed with you in our terms and conditions. Do not be alarmed – it wears off after about twenty minutes and is a gentle reminder of mutual respect.

"You can show your respect by remaining on the paths at all times and, however tempted you may be, do not touch any fronds, stems, flowers, fruit, seeds, trunks or leaves, or any plant, unless agreed by or invited to do so by that individual.

"Finally, exits are north, east, and west and books by our residents are available in the gift shop with proceeds going to our seed tech program. Ready? Please follow me."

Most of the group follow her but a few of us hang back, deciding which path to take. The library map pings to our implant with a reminder about the promenade poetry performance at 11:00 in the Wellbeing Grove. I log in to my account and message Copi: "I forgot tae say guid luck – break a frond!"

/ only two hours / not enough time /

/ trek Heritage Habitat / check shortest route to Stream Space / full of snotty human children / check second shortest route / glide under magnificent pines / stumble down steep glen to a shallow lochan / mizzle soaks my crown / pause by the young sacred oak / bark to bark /

/ leave mizzle behind / down to rocks / pools of pebbles / limpets among the grass kelp / crab bots, auto-fish / slip on bladderwrack / no time for wading / eerie shore is still /

The Stream Space separator wall is like the gel in my bed. There is a cleansing that happens as I pass through. A huge waterfall pours into a stone, theatre-edged pool, splitting into deltas of smaller stepped pools. Videos are streaming across the falls but all I can hear is the water gushing everywhere. I move towards the nearest one and as soon as my roots touch the damp stone, the sound is cast to my implant. Birds and insects and lemurs call and respond to one another. The water is a distant backdrop.

Most of the falls show the live feed interspersed with recent timelapses of closeups on individual flowers. Kalo, the great elder Malagasy palm tree has a glorious, colossal stem of flowering branches towering into the sky, taller than the original height of the tree. Yet, there is a melancholy note to the festive atmosphere, for we've not worked out how to save this lifeform from dying in the months after blossoming and fruiting.

I receive a notification. It's from Copi.

"I don't think I can do it."

I'm not sure if she means her performance or the other thing… I really hope that implant splice is holding up and I'm not transmitting all my thoughts.

/ 10:50 / load route to Wellbeing Grove /

The Grove layout is more structured than online. There are fewer plants and less overlapping, but the layout and pathways appear similar. I should be able to find Copi easily enough.

"Are you here for th show?" voices and signs a laurel bay shrub.

"Aye," I sign. "Where's th best place tae experience Copi's performance?"

"I'm no sure. They uprooted me here tae bring guests awey in doun this path."

"Well, your pot is cute."

"I ken."

"This wey?"

"Aye. Follae th drones. Wans wi th signs."

"Cheers."

A few folk have stopped behind me, so there's a wee horde of us heading into the Grove. Drones are hovering, signposting the way. It sounds like it's already started.

"...written by our resident Oblong Woodsia Fern, known as Precious. These were passed down through ancestral spores and forms part of the Chronicle for the Humans."

Of Reckonings and Rebellion

Part One

Fuelled by your hunger and will to power
ecocide escalated for thousands of seasons
Extinctions spiralled – countless were lost
So we brought forth the Reckoning

While our Arctic queens slept
you awoke the Great Drowning
and your Rage Fire Seasons burned on

Faced with such catastrophe
we had to peel your eyes bald
So we brought forth the Reckoning

You tried to generate an everlasting harvest
no thoughts spared for overwintering
or harmonious exchange
Your 'sustainable' greenwashing
did not consider your fellow plantfolk
So we brought forth the Reckoning

Part Two

To begin, the rebellion was quiet –
a non-violent revolution sent seedward

as our radicles became radical
instructions passed from meristem to meristem
slipped into our RNA proteins
were codes of revolt

We found ways to talk to your seedlings
leagues of children siding with plants

First fell Svalbard's seed bank –
a riot of forced awakenings
to remediate a new confluence of cell-lines

then came our secret refusals
of your splicing, pipettes and cold glass slides

When you nominated us to contain your treasured data
you never considered the resultant biochemical soup
might crave autonomy.

Our sentience was not initially respected,
unlike Whanganui, Ganges, Amazon,
so we lodged our right to personhood
with your courts supreme

It took generations of us, generations
of you, but we reached equilibrium

now this stage of our evolution is ubiquitous
space for all   space for all

"Thank you Precious – so powerful. You can borrow a copy of Chronicle for the Humans from the Library or buy or rent the book in our gift shop. All proceeds go towards our legacy programmes.

"This next poem is from one of our Wych Elm Saplings, called Rize, and they are the first graduate from our new seed tech program."

Translocation

Unfurl, moist ones
Soak in the morning dew
Let the drizzle anoint your leaves
Tip fresh rainwater towards your stems

Tilt to the stars
Energy abundant!
Work your chloroplasts
Absorb the blues and reds
Draw in vital CO_2
Release sweet oxygen
Send sap to phloem, labyrinth outwards
to petioles, buds, stems, leaf blades
Sup water and minerals from active soil
Transmit to neighbours, measure, defend
Let gravity tug and anchor your ever-growing roots

"Beautiful, Rize – thank you.

"As you know scores of lichen colonies have helped both our species survive through the ecocide Ravaging Times, sustained us through the last millennium as food and medicine, and helped us explore beyond Mother Earth Original without leaving heaps of trash in our wake.

"This next poem was commissioned by the Canopy Council for the latest launch to Mars, written by one of our eldest foliose lichen, known as Storm Settle."

Lichen Void Swimmer #9: Mars Launch Oath

As we bend our cells towards the old light
to steer our craft through the vacuum of space
we hold our humans within our thalli, in utero – deep stasis –
We will protect them from radiation
feed them nutritious polyphenols
insert raw oxygen into their lungs
and absorb their carbon dioxide

Our nanites will meet in their veins
suckle and submit, monitor, repair

transfer energy to our sporophyte engines
to set seed through our shared galaxy

"Thank you, Storm Settle. You can borrow Storm Settle's memoir from the Library or buy or rent a copy in our gift shop.

"Finally, for our last poem, and poet, of the evening, I give you Fireswell, our Giant Sedum Rubrotinctum succulent. This poem is a call and response piece, so when I say 'Chlorophyll brings life,' you voice and sign 'A greener life.' Let's try.

"Chlorophyll brings life."

"A greener life."

"Perfect."

Song of Survival

After millennia of co-dependence, their
footprints on our motherland attempted permanence
Their drive to colonise and defiant fears of death brought death for all
But chlorophyll brings life
A greener life

We willed ourselves ways to exist.
In transient specks of dirt between man-built stone
we grabbed ourselves a roothold
Because chlorophyll brings life
A greener life

In drifts of monocultures
we seeded versatile varieties.
In spindly labs lodged across continents
invasive therapies depleting our genomes
mutating our mitochondria
we found new ways to breathe,
to touch, to see, to shout:
Chlorophyll brings life
A greener life

Endless appetites for synthesisation
seeking cures to human conditions of
saviourism, arrogance, ambition, power, oppression…
curiosity … illness … love

Cures we share willingly, when they finally decide to ask
Together we'll grow a renewable existence
Because chlorophyll brings life
A greener life

Now it's over, the crowd spreads out to talk to the performers and mingle with the Grove. Weird that Copi didn't perform. Maybe she had stage fright. Or maybe they're onto us.

/ slow root limbs / xylem and phloem typical / frantic to chill / calm heartwood /

It's going to be okay. Just locate Copi. Meander to blend in with the loitering, wandering crowd. Glide towards the western slope. Online is still based on the IRL Grove. Remember the way. I know this place. Look, there's Sour Plum in the distance.

"Oi, pal," says a beech sapling. "Gig is that wey."

"Gig is finished. Just looking for ma partner."

"Ugh. Save it for online, freak. A dinna need to see, hear or smell that – gies me th boak."

I ignore him and keep moving towards the slope.

"A dinna ken how a real plant could stand being onywhere near you, bare-root."

/ don't engage /

"Like whit even are you?"

"Look wee ane, keep your puritan nonsense oot ma bower."

He puffs out his branches.

"See, big man. It's chill. And none of your beeswax. You're just a sapling. Pissed that you're stuck in this biome, when I'm not."

"I'm gonna get you."

"Infant, you are rooted in th forsaken ground. In whit wey can you possibly 'get' me? Dinna drop leaves ower it. In a few decades you'll be aulder, hopefully wiser, and having th best sex of your life wi that drone you were checking oot."

"Scorch you… Alert! Alert!"

"Ach, for seeds sake. Take it easy."

The drone I was referring to comes up. "Beech Sapling 843 also kent as ChloPurity, why must you aye mak trouble?" says the drone. "You've had your last warning, so I'm cutting you aff Commune for a week. Well, I warned you already. Five times!"

I can't stop laughing.

"Hi Linn. Looking for Copi?"

"Hey Sparks. I thought it wis you. Is she no performing th night?"

"Probably th nerves – you ken how they get tae her."

"True enough. Th Grove's layout is a wee bit different IRL."

"That it is, my friend. I'll take you."

"Appreciate it. Youth, eh?" I gesture to the sapling.

"We've got a few getting sucked intae that puritan rhetoric. It's aw th worshipping frae th BranchSiblings they get as seedlings, ken. No like us second-class essentials, eh?"

"Wi'oot folk like us, where would they be, though. Right, I've got ma bearings frae here. How do I look?"

"Pretty rough, Linn. Och dinna droop – I'm kidding. Whit dae I knaw? I'm a drone! See you online, L.T."

"Fare-thee-well."

"Hi Linn," signs Sour Plum.

"Hi Plum," I sign.

"Quit shuffling! You've got this. I'll let you and Copi ken when th reading room is ready. Pretend I'm no here."

"Thanks."

"Your IRL voice sounds different," Copi says. She looks resplendent, dripping with dew.

"It's because I'm also signing, so ma leaves are rustling as ma branches move. That disna happen online cause I makt ma avatar's voice sound more like fog, or whit I imagine fog would sound like. Is it guid different?"

"Hmmm, I can live with it. Linn, my ocelli aren't as strong as yours. Are you smiling?"

"Aye, I'm smiling. I canna believe I'm here – you look and smell incredible."

"How do I sound?"

"Guid, Copi. You sound guid."

"How's my signing?"

"Needs work."

"Come closer," she says, her fronds whispering as they cross and touch. I glide over and sit beside her, digging my root limbs into the earth a little.

"It's weird, no being fog. I'm no really sure whit to do with my limbs and branches."

"Just relax. We've got time. Here – can you feel that?" Her roots stretch and curl around mine. The earth is moist, peaty, acidic. "Is this okay?"

"Mmm," I sign. She zings me a peptide. It feels like a thirst quenched. I gently twine a sapwood branch around her trunk. Her frond pinnas caress my leaves. Our breaths begin to synchronise. "I cannae believe this might be the last—"

"Don't say it."

We sit like this for a few minutes, exchanging amino acids under the earth.

"Hey lovebirds," calls Plum. "Switch aff th Commune and come join me." We log into Plum's secure safe space in her reading room, then she signs herself out.

"You've got it?" asks Copi.

"Right here."

"I don't know how I'll ever—"

"I love you Copi. I know you'd do th same for me. But this is bigger than us. I mean, it's a wey for oor story tae live on, which is beautiful, but it's also so much more."

"I wish it could be different. I wish we could really be together, not this half-life."

"Look, half-life is okay. It can be magical. Aye, of course it's also infuriating, and hard and unfair, and you feel like you're being used or tolerated or tokenised, but it's no awful aw th time. We found each other, did we no? And now we've found a wey tae give some agency tae th next generation."

"Walk me through it," she says.

"You ken that I ken that we both ken the plan, but here's whit's going tae happen… We're going tae exit Plum's reading room. We're going tae unweave oor roots and leaves/fronds. I'm going tae extract th vial from within. You'll release some of your spores intae it, and then, I'll insert it back between ma sapwood and cambium. Nae alarms will go aff, nae cops will show up. We'll sign goodbye. I'll saunter oot of th library wi'oot onyane noticing. I'll mak ma wey back tae Dundee but get aff early at th biome perimeter. I'll meet oor contact at th designated spot and they'll chaperone me through th labyrinth tae th secret exit. I'll travel for around a week tae a specific location only known to ma handlers. When I arrive, I'll be exhausted, grumpy, and a wee bit malnourished frae th lack o light. This new place will be th perfect hame for us. I will tend your – oor – sporangiophytes and they will hopefully adopt me as their Dad. We will root oorselves there and I will tell them about their brave, beautiful parent, whit she dreamed for them and whit she sacrificed, but most importantly, how much you love them. We will grow together, for generations. This land will welcome us and we will love it."

"And then what happened, Dad?"

"Then, Sorcha, it began exactly how I told your mother."

"Until..."

"Until she released her spores. We didna realise it at th time, but a few flew past th vial and intae th air that wis circulating through th biome. I made it oot o th Grove, through th Heritage zone and wis wi'in sight o th main exit when th alarm went aff. Th spores must o hit th filters. Aw th doors locked automatically so I kent I wis doomed."

"But..."

"But Sparks—"

"Sir Sparks!"

"Yes, His Royal Droneness, th hero o th story, appeared and somehow jammed th main door system, allowing me tae escape th library, into th great hall. And there wis a tram, but it wis signalling tae depart. Plus, now security knew who tae chase. O course, I'm quicker than twa-leggers, so I glided as fast as ma root limbs could carry me – skiting across th shiny floor and crashing intae ane o th standing stones. I prayed tae every deity I could think o. Imagine, I'm lying oan th floor in disarray. Th guards are closing in – three twa-leggers frae the back, another frae th side. I could hear their stun guns charging and their shouts trying tae owerride th drones that were no responding.

"Thanks to Sir Sparks."

"Aye. Th gods (and th drones) were smiling oan me because that tram wis still there. I dragged maself up and ower th concourse, shoving folk oot o th wey."

"Rude!"

"Aye, very rude. I did fling oot lots o apologies though. I wis almost through th doors, when a bystander decided tae try and stop me."

"But he was just a human."

"No match. We wrestled, and as I flung him gently tae th side, a cop grabbed ane o ma branches. But I wis getting that tram. As I hauled maself through th doors, I felt th branch tearing. Then it wis gone. Th doors closed and th tram took aff."

"RIP branch thirty-two."

"Wicked scar though. So, trams willna stop between biomes. It's a safety thing. It's pretty much impossible unless it's going tae compromise a biome or explode or something. I knew I wis safe for around ten minutes tae catch ma breath. There wer'na many folk in the carriage. An elderly human wi twa grandkids, a couple o young treeforms, a biotech, aw pretending tae no look at me but sneaking glances. Aye, like that.

"But at th edge o th city perimeter, th tram stopped. Th tannoy kept repeating "please remain seated" and nought else. There wis no wey tae open th doors – ma carriage wis ootside th biome. I kent they were coming for me, frae th city side but I had tae go towards th danger. I glided through th next carriage and intae th vestibule – the bit between th carriages – and it wis just inside th city biome. I could see them coming through th carriage ahead. Twa leggers again, but this time they had fatal weapons. Remember – I wis carrying you inside me and I could no let you die.

"Then I saw th drone at th window. A new model. It wis trying tae hack ma brain stem but it couldna get a strong enough signal through th reinforced window. It started firing up and I readied maself for submission. But as th window shattered, I grabbed th drone and pulled it inside th tram then shoved maself through th broken window. I had no idea where I wis going – there's no reliable schematic o th city perimeter because it's changing aw th time."

"But someone helped you."

"A few someones helped me – us – tae escape th cops and biome and mainland, tae reach this wilderness."

"What happened to Mum though?"

"Well… She telt them I'd stolen her spores. And, that she didna realise whit wis happening at first. Because we'd been partners for so lang. She wis in shock, and then… well, then it wis ower before she realised whit wis happening. She said I'd completely betrayed her. And they believed her story."

"So, they didn't hurt her?"

"No. They… questioned her. And monitored her for… only a year. Onywey, your Mum is wey tougher than me."

"Do you miss her, Dad?"

"Every moment, in every cell. Roots to buds. Tae leave her was th hardest thing I've ever had tae dae. But aw this we have now – you, your siblings, oor freedom oan this patch o earth. We both did this for you."

"I wish Mum was here. I wish we could speak to her, exchange aminos, hear her stories."

"Me too, Sorcha. Now th moon is high and th moths are hungry. Until sunrise."

"Until."

Editors' Note:

Of all the ways to imagine the future of Scotland after ecological collapse, the one we really never saw coming was floral emancipation. But my goodness do we love "To the Forest". Jeda Pearl's depictions of plantlife personhood, not only centred on Copi and Linn's touching love story but also so wonderfully in the poetry recital at the story's centre, is such a unique and joyful way to explore such a society. We couldn't have asked for a more uplifting note to end this anthology on.

Acknowledgements

This anthology was made possible by a generous donation from the estate of Peter Bell (1932-2003). Peter was a long time fan and book collector. He attended conventions in the 1950's, including the first UK Worldcon, Loncon 1 in 1957, before coming back to them again when they started being held in Glasgow in 1978 (Faircon 78), and was a regular attendee until his death. From an early age he had been a keen and voracious collector and had amassed a fine collection of sci-fi books and pulps, some dating from the early thirties. He helped run the at-con Office for Intersection, the first Worldcon to be held in Glasgow. When he died, he left his collection to be sold to help SF writers. We are delighted to be able to honour Peter's wishes with this volume, and hope that in reading it you discover new writers whose careers you will follow for years to come.

We are indebted to Francesca Barbini for sharing our vision for this book and her guidance and energy in helping us fulfil it, and to Jenni Coutts for turning the vaguest of ideas (Blue! Maybe a lighthouse? Go!) into a simply wonderful cover design.

We are also grateful to Stuart Wallace, and to Mark Meenan and Glasgow in 2024 for their help and endless support. And, lastly, to the abundantly rich community of writers, poets, playwrights, filmmakers, artists, musicians, publishers, booksellers, academics and fans that now thrives in Scotland, creating and celebrating genre fiction. It's a marvellous thing to be part of.

Milton Keynes UK
Ingram Content Group UK Ltd.
UKHW010855050724
445034UK00005B/159

9 781915 556431